LOVE ON THE RUN

A SMALL TOWN CHRISTIAN ROMANCE

LOVE IN BLACKWATER
BOOK FIVE

MANDI BLAKE

Love on the Run
Love in Blackwater Book 5
By Mandi Blake

Published in the United States of America
Cover Designer: Amanda Walker PA & Design Services
Editor: Editing Done Write

CONTENTS

CHAPTER 1

ANNA

"I got the goods!" Olivia held a can of soda over her head as she closed the door behind her.

Anna reached for the drink and popped the top. "You're a lifesaver." Her stomach had been rolling all morning. Too bad bubbly drinks weren't an actual cure for wedding jitters.

Olivia brushed her hands down the sides of her navy dress. The torso was fitted, and the flowy skirt fanned out from the waist. It flattered Olivia's figure perfectly. "Are you ready to get into the dress? I saw your mom on a warpath, so I sent her to the reception hall to handle a fake catering emergency."

The mere thought of her mother sent Anna's stomach into another riot. Her mom had been shouting and seething since the rehearsal dinner.

Anna set the soda on the vanity. "Let's get it over with."

"Don't sound too excited to get into your wedding gown," Olivia whispered.

She was right. Anna should be giddy to slip into the custom gown. It was gorgeous and everything she'd ever hoped to wear on her wedding day.

Except, the nerves were eating her on the inside. Getting married was one of the biggest decisions of her life. Less than an hour before the ceremony wasn't the time to get cold feet.

She was marrying Dean Simmons. He was successful, handsome, wealthy, and socially connected—everything her husband was supposed to be.

Well, he was everything her mother said he was supposed to be. He claimed to be a Christian too, but he rarely went to church with her or prayed. They spent so much time apart, it was tough to find time to talk about anything. For the last few months, Anna and Dean had done little except argue and plan the wedding.

"I'm sorry," Anna whispered. "I really am excited to wear it."

It was half the truth, and Olivia knew it. The dress fit Anna perfectly. It was the groom that might not be the best fit.

Maybe it was Anna's fault their relationship had been rocky lately. Maybe she was the problem like her mother believed. According to Catherine Harris, Anna should support her husband and care for him no matter what. It was the epitome of selfishness that Anna wanted Dean's devotion and attention.

Olivia turned to Anna and rubbed a hand up and down her arm. "Are you sure about this?"

Anna gave her friend the standard "I'm okay" smile—the one she used to hide behind when she wanted everyone to think she was fine. "Of course."

Olivia's eyes narrowed. She knew the truth. Now, Anna was lying to her best friend.

Without arguing, Olivia reached for the dress. "Then let's do this."

Anna slipped off her robe and draped it over the vanity chair. Olivia carefully opened the top of the dress for Anna to step in.

As the dress rose around her, so did the invisible trap. It was easy to imagine one of those coil spring traps closing around her like a predator's teeth. She sucked in deep breaths as if she could fight off the panic coming to claim her.

Good grief. This was her wedding day, not a prison. Thinking of being confined had her adrenaline rushing through her system in heavy pulses.

"Anna–"

"I can't talk," Anna whispered. "Let's just do it."

Olivia's chin quivered, and Anna's throat tightened. She had the best friend a woman could ever ask for, but no one could save her now.

"I love you," Olivia said, blinking back tears. "I love you so much, and I'll always be here for you."

Anna nodded, unable to speak around the knot in her throat.

Staring at the wall as Olivia secured the buttons, Anna blocked out all the doubts and said a silent prayer. *Lord, help me. Please, help me. I'm drowning. I don't know if I can do this. Why do I feel this way?*

There was a knock at the door, and Olivia's hands stilled on the buttons. "Should I let them in?" she whispered.

"Yeah. It's fine."

There was one thing Anna knew for sure—whoever was on the other side of the door wasn't her mother. Catherine Harris would have barged right in.

Olivia opened the door but not enough that Anna could see the visitor. "Can I help you?"

"Can I see the bride?" a woman asked.

Olivia glanced at Anna who pasted on her signature smile. "It's okay."

Olivia moved to the side, and a beautiful woman with dark hair stepped into the room. Her cream sweater and jeans complimented her dark hair and skin. The mystery woman was beautiful, but she wasn't dressed to attend a wedding.

Twisting her fingers, she raked her gaze over Anna's dress before tucking her chin again. "I know you don't know me, but I'm Misty."

When Misty paused, Anna lifted the skirt of her

dress and stepped forward to extend a hand. "I'm Anna. It's nice to meet you, Misty."

Instead of taking Anna's hand, Misty shook her head. "I'm here because I couldn't let you marry Dean without knowing about us." She lifted her chin, channeling a resolve that had her shoulders shaking. "We've been seeing each other for months, and I'm sorry for that. But... I'm not really."

All of the air in Anna's lungs was sucked away. Her chest ached as she tried to breathe through the kick she'd just taken.

Of course. Dean would be interested in Misty. She was gorgeous. But that wasn't where things ended. He'd been seeing another woman for months. It wasn't a fling or something that happened once.

"You what?" Olivia shouted.

Misty jerked away from Olivia. Her hand shook as she wiped her cheek. "I–I–"

Olivia took a step toward Misty. "Get out."

"No." Anna lifted a hand. After a shaking breath that tore her insides, she managed to speak. "I want to know more."

"Anna, you don't have to listen to this," Olivia reminded her.

"I need to hear it." The pain was already spreading. Why not let it consume her?

Misty held her hands out as if pleading. "I love

him, and he says he loves me. I just know that if you marry him today, he'll never be mine."

"Oh, you can have him," Olivia spat. "He's a lying jerk, and you deserve each other."

Misty ignored Olivia and stared into Anna's eyes. "Please. I can't live without him. I love him."

Olivia turned and threw her hands in the air. "He's not going to be around to love you back because I'm going to tear his limbs off and feed him to my chickens."

"Wait!" Anna stopped Olivia on her way to the door. "Just wait a minute."

"You'd better hurry," Olivia said, crossing her arms with a huff. "I have friends to round up. They'll want to take their shot at Dean too."

Anna looked back to Misty. "How long have you been together?"

Misty sniffed, clearly upset at the thought of losing her one true love. "Nine months."

The pulling in her chest deepened. He'd been seeing another woman when he asked Anna to be his wife.

Flipping through her moments with Dean, she filtered them through the new information. A carousel of memories flashed, and she wanted nothing more than to jump off the ride.

Everything had been innocent until now. Now she was on the verge of sickness as the memories turned to internal screams.

"Are we done here?" Olivia asked. The sass in her tone meant she was ready to claw Misty's skin off if she hung around much longer.

Anna raised her chin and channeled the smile that protected her heart. "Don't worry. I won't be marrying Dean. Now or ever."

Misty covered her face with her hands and sobbed. If only Anna could taste just a little bit of that relief.

"Okay, time to go." Olivia opened the door and stepped to the side. "Have a nice life. Don't let my foot hit you on the way out."

Misty took a step closer to Anna. "Thank you."

Anna held her smile in place and nodded for the woman to leave.

As soon as Misty was out the door, Olivia slammed and locked it.

"Can you believe the nerve of that woman?"

Anna dropped the act and clawed at the neckline of her dress. "Get me out of this."

Olivia was behind her in a second, ripping the line of buttons apart. When the dress pooled around her legs, Anna fought to breathe.

"Slow that breathing down, babe. I don't want you to pass out." Olivia grabbed the cute, white dress Anna had planned to wear for the last part of the reception. "Here. Put this on."

Anna slipped the silky fabric around her and lifted her hair so Olivia could zip the back.

She led Anna to the chair in front of the vanity. "Sit." Her friend grabbed the soda and shoved it at Anna. "Drink."

Olivia was getting a friend promotion. She was the perfect woman to have by Anna's side at a time like this. "Thanks."

The electricity coursing through her eased when Olivia wrapped her arms around Anna's shoulders. Maybe she'd needed a hug instead of a soda all along.

"Don't worry," Olivia said, releasing the hug to morph into business mode. "I'm going to handle all of this. Here's my plan." She ticked off items on her fingers. "First, I'm going to have Dawson and Travis tie up your mom and hide her in a closet until everything is over. Or forever. Second, I'm going to make sure Dean gets at least one good punch from all of the guys. Third, I'm going to slip you out of here unnoticed."

Anna shook her head. "All of that sounds good, but I want out of here *now*."

"Okay. Okay." Olivia patted the sides of her dress. "Dawson has my keys. I'll be right back. You'll be okay for a few minutes? I'll send one of the girls in here as soon as I find them."

"I'm okay," Anna said. Oddly enough, the sickness that had been bubbling in her middle all day was starting to ease.

Olivia turned at the door and flashed Anna a

tense smile. "I love you, and we're going to get through this."

"I know." Anna nodded. "You're the best."

With a wink, Olivia disappeared, leaving Anna alone in a quiet room. Chairs were stacked in the corner of the Sunday School classroom, and a dark-purple stain slashed across the worn carpet.

She couldn't just sit here. She wasn't getting married, and she wasn't a bride.

Shooting to her feet, she paced the small room in the church building where she worshiped every chance she got. She'd welcomed Dean into her life. She'd trusted him. She'd planned a future with him. She'd been prepared to give him everything!

He'd played with her heart and hadn't cared about the fallout.

Anna stopped pacing and looked in the mirror. She was all done up for her wedding day, but her life was crumbling around her.

She'd been living under other people's thumbs for years, and she was finally free. Dean wouldn't tell her what to do. Her mom wouldn't make her feel like she was a bad girlfriend.

No. She was going to live her life for herself. Well, not completely for herself. She would live her life for God first and foremost. All of the joy in her life was because of Him, and she couldn't forget that.

Maybe this was even a part of His plan. Maybe

she was supposed to reinvent herself and become the woman He wanted her to be.

In the mirror, the woman staring at her was fierce and confident. Her hair was styled, her dress fit perfectly, and she was beautiful without a stitch of makeup on her face. Yes, she could do this. She could do anything. She had a group of friends who loved her. They would help her through this.

And she would never make the same mistake twice.

Slipping her feet into the white tennis shoes she'd worn to the church, she grabbed the small clutch that matched her dress and walked out the door.

CHAPTER 2

BEAU

The small parking lot in front of the church was packed—even more so than a typical Sunday morning. Apparently, Anna and Dean knew how to draw a crowd.

Money did that. Money brought people swarming in on all sides, and it only caused problems. For Beau, those problems were usually in the form of unbalanced accounting records. Mechanics weren't built to handle money, and he'd gladly fix a car over reconciling statements any day.

He usually parked on the left side of the building, but that section was full because it was closer to the dining hall. Catering trucks blocked most of the area by the side entrance.

It was a good thing his motorcycle didn't need its own designated parking spot. He parked on the right side of the building in front of the first row of vehicles and popped the stand.

He pushed back the sleeve of his leather jacket to check the time. The wedding hadn't started. Why did it look like he was one of the last to show up?

Whatever. He'd find a seat at the back and slip in without having to make boring conversation with anyone. Then, he would sneak out while everyone got excited about the reception.

He pulled off his helmet and gloves and stowed them in the side bag. After running a hand through his short hair, it was time to face the music.

Olivia promised the ceremony would only last about fifteen minutes. He could sit still for a quarter of an hour. At least, his sister assured him he'd survive.

Olivia also claimed weddings were beautiful and thought he should be actively working to find a woman who would entertain the thought of spending her life with him.

That's where she lost him. He had no desire to get married or commit to any other relationship titles people used these days.

He wasn't interested in "hanging out."

He didn't care to "date."

"Getting to know someone" wasn't for him.

He needed a wife like he needed a toe fungus.

His black boots were a stark contrast to the

white stone steps leading to the side entrance. Maybe he should have worn something nicer.

He was halfway up the stairs when a blur of white burst through the door. Anna held a small purse in one hand and pressed the other over the skirt of her dress as she flew down the stairs.

Anna Harris was a force to be reckoned with. The bride had been best friends with Beau's sister since they were in middle school, and he'd gotten a front-row view as she'd carefully picked her way through life one perfect piece at a time.

Graduate with honors.

Become a successful attorney.

Help the community.

Volunteer at church.

Find a boyfriend.

Fall in love.

Get married.

Live in the suburbs with a picket fence.

Have pretty babies just like her.

Yeah, Anna's list was generic, but one item on her list meant more than all of the others.

Fall in love.

The woman had been walking around with stars in her eyes since they were kids. Everything she did revolved around love and building the perfect family.

Now, she was barreling out of the church on her wedding day.

Her attention focused on her feet bouncing down the stairs until she was three steps from him. When she finally looked up, her eyes widened a mere second before her foot slipped off the step.

Poised and ridiculously perfect, Anna Harris even tripped gracefully. The whole thing happened in slow motion. Her foot landed unevenly, her shoulders pitched forward, and her arms reached toward him.

Then, someone hit fast forward. Beau opened his arms, and she tumbled right into his chest. Wrapping her up, he took a step down when the force threatened to send them both falling. Turning, he held her suspended above the stone stairs.

And that's how Beau ended up dipping the bride on her wedding day.

Anna clung to his back and shoulders, huffing quick, loud breaths. "I—I almost fell."

"Yep. But I caught you."

Please don't panic. Please don't make a big deal out of it. Please don't cry. For the love of all things good, please don't cry.

Beau raised her, holding her steady until she balanced on her feet. "Are you okay?"

Anna brushed her hands down her dress. The purse she'd been carrying was at the bottom of the stairs. "Um, I think so. You caught me."

"Yeah," Beau drawled. "We covered that." Did

she really expect him to just let her fall? Of course he would catch her. “You’re all good?”

She nodded quickly, still gasping for those quick breaths that were doing nothing to calm her.

“Breathe. I need more words, Anna.”

She looked up at him, and a wave of dread slid down his back. Her wedding started in fifteen minutes, and her hair was escaping from the pins holding it up. Was she wearing any makeup? Why was she in running shoes?

Shoot. She was running.

Granted, she needed to run. She needed to run as far and as fast as she could from Dean What’s-His-Face. That guy was the definition of a loser.

She tucked a stray hair behind her ear and closed her eyes. “Yes. I’m okay.” She swallowed hard and looked him up and down. “Where are you going?”

“I don’t know. I thought I was going to your wedding, but since it looks like you’re not going to your wedding, I guess I’m free.”

Anna turned to the building. Her blonde hair flared around her, still looking great despite being a little messy.

Satisfied that no one was coming after her, she grabbed Beau’s hand and continued down the stairs. “Good. Let’s go.”

Beau tugged slightly on her hand. Holding hands was one of those weird touchy-feely things people did in relationships, and he didn't like the idea of being led around by Anna. "Whoa. What are you doing?" She'd been about to marry the world's biggest moron. Did he really trust her judgment?

Anna stopped and turned to him, still gripping his hand. "I have to get out of here, and I need a ride."

Beau took in her outfit. "You can't get on my motorcycle like that."

Anna looked down at her short dress. It was cute. Well, it was something other than cute, but Beau wouldn't be analyzing it any more than that.

When she looked up, it was her sincerity that struck him. "Why not?"

"It's fifteen degrees out here. You'll freeze. And no skirts on the bike. That's dangerous."

That was a new and unexpected rule. Who would have thought he'd be laying down laws about skirts on his bike today or any other day?

Anna's shoulders sank, and her blue eyes narrowed. "I really need your help."

Oh no. She would not lure him in with a pitiful pouty face. He was immune to feminine wiles, and she was wasting her efforts to suck him into a situation that wasn't any of his business.

"Anna!"

Beau turned at the sound of Dean's sharp tone itching for a fight as Anna whispered a clean curse under her breath because the woman was as sweet as cotton candy and didn't have a mean bone in her body, but Dean was Beau's least favorite person on the planet. It was easy to daydream about thumping him off a cliff, but Beau had done a fantastic job of staying out of Dean and Anna's business since day one.

How exactly did he end up standing between the runaway bride and her ex-groom?

"Dean, she told me. I think it's only fitting that you be the one to explain to everyone why there won't be a wedding happening today." She pointed at the woman trailing Dean like a puppy. "Misty is good at telling the story."

"You can't be serious. It's our wedding day. Get back inside!"

Beau straightened his shoulders when Dean stalked closer, but he didn't have a chance to take one step toward the guy before Anna pointed a manicured nail in Dean's face.

"You think that's going to work on me now? I can't believe that all those trips you took were for her." She turned the finger around on herself. "I begged you to spend time with me."

"That's the thing. You're not begging. You're nagging," Dean said.

Misty looked like she'd been through the wringer with black makeup smeared from her nose to her hairline and all down her cheeks.

Why wasn't it surprising that Dean had a

woman on the side? Few people had ever seen him treat Anna with respect. Why did he ask her to marry him if he didn't want to be faithful to her?

Dating had never been at the top of Beau's to-do list, but it made sense that you wouldn't ask a woman to spend the rest of her life with you if you didn't want to spend the rest of your life with her.

Misty pulled on Dean's arm. "Please. Let's go. She said the wedding is off."

Dean shoved her off and focused on Anna. "You think you can just leave?"

Anna crossed her arms over her chest. She had to be cold, but she didn't look like someone protecting herself from the weather. It was a stance of defiance. "Did you cheat on me with Misty?" she asked calmly.

"What? How can you even ask me that?" Dean spat back, as if surprised she'd have the nerve to even ask.

Anna huffed. "Yeah, this conversation is over. I'm not marrying you. Misty can have you, and I wish you two the best. Oh, and you'll be getting the catering bill. Be sure to tell everyone to stay and enjoy the food."

Dean's chest rose and fell as he took deep breaths. His face was turning a scary shade of red that didn't look healthy. "Get. Back. Inside."

"Absolutely not," Anna spoke calmly with her chin slightly lifted. "I don't have to stay with you. I didn't stand up in front of God and the people of this town and make vows to you."

"This is ridiculous. I—"

"Dean," Misty whined, still pulling on his shirt.

Dean rounded on her, and she shrank back. "Shut up. This is all your fault."

"Don't talk to her like that," Anna said.

Dean threw his hands in the air. "Why do you care how I talk to her?"

Anna clenched her fists at her sides. "Because you talk to me the same way. You don't have to say it. I know you've been seeing her."

Beau crossed his arms and eyed that little bit of tension in her hands. Good for her. She needed some fight in her after putting up with loser Dean for so long.

Dean took a step toward Anna and lowered his voice. "I swear, if you don't get back in there—"

"You might want to take a quick second to think about how you want to finish that sentence," Beau said.

Great. Why'd he have to say something? It was like the words just popped out.

Getting involved in this marital tiff was about as appealing as licking wet paint, but apparently there was a tipping point to Beau's indifference.

Anna grabbed Beau's hand and pulled him toward the parking lot. "Let's go, *please*."

She hadn't cried yet, but the last word was

drawn out and a little shaky. That was the only reason he let her lead him away from the church.

"You're leaving with *Beau*?" Dean spat.

"I'm just leaving you. That's the whole point of this exit," Anna snapped back.

Thank goodness. She didn't want him involved any more than he wanted to be.

Dean and Misty shouted at each other as Anna blazed a hot trail for Beau's motorcycle, stopping only to pick up her purse. By the time she stood beside his bike, her whole body was shaking.

"You're freezing. Let me get someone's keys and we'll take a car."

"No." Anna grabbed his bicep with enough force that he heeded her word. "I need to go now. My mom will figure out what's going on soon, and I can't be here when—"

Beau held up a hand. "You need pants."

"I don't have pants."

Beau reached into his side bag and pulled out a pair of black sweatpants he'd intended to wear at the gym and handed them to her. "You're lucky they're clean."

Anna didn't waste a second as she handed him her purse. She hiked her leg up, exposing the pale-blue garter snugly wrapped around her thigh and shoved her feet into the pants—shoes and all. With the other leg in, she jerked the string around the waist to its max and knotted it.

Okay, he'd expected a little pushback on the pants. At least she was making this easier. "Tuck the dress in."

"What?"

"I'm serious. I don't want your skirt getting caught in anything."

Without a word, she shoved the ends of the dress into the waistband of the pants. "Good?"

Beau stowed her purse in the saddle bag and handed her the helmet. She shoved it over her hair without missing a beat.

She really wanted to get out of here.

"What about you?" she asked, her words muffled through the helmet.

"I didn't really expect to have a passenger today."

She reached to take the helmet off, but Beau put his hand on top of it. "Nope. This isn't negotiable. You have to wear it if you're riding with me."

Anna lowered her hands and rested them on her hips, showing off her bare arms.

That wasn't going to work either. Beau slid the leather jacket off his back and held it open for her.

When she hesitated, he shook the jacket. Surely, she wouldn't fight him on this too. "This isn't negotiable either."

Anna turned around and slipped her arms into the sleeves. Shivering, she wrapped it tight around her front. "Thanks."

Dean and Misty were still arguing on the steps, but it wouldn't be long until someone came looking for the bride and groom. He shoved his gloves on and focused on Anna. "Have you ever been on a bike before?"

Anna shook her head, but he couldn't see her face through the helmet. As long as she didn't puke, they should be okay.

"This is a first for both of us." He slung a leg over and settled in. "Rules. Hang on tight, and lean when I lean."

"What?" She was still shaking, but was it from the cold or fear?

"When we lean to turn, don't try to balance by righting yourself. You have to lean into the curve."

Anna glanced at the church then straddled the bike behind him. Her body pressed against his back, and her arms wound around his chest.

At least she was taking rule number one to heart. She'd cut off his air supply hanging on like that.

He tapped her hand. "Not that tight."

Her grip loosened, but only a little.

"Where are we going?" he asked, keeping an eye on Dean and Misty.

"Your garage," she said as she pressed the side of her helmet to his back.

As soon as he started the bike, Catherine Harris

stormed out the door with their friend Hadley on her heels.

“Go!” Anna shouted behind him.

He didn’t need to be told twice. Catherine Harris wasn’t his favorite person, and he’d do just about anything to avoid her, including riding off with Anna on her wedding day.

CHAPTER 3
ANNA

Every muscle in her body ached and spasmed by the time Beau parked in front of Blackwater Automotive. Her heart threatened to beat out of her chest even after the roaring of the engine died. Vibrations continued to surge through her body long after the silence engulfed them.

That wasn't the kind of excitement she expected on her wedding day. It wasn't even on her bucket list.

When Beau stuck his hand out to the side, she slowly peeled herself away from his back and placed her hand in his. Her arms and legs shook as she carefully crawled off the bike.

Beau stood in front of her by the time she removed the big helmet from her head. Wisps of her hair flew in front of her face.

He reached for the helmet, and she handed it

over. Without something to hold onto, her hands shook even more.

Beau pulled her clutch out of the side bag, and she took it from him. He jerked his head toward the garage. "Let's get you inside."

The cold breeze stung her cheeks, but his jacket and sweatpants covered the rest of her body. She followed him through a side entrance, and warmth greeted her as soon as she stepped into the building.

She spent plenty of time at Beau's garage. All of their friends did. It was a central hangout since Beau and Gage worked there, Asa and his son fixed up old cars, and Olivia made sure her brother and his employees always had good food to eat.

Beau led her to the break room and pulled a seat out at the table on his way to the refrigerator. "You hungry?"

Anna settled into the seat, and her shoulders rounded forward. The ache in her middle had subsided, overridden by the adrenaline rush of riding Beau's motorcycle. "I don't think I could eat."

"Ginger ale?" he asked.

"That would be great." The rolling in her stomach had started to ease, but a ginger ale would help a little too.

Dean cheated on her. The blow still hadn't fully registered. She wasn't getting married today. The future she'd planned disappeared into a cloud of smoke.

Oh, and she'd commandeered a ride from Beau. On his motorcycle! She'd never even considered getting on the back of a bike before, but today, she'd been all too eager to jump on to escape the disaster waiting inside that church.

Beau passed her a can and rested against the counter, crossing his arms over his broad chest. His pale-blue collared shirt only reminded her that they'd both planned to be at the wedding today.

"You need anything else?" he asked, looking down at his boots.

She placed the cold can on the table and wrapped her arms around herself, unwilling to give up the jacket he'd let her borrow. "I think I'm okay. Thanks for helping me get out of there."

Beau didn't say anything, which was exactly what she expected. He'd probably used up his allotted words for the day going back-and-forth with her about the escape.

The phone in her small clutch vibrated, and she reached for it.

A photo of Olivia with her arms wrapped around Anna's neck smiled at her from the screen. "Do you mind if I answer this? It's your sister."

Beau pushed away from the counter and walked right out of the room. He'd probably been itching to get away since the moment he saw her running out of that church.

He'd caught her. It was a cruel parallel but a

stark contrast from her first encounter with Dean. She had pretended to trip in front of him to get his attention, and he'd almost let her hit the ground—only catching her at the last second.

The relief in that moment when she realized Beau hadn't let her fall on the stairs still lingered, helping her keep her chin up. Beau had saved her more than once today, but he probably wouldn't see it that way.

Anna answered the call. "Hello."

"Anna, are you okay? Thank goodness you answered. I've been looking all over for you."

"I had to get out of there. I'm so sorry I—"

"Don't worry about it. I'm just glad you're okay. I've taken care of everything here, including your mom."

"Oh no." Catherine would be absolutely livid.

"I'm not saying she won't let you have it when she sees you though. She's furious. I hope you didn't go home."

"No. Beau took me to his garage."

Anna traced a finger over a line on the wooden table. She liked hanging out at the garage, but this wasn't how she'd expected to spend her wedding day.

"Thank goodness. Okay, I'll be there in ten minutes. Just sit tight."

"Thanks, Liv. I don't know what I'd do without you."

"You'll never have to find out. I'll see you in a minute."

Anna cradled the phone in her hands, but it immediately started vibrating again. Her mother's photo filled the screen. Catherine's headshot from the law firm's website.

Her blonde hair that matched Anna's hung in her usual wavy curls over her shoulders, and she wore a black suit. Her smile was friendly enough, but it wasn't an expression she used around Anna often. Smiles were reserved for clients and influential friends.

Anna stared at the phone, but her fingers wouldn't budge to answer it. When the vibrating ended, it started right back up again.

A sinkhole opened in her chest, and everything collapsed into it. She'd trusted Dean, but she'd done it blindly. She'd wanted love, but she'd been taught a lesson instead.

A tear tickled her cheek, and she wiped it away before standing. She couldn't sit here any longer.

Anna inhaled a deep breath, and the smell of grease and exhaust fumes filled her nose. For some reason, the familiar scent chased away the tension she'd been holding in her shoulders.

She was still wearing Beau's jacket. And his pants. A small chuckle crept up her throat as she looked at the ridiculous outfit. She had the skirt of her dress tucked into Beau's sweats! The image was enough to send her into a laughing fit.

"What's wrong?" Beau barged into the break room, stopping by her side in a second.

Anna wiped at the tears on her cheeks as she gasped for breath. "Nothing. I was just laughing at myself." She held her arms out at her sides. "I look ridiculous!"

Beau's gaze moved from her head to her feet and back up again. The intensity in his stare as he looked her over sent a tingling down her spine.

"You look fine. You don't have to impress anyone here. Do you want me to call Olivia and tell her to bring you some clothes?"

Anna shook her head. She needed to forget about Beau's stare as much as she needed to focus on their conversation. "No. I'll figure out how to get clothes later. My mom will harass anyone who shows up there, and I'm not ready to face her yet."

Beau shrugged one shoulder. "Suit yourself."

Anna tugged the jacket off her shoulders. "You can have your clothes back now."

Beau held up a hand. "Keep them on until you get something else."

"I'm wearing a dress. I'm fully clothed."

"You might get cold," he said, dry and matter-of-factly.

She positioned the jacket over her shoulders. "I'll leave this on, but I'm taking the pants off."

Beau didn't try to change her mind again. He walked straight over to the coffee pot and started gathering the things needed to brew a pot.

She clumsily removed the pants and hung them over the back of a chair. The jerky movements and lack of balance didn't feel right. It was usually easy to be graceful.

Not today, apparently.

Her phone buzzed again, and she left it bumping over the table. Talking to anyone right now would only end in tears.

"Should I turn it off?" she asked.

Beau propped an arm against the counter by the coffeemaker. "If you want to."

Turning off her phone wasn't something she ever did. She had clients, friends, and family, and she liked being available to them all the time.

Well, some of them. Her mom's calls tended to summon red splotches on her chest and neck.

Did she want to turn it off? She couldn't remember the last time she'd done that. Wasn't it rude to ignore the mess she'd have to clean up today?

The screech of a metal door opening jerked Anna's attention from the phone, and the clicking of heels sounded down the hallway.

"Sounds like reinforcements are here," Beau said as he slipped out of the room without waiting for the coffee to finish brewing.

CHAPTER 4
ANNA

Olivia launched herself at Anna. "I'm here. It's going to be okay. I promise."

Her friend's embrace was enough to send her over the edge. Anna never let the world see her feelings unless it was happiness.

But Olivia? Olivia was Anna's safe place, her shoulder to cry on, and her midnight call. Olivia was the one she could count on to be there for her through anything.

"It's okay. I promise. We took care of everything and also managed to have Dean escorted out by Asa and Dawson."

A laugh broke through Anna's tears. "I wish I'd been there for that."

"It was glorious. He was furious, and Misty cried enough to fill a kiddie pool."

The unease was back. Misty had won in a way. Why did she feel sorry for the woman?

Relief and a gut-wrenching sadness warred within her. Dean hadn't respected her enough to remain loyal. She might have high expectations for love, but Scripture said love was faithful.

She could have been trapped in a marriage with him. Yes, trapped would be the appropriate description of a relationship without fidelity.

"Back to square one," Anna whispered.

"Stop that," Olivia said, breaking the hug to look at Anna. "You're an amazing person, and I know God has the perfect man for you out there."

A chuckle shook Anna's shoulders. "He got lost."

Olivia laughed too, but it lacked mirth. "He's not lost. God knows the timing too. It's just not right this minute."

Anna sighed. "I know. I'm trying really hard to be patient."

Olivia rubbed her hands over Anna's shoulders. "You're doing great. Patience is tough. Just ask Dawson."

Dawson had waited very patiently for Olivia to open her heart to him. He never pushed, but he never gave up either.

Now, Dawson and Olivia were being made to wait for a child to grow their family, and they were handling it well because they trusted God.

Why couldn't Anna be that patient?

Anna wiped her face, grateful that she hadn't put on a ton of makeup before Dean's secret came out. "How many men do I have to share my favorite color with before I find my person?"

Olivia's lips pressed together in a thin line. "I don't know."

"That was a joke. You were supposed to laugh and tell me something encouraging."

"Oh, I'll be encouraging, but I think you need something a little different. You've always wanted to find love and live happily ever after, but what else do you want?"

Anna narrowed her eyes at Olivia. "What do you mean?"

"You've been so focused on finding someone and making sure they're happy enough with you to stay that you might have lost sight of what makes *you* happy."

Anna swallowed. What made her happy? It wasn't Dean. She hadn't been truly happy in their relationship for a while. Hindsight was 20/20.

She loved her job, but it wasn't always fulfilling. Clients at the law firm rarely thanked her for the things she did for them. Sure, she earned plenty of money, but what was she even doing with it?

Her fashion vlog was definitely a passion project, but that could all fall apart when her wedding sponsors found out she wouldn't be wearing and featuring the custom gowns they made for her.

She'd have to pay them back. That was one thing she'd be doing with her money.

"Maybe you're right," Anna admitted.

Heels clicked rapidly down the hallway seconds before Hadley and Lyric entered wearing their navy bridesmaid gowns.

"Are you okay?" Hadley asked as she greeted Anna with open arms.

Sinking into the embrace, Anna took a stinging breath past the tightness in her chest. "I'm okay. Thanks for all your help today."

"Don't mention it. It was our pleasure," Lyric said as she rubbed a hand over Anna's back.

"Yeah. I'm so sorry you're having to go through this, but I really enjoyed seeing Dean getting put in his place," Hadley said.

"We're here for you, Anna. Anything you need," Lyric added.

"The other ladies are too," Hadley said. "Everly Lawson stepped in and took over as your wedding coordinator. That other lady was still taking orders from your mom, and Everly spoke up for you and put her foot down on a lot of things."

"I wanted to hire her in the first place. Mom wanted someone else, and Everly was already busy planning weddings at Wolf Creek Ranch."

Lyric continued rubbing Anna's back. "We all pitched in to wrap things up. Everly told the guests to stay and eat since the food was already paid for."

"Good. I wouldn't want it to go to waste," Anna said, relaxing a little with her friends around her.

Hadley gasped. "Wait. What about your honeymoon? You should totally still go!"

"Definitely," Lyric said. "You spent as much time planning the trip as you did the wedding. You deserve it."

Anna's spirts fell. Not only had she been planning the trip to Freedom, Colorado for months, she'd booked a bunch of extras she'd always wanted to do. She called it her bucket list. "My honeymoon? I can't go on my honeymoon alone."

"Bring someone with you," Lyric said. "It's within driving distance, so it's not like they'll need a passport or anything."

That was one of Anna's stipulations. Her crippling fear of flying had kept her from traveling with Dean. Maybe she'd have discovered his affair sooner if she'd been able to spend more time with him, but knowing she was afraid of flying hadn't stopped Dean from jet-setting without her.

Now that the idea was in her head, missing out on the perfect trip she'd planned for their honeymoon would just be another crack in her breaking heart.

Anna threw her hands in the air. "Why would I bring someone with me? Because misery loves company?"

Hadley grabbed Anna's hand and bounced on

her toes. "No, you'll be happy having fun and knowing you don't have to put up with Dean's bad attitude and philandering anymore."

In theory. Anna had been looking forward to the things she'd planned for them. Was she really going to miss out on all of the fun she'd been looking forward to doing?

"Would anyone want to go with me?"

Olivia groaned. "I have to work. I already offered to cover three shifts for someone else this week."

"I can't. I work every day next week," Hadley said.

"Jacob has basketball tournaments," Lyric said. "I'd love to go, but I can't miss his games. They have a shot at the championship."

Olivia rubbed a hand over her chin. "Bella is super pregnant. She won't want to be away from her doctor. Who else?"

Anna had plenty of friends but not many she would just call up and ask to go on a spur-of-the-moment trip with her. "I think that's a sign. I'm not supposed to go."

Olivia grabbed Anna's hand. "Wait. Don't give up yet. I'll be right back."

She darted out of the room with her heels clicking on the floor and her dark hair flowing.

Anna shook her head. "It's fine. I have a big mess to clean up here anyway."

Hadley spotted the coffee pot and pulled a mug

from the cabinet. "I'm serious. Everly took over. We told her what happened, and she immediately turned on her professional face."

Lyric appraised Anna with raised eyebrows. "You look great by the way. Beau's jacket gives that hot dress a new edge."

Anna gripped the lapels of the jacket and pulled the two sides tighter around her. It was officially becoming a source of comfort when everything was falling apart around her.

"It's too big."

Lyric grinned and gave Anna a playful wink. "Sure, but it looks good on you."

The memory of wrapping her arms around Beau as they drove away from the church sent her heart racing again. Would she have been brave enough to leave if he hadn't been in the right place at the right time?

Hadley raised a mug of steaming coffee. "I'm going to check on Olivia. I have a feeling she needs help."

CHAPTER 5
BEAU

Beau stared at the laptop screen while a mechanic pointed at the high-pressure oil pump and talked through the steps to change the gaskets on a Duramax engine. It was his second time watching the video, and he'd still only caught bits and pieces.

Resting his forehead in his hands, his fingers threaded into his hair. Why did he have to get involved in Anna's business? Why didn't he turn around and head home when it was clear the wedding wasn't happening?

If he'd done the smart thing and walked away, he wouldn't have heard all about how Dean had cheated on Anna. He also wouldn't know what it felt like to have her arms wrapped around him, she wouldn't be wearing his clothes, and he wouldn't have had to see so much of her in that short, white dress.

How in the world was he even thinking about her legs while an old, bearded man pointed to a greasy oil leak?

Something was wrong with him. He either needed sleep or a slap in the face. He hadn't decided which would help the current problem.

Olivia burst into his office and closed the door behind her as if she were running for her life. The desk in front of him rattled as she slapped her hands on it.

"What are you doing? Is someone chasing you?" he asked.

His sister leveled him with a serious stare. "Beau, I'm going to ask you to do something. If you really love me, you'll say yes."

"Who said I loved you?" Beau returned his attention to the computer.

Caring about his sister was the single most destructive thing in his life. Sometimes he wished he cared less, then he wouldn't get roped into doing things for her all the time.

"Please, please, please," she begged.

"I'm not committing myself to anything you want." He clicked random buttons on the keyboard. "I'm busy."

"I need you to go with Anna on her honeymoon," Olivia said quickly.

Ha! That was the worst idea he'd ever heard.

"Not a chance. Now get out."

"Beau Lawrence, I have not been doing random acts of kindness for you your entire life for no reason. I need your help right now, and you're going to listen to me."

"Sounds like that's your problem, not mine. I didn't ask you to bring me lunch every day."

Olivia slapped her hand on his desk again. "I'm serious! Beau, Anna needs this. She's been so excited for this trip—"

"Her honeymoon? Yeah, I can imagine why she was excited about that."

"Her loser fiancé just cheated on her. She needs something to cheer her up."

"Then go on a girls' trip. Have fun. The door is that way." He pointed toward the exit and unpaused the video he'd been pretending to watch.

Olivia continued to stare as if she could burn a hole through him with her laser beam eyes. "I can't go. Neither can Hadley, Lyric, or Bella. Anna needs to get away from her mom for a minute, and *you* need to take a break."

"Why would I need a break?"

"Because you work *all the time*."

"So? Why don't you mind your own business?"

Olivia scoffed. "That's no fun. Who would take care of you?"

A retort sat on the tip of Beau's tongue, but he

swallowed it back. Ever since their mom died, Olivia had treated him like a child. At first, it didn't bother him, and he assumed it was one of the ways she was coping with Mom's death.

As time went on, Olivia kept doing things for him. She brought him food, stopped by the apartment where he lived in the back of the garage to make sure he wasn't growing mold on any food he'd forgotten to throw away, made sure he visited the dentist for a cleaning twice a year, and cut his hair every few weeks.

He'd thought about asking her to stop multiple times, but he always chickened out, worrying she'd think she wasn't needed and have a breakdown over losing their mom.

He let her walk around in his life because he thought she was lonely. Now, she was married to Dawson, and there wasn't any reason for her to be checking up on him.

"Liv, I don't need anyone to take care of me. I'm a grown man. I own a business. I pay my taxes. I even wash my own clothes. I'm grown. You can stop worrying about me."

Funny, he'd been worrying about her for years, but she'd been doing the same for him. Maybe he should have taken her up on that family therapy session years ago.

"You're all alone," Olivia said.

"Happily. I like being alone."

"Well, then you can go on this trip with Anna. You two can be alone together."

Beau replayed her words, but they still didn't make sense. "Huh?"

"Just trust me on this one. The guys are more than capable of handling the business while you're gone, and Anna can go on her trip."

"She can go by herself."

Olivia propped her hand on her hip. "Do you know how dangerous it is for women to travel alone?"

Hmm. She had him there. People tended to clear a path and look away when he walked down the street. Fear wasn't something he understood. The realization that Anna might feel better just having him around was unsettling.

The door opened, and Hadley slipped into his office holding a cup of coffee. She greeted Olivia with a huge grin on her face. "I knew I'd find you here!"

"Tell him it's a good idea," Olivia said with a jerk of her head toward him.

"It's a great idea. Anna won't be worried about traveling on her own, and you'll get to do all kinds of stuff she's already booked."

"No, thanks," Beau said, thinking about the kind of things people did on their honeymoon. He tugged on his hair until his scalp hurt. Why couldn't they leave him alone?

Hadley set the mug on the desk next to the group of circles that stained the wood. “I brought you a peace offering.”

Olivia rounded the desk and dropped to her knees beside his chair. Clasping her hands to her chest, she pleaded, “Please. Beau, this is my best friend we’re talking about. I’m worried about her, and I don’t want her to let that jerk’s actions ruin her self-esteem. She needs some joy in her life after spending so much time with that troll.”

“Amen,” Hadley said.

“And you think I’m the key to happiness?” Beau asked. “Yeah, I think you need to try again.”

Olivia looked at him and sighed. “I will love you forever if you do this for me.”

Beau shook his head. Good grief, why was she laying it on so thick? He’d done plenty of things for her before. Why did she think he was even a good option?

He’d been thinking about a vacation, but his work was his life. Every time he thought about taking time off, the list of things he wanted to do was inconveniently blank. “I want a vacation, but I have no desire to take romantic walks on the beach.”

Olivia perked up with wide eyes. “Good, because I know for a fact she’s planned to go snowboarding.”

“What? Does she even know how to snowboard?” Beau asked. Snowboarding was incredibly dangerous if she didn’t know what she was doing.

"No, but that's the point. She planned a bunch of things she's never done before because she wants to be adventurous. I bet you could even convince her to go ice fishing."

He could get on board with ice fishing. Snowboarding was fun, and he could think of a few more winter activities he'd enjoy.

"What kind of romantic things does she have planned? I don't have to do those, right?"

Olivis shrugged. "Probably not, but I'm guessing it would include reservations at awesome restaurants. I know you like to eat, right?"

Pinching the bridge of his nose, Beau counted backward from ten. It was a stupid idea.

"Come on, Beau. You could save the day and have fun. Win, win," Hadley said.

Letting his hand fall to the desk, he asked, "How much is this going to cost me?"

"What if you let her cover the activities she's already pre-paid and you pay for the meals and extras?"

"Paying for meals makes it seem like dates," Beau added.

"But we all know they're not dates. You're both just on an adventure together. Who cares what anyone else thinks?" Hadley asked.

There were dozens of reasons he kept his distance from Anna, and this was the absolute worst time to get involved. "Is her mom going to slash my tires while we're gone?"

A wicked smile grew on Hadley's lips. What had he just done?

"No! I promise to keep an eye on her," Olivia said as she scrambled to her feet. "I'll take care of all the wedding mess, keep her mom distracted, and I'll clean your apartment for a month."

Two knocks sounded at the door before Gage walked in with a navy tie hung around his shoulders. "What's up?"

Hadley pointed an accusing finger at Beau. "We're trying to convince him to go with Anna on her honeymoon."

Gage's wide eyes jerked to Beau. A floating light bulb might as well have turned on above his head. "That would be awesome."

"Nobody asked you," Beau said, leveling Gage with his signature "tread carefully" frown.

Gage went on as if Beau weren't trying to burn a hole through him with his stare. "I bet she has reservations at the best restaurants."

"That's your reasoning? Food?" Beau asked.

"Filet mignon," Gage slowly enunciated.

The argument with Gage was lost. Hadley had won his heart with food.

Beau wasn't so easily bought. "I can afford my own steak."

Olivia clapped her hands, clasping them to her chest. "So it's settled."

"The only thing that's settled is that I'm not going."

There. Foot down.

Gage scooted to Hadley's side and wrapped an arm around her. "Come on, man. I can handle things here. It's just a week."

Beau glared at his traitorous friend. "Whose side are you on?"

Gage tilted his head toward Hadley who sported a closed-lip grin.

"I don't need a break or a vacation. I like my job. Everything is great."

That was true enough. Life was a walk in the park. There was absolutely zero reason to shake things up, especially with his sister's best friend..

Gage pulled Hadley tighter to his side. "But Anna does need someone to go with her. Even if you don't need this, she does, and it wouldn't kill you."

Beau rubbed the back of his neck beneath the stiff collar of his shirt. "How far away is this place?"

"About an eight-hour drive," Olivia said.

Eight hours. Eight hours stuck in a car with a woman who just found out she got cheated on minutes before her wedding.

"That sounds like an absolute nightmare."

Olivia bent down beside him to whisper, "Beau, please do this. Anna is my best friend, and she needs this trip, and she needs someone with her. You don't have to do anything you don't want to do."

"Except go," Beau added.

Olivia's eyes drifted closed. "Please," she begged again.

Why was he considering this? Anna's problems weren't his problems, but it was hard to ignore Olivia whenever she was worried about her friend. His sister was the kind of person who would do anything for anyone. She'd give everything she had to help others.

Olivia got that from their mom, but that selflessness hadn't been passed down to him. Still, a tiny, nagging voice in the back of his mind said he should try to be more like his selfless sister.

Beau's chin fell to his chest. Olivia wouldn't let it go until he gave in. "Fine. I'll go."

Olivia and Hadley bounced up at the same time with matching whoops.

Gage walked over and slapped a hand on Beau's back. "Thanks, man. I think this will be good for both of you."

"Don't talk to me. You're cleaning toilets until further notice."

Gage rolled his eyes. "Yes, boss."

Olivia and Hadley darted for the door at the same time. "Start packing. We'll be back in an hour with Anna's bags."

Beau shook his head as the door slammed closed behind them.

Gage picked up the mug of coffee Hadley had brought Beau and took a sip. "Time for a vacation."

Vacation. How ridiculous was it that Beau had no idea how to go about taking a break. "Maybe they'll tell Anna the idea, and she'll shut it down."

Gage shrugged. "You're right. Who wants to go on a vacation with the Grinch?"

There. Beau wouldn't start packing until he knew for sure he was actually required to go.

Gage chuckled as he headed for the door. "You need to borrow a suitcase?"

CHAPTER 6
ANNA

The weight crushing her chest followed them out of Blackwater, Wyoming. Even with four hours between them and the chaos she left behind, the ghost of her mother's hands might as well be wrapped around her throat.

The emails. The messages. The voicemails. Trying to manage them was like trying to drink from a firehose.

Add in the slight nausea from looking down at her phone while riding, and she was five minutes away from full-on motion sickness.

Dropping the phone onto her lap, she rested her heavy head back and closed her eyes. Beau was a surprisingly good driver. He obeyed all traffic laws, including using his turn signals and maintaining a speed within the limit.

It was unexpected from someone she'd always

assumed lived by his own rules. Not that Beau had ever been a troublemaker. He just didn't care much about what other people thought.

At least, that's what she thought he thought.

Okay, that was getting confusing. She'd assumed a lot of things about him over the years, knowing he wouldn't give her an answer if she straight-up asked.

Now, he didn't have much of a choice but to talk to her. Well, he could ignore her, but maybe if she didn't push too far, he'd talk to her long enough to help the nausea ease.

Twilight settled like a blanket over the land around them. Shadows of forests and rocks crept over the hills and valleys. It really was beautiful.

She'd been looking forward to the drive to Colorado. Too bad she'd been too busy to look up and see it until it was almost too late.

The man beside her hadn't said a word unless spoken to since he got in the car. His long arms were relaxed with hands placed correctly at the ten and two on the steering wheel. Anna turned her attention to him, "What are you thinking?"

Beau kept his attention on the road ahead. He'd changed into a gray, long-sleeve thermal, jeans, and worn boots before tossing his duffel bag into the trunk of her car.

He hadn't put up a fight at all when she suggested they take her car instead of his truck. She felt bad enough for dragging him along with her. The last thing she wanted was to put miles on his vehicle.

"I'm not thinking. I'm driving."

"Doesn't that require thinking?"

Beau shrugged.

Anna picked up her phone and opened the Instagram app. The nausea had dissipated enough. "Nice talk. We should do this again sometime."

The flood of messages brought the nausea back. One of the drawbacks of being followed by hundreds of thousands of strangers on social media was that they all wanted the inside scoop. Everyone wanted a piece of her life that no one else had, and that meant plenty of people had zero qualms reaching out and asking how her wedding went.

It didn't matter that as far as they knew, she should be spending this time with her new husband.

It didn't matter that what she'd thought would be the best day of her life turned into the worst.

It didn't matter if she wanted to share the most private parts of her life or not, someone was going to find them and exploit them.

There were also plenty of wonderful people out there who genuinely wished her the best. Those were the ones she appreciated. If only she had time to cultivate all of those sweet friendships the way she wanted to.

Her phone rang, displaying the name of the wedding florist. She answered the call and pressed the phone to her ear. "Hey, Fiona."

"Hey. How are you doing?" Fiona asked, lacing her soft words with pity.

"I'm okay. Thank you for asking."

"You know I'm always here for you if you need anything, and I'll be praying for you during this hard time."

Anna turned toward the passenger window. Another kindness to be added to the day.

As much as she wanted to say Dean had crushed her, it wasn't true. In fact, his infidelity had opened her eyes to the goodness of her community. Mixed in with the snide comments of people on the internet were prayers and kindness from so many people she'd grown up with in Blackwater.

"I appreciate that so much."

"Well, I also wanted to reach out and let you know that Hank and I have decided to void your bill."

Anna sat up straighter. "No! I'm paying you. Those flowers were gorgeous, and what happened wasn't your fault."

"I know, but I wouldn't sleep well at night knowing I'd added to your distress. Honey, you deserve a wonderful man who will love you and only you for the rest of his life."

"Fiona, I had no idea you were such a romantic."

The older woman giggled, and the sound chased away some of the darkness that had settled over Anna throughout the day. "You don't become a florist without believing in love."

"I still want to pay you for the flowers," Anna said.

"Don't take this blessing away from me. I'm a grown woman, and I say your money isn't any good here," Fiona said, stern and proud.

Anna gulped down the emotion threatening to clog her throat. She'd find a way to help Hank and Fiona someday. "Thank you. That's so kind of you."

"Keep your chin up. God has this all figured out."

"I know He does." Knowing was one thing. Being patient enough to trust Him was a different ball game. Easier said than done.

Anna ended the call and immediately made another call. Everly answered on the second ring.

"Hello."

"Hey, girl. I had to call and say thank you for everything you did today."

"No problem at all. I know exactly what it feels like to have the rug ripped out from under you like that, and I wouldn't wish it on my worst enemy."

Anna hadn't known Everly before she married Blake, but knowing others found love after betrayal kindled a spark of hope. "I'm so sorry, friend."

"Don't be. It was for the best. The Lord had a plan for me, and it included Blake."

Anna glanced at her bare finger. Maybe some good would come out of this mess. At least she found out about Dean's affair before she married him.

"I'm so happy for you," Anna whispered. It was easy to mean it. Everly's happiness didn't have anything to do with Anna's low moment.

"You have a group of people praying for you, girl."

The tension in Anna's chest released. Maybe that was what she needed. Faith, hope, and trust. "Thanks again. You have no idea how much you helped today."

"Get some rest, and call me if you need anything else."

Anna pressed the microphone on her phone and spoke a note to her to-do list. "Send Everly a gift basket. Ask Haley Harding to design an ad for Fiona's Flower Shop. Call the Blackwater Messenger and ask about ad space."

When she raised her head, Beau was looking at her.

"What?" she asked.

He returned his gaze to the road. "Nothing."

"Why did you look at me like that?" It was the first time he'd noticed her at all since they started driving.

It was not the first time she'd noticed him though. It was difficult not to look at the quiet man that took up too much space in the cab. She'd be sharing more than the console between them for the next week. Would traveling with Beau be easy?

"I just figured you'd have someone else handle that stuff for you."

Anna scoffed. "This is my mess."

"Agree to disagree," Beau said stoically.

"You think Dean is going to care about any of this? All he needed to do was show up. Well, and be faithful, but silly me thought that was a given."

She scrolled through the messages, but most had little to do with him. "Not getting married today really did a number on my social platform. Designers and boutiques made custom pieces I was supposed to wear. Now, I have to find a way to tell them that the expensive clothes they gave me won't be featured in my beautiful wedding photos."

Her phone rang again, and she quickly answered. "Hey."

"Hey. What are you doing?" Olivia asked.

"Oh, just burning bridges. The usual," Anna said.

Beau made a noise, and she looked over at him. Was that a chuckle?

"You like it when I'm melodramatic?" she asked.

Beau didn't respond, but his mouth lifted in the slightest grin in the fading sunlight.

He was actually grinning. Why did that small expression trigger her own smile?

Olivia huffed. "Tell him not to be a jerk."

"I'm not being a jerk. I'm minding my own business," Beau said loud enough for Olivia to hear.

"That's true. He hasn't said two sentences before now," Anna confirmed.

"Tell him not to be a knot on a log either," Olivia added.

Anna glanced at Beau, but he ignored his sister's correct assessment. "I'm going to go out on a limb and say he heard you."

"I just wanted to check in. You two behave and play nice."

"Yes, ma'am," Anna and Beau answered at the same time.

Olivia's laughter surrounded her quick "Bye" as she ended the call.

Anna checked the map on her phone. "It looks like we're about five minutes from the resort where we're staying tonight."

"Just tonight?" Beau hadn't asked many questions about the trip, so she hadn't felt the need to offer anything.

"Yeah. We still have a few hours before we get to Freedom where we'll stay the rest of the week. We have a few things planned for tomorrow, but we can talk about what you want to do after we have dinner. We have reservations at the resort restaurant. It's supposed to be amazing, but we can go somewhere else if you want."

"It's fine with me," Beau said.

"You don't even know what it is."

Beau shrugged. "I don't care. I assume they'll have food, so that's all that matters."

Hmm. No push-back on the restaurant. That was new. Dean liked to make most of the decisions, and he'd been particular about the places he ate, so planning a lot of the honeymoon had been stressful.

All of the worrying she'd done over this trip with her future husband was wasted. Anything she'd planned with him in mind was like a slap in the face.

A few minutes later, the Snowy Peak Ski Resort came into view. White lights twinkled over every tree, column, and awning. Wreaths were hung in every window, covered in a light dusting of snow, and the moonlight shone bright over the mountains in the distance.

Beau parked in front of the stately entrance and turned to her. "This is it?"

Anna looked at the lodge. What had Beau expected? A quaint B&B? A roadside motel? The question didn't hold judgment, but was there a little bit of awe in his tone? She'd chosen the luxury hotel thinking it would be the perfect place to spend her wedding night.

That vision went up in smoke hours ago. There would be no honeymoon activities tonight.

"Is this okay? It's already paid for."

Beau nodded once and slipped out of the car just as a doorman wearing a long black coat and hat opened her door. Taking his hand, she stepped out into the cold night.

Another doorman met Beau at the trunk and reached for their luggage.

"I got it," Beau said, shouldering both bags with ease.

Anna pressed her fingers over her mouth as her lips spread into a grin. This was going to be a fun trip.

CHAPTER 7
ANNA

Beau stepped to the side at the door to their room, motioning for her to enter first.

Anna knew what to expect as she stepped inside. An open entryway spread into the common area with a sectional sofa, a sleek television disguised as artwork, and a minibar in one corner.

It was lavish and outrageous, but nothing inside the room compared to the view through the floor-to-ceiling windows that led onto a private balcony.

Anna stepped inside and turned to study Beau. He followed her in but didn't put their luggage down. His gaze swept over the room, and his chest rose and fell in a deep breath.

What was he thinking? His expression gave nothing away. Would he see the whole thing as outrageous—a gross waste of money?

Anna saw it that way, but Dean had expected

nothing less than lavish for their honeymoon. Status mattered to him in a way it never had to her.

Setting her jaw, she pushed thoughts of Dean out of her mind. “The bedroom is this way,” she said, heading for the open door near the sofa.

Beau followed her into the room and looked around. “Where do you want your bag?”

Anna pointed to a spot beside the bed. “You can just leave it there. Thanks for bringing it up for me.”

“No problem.” He turned and started for the door.

“Where are you going?”

Beau’s brow lifted as he pointed to the common room. “The couch.”

Oh, of course. There was one bed—a king—in the large bedroom. “Well, you can leave your bag in here.”

“It’s just one night. I’ll let you have your space.”

Space. She had a lot of space in the big bedroom by herself.

“What time are the dinner reservations?” he asked.

“Seven.”

The whole interaction had her skin crawling. Why did things have to be weird?

Because she was on her honeymoon with a man who wasn’t her husband. Things were bound to be awkward.

Beau glanced around the lavish room. "What's the dress code?"

"Business casual." Hopefully, Olivia had prepared him for some of the nicer activities Anna had planned. If not, he could wear what he wanted and that would be it.

Beau nodded and left, shutting the door behind him.

With thirty minutes until they needed to be downstairs for dinner, Anna opened her suitcase and unfolded the garment bag. Carefully, she picked through the outfits she'd brought. The sleek, white gown she'd intended to wear tonight mocked her as she pushed it aside.

Every piece of clothing she'd packed had been sent by boutiques from all over the world. Her agreement with each boutique stated she would wear the free clothing and share photos on social media in exchange.

Rubbing the back of her neck, she stared down at the dresses, sweaters, and coats. She couldn't wear any of it, and she'd have to send every piece back. If pictures circulated of her on her honeymoon with another man, it would do more harm than anything.

The outfit she had on would have to do. Shoving off her coat, she tossed it onto the bed and stepped in front of the large mirror by the closet. Her hair needed attention, but the fitted, scoop-neck sweater would have to do. The blush color highlighted the blue in her eyes, and the tailored charcoal slacks gave the outfit a business casual air.

The crushing silence settled on her shoulders. Who cared what she looked like? Everything seemed so unimportant in retrospect. She wanted a warm meal and twelve hours of uninterrupted sleep. As if that would make today disappear.

Opening the bedroom door in a rush, she stopped short when she spotted Beau lowering his arms after removing his shirt.

Thankfully, the white undershirt he wore was still tucked securely into the waist of his jeans or else she would have witnessed a real show.

It had been a while since she'd seen him in a short-sleeve shirt—at least a few months. Had his shirts always pulled tight over his shoulders and back?

"Um... sorry. I should have knocked or something," she sputtered.

Beau tossed his shirt onto his duffel bag and grabbed a gray button-up. "Just changing shirts. What's up?"

"I was thinking we could see if they'll seat us early for dinner. If you want."

Beau gave her his signature nod, and that was all. As much as she loved to talk, his simple gestures were much better than Dean's constant protests and complaints.

Three minutes later, Beau was dressed in a gray button-up and black slacks.

Okay, so the man could pull off grease monkey and urban chic. His olive skin paired with thick, dark hair and a neatly trimmed beard was the perfect mixture of masculinity and style. He'd be a great model if she ever decided to expand her social media platform to include men's fashion.

As if Beau Lawrence would ever agree to be her model. He'd never commented on her influencer status, but he probably thought it was silly.

Fireside was the most formal of the three restaurants in the resort. The dark ambiance was broken up by white tablecloths spread throughout the room and flickering candlelight. The dark night through the large windows featured the Rocky Mountains bathed in the glow of the moon.

A host wearing all black greeted them with a subdued smile. "Good evening."

"Reservation for Lawrence," Beau said, stepping up beside her.

Lawrence? She'd booked the reservation under Dean's name, assuming she'd be Mrs. Simmons tonight.

"Right this way," the host said as he gestured toward the dining room.

Leaning closer to Beau's side, Anna whispered, "Lawrence?"

"Olivia texted earlier that she changed all of your reservations into my name."

Anna lifted her chin as she wove through the dining room. Olivia had outdone herself. All of her friends had come through today. What could have been an awful day was reminding her of all her blessings.

The host recounted the specials and quietly slipped away.

Despite the gentle gnawing in her stomach, Anna couldn't tear her attention from the beautiful view. Snowflakes slowly drifted to the ground in front of a peaceful mountain scene.

Beau didn't look up from the menu until a young waiter appeared beside their table. "I'm Grayson, and I'll be at your service this evening. Can I start you off with a glass of our house wine?" He showcased the bottle as if it were a priceless relic that belonged in a museum.

After they both declined the wine and requested water, the waiter took the wine glasses from the table. "Do you have any questions about the menu?"

"I don't. What about you?" she asked.

Beau shook his head and lowered his menu.

Hmm. Everything on the menu appealed to her in some way. Deciding would be difficult.

Beau's hand slapped onto the table, and Anna jerked, startled by the thud and the rattling of the glass candle holder in the center of the table.

The breath halted in her chest as her attention jerked up to Beau. His stern expression had her heart pounding, but his focus was fixated on the young waiter.

"Eyes up here, buddy."

The waiter's eyes widened, and the wine glasses he held in one hand clinked together. "I—I'll just give you some time to look over the menu."

The terrified man sped toward the kitchen as if Beau might come after him. Couples turned in their seats to find out the cause of the commotion.

Anna leaned forward, pressing the menu to her chest. "What was that?"

"He was looking down your shirt," Beau explained as he resumed browsing the menu.

Her neck and cheeks heated as she glanced down at the scoop neck of her sweater. It wasn't a revealing top, but from the waiter's angle, he probably had a nice view of her cleavage.

"You're kidding," she whispered as the heat spread up to her ears. She took great pains to make sure her clothing was modest and tasteful. She hadn't thought twice about the sweater. It seemed safe enough.

"Wish I was," Beau mumbled, engrossed in the descriptions of the food printed in front of him.

The people around them lost interest, but Anna's heart still pounded as if she'd tripped in front of everyone in the restaurant. “I’m sorry,” she whispered.

Beau still didn’t look up. “It’s not your fault he decided to oggle you. Men are pigs.”

The tension in Anna’s forehead eased, and the ache in her chest lessened. Beau’s defense of her might have drawn too much attention, but at least he’d been looking out for her. Maybe Olivia had been right to suggest he come along on the trip.

“All men? Are you a pig too?” she asked with a grin.

“I’m ordering the mud pie,” he said dryly.

A chuckle bubbled up her throat before she could stop it. The more she tried to rein it in, the more forceful the laughter became.

Beau looked up as she pressed a hand over her mouth, but she couldn’t hold it back. His self-deprecating joke let loose a different kind of hysteria than she’d been trying and failing to hold at bay.

A slow smile lifted on Beau’s lips as she covered her face with the menu. People were starting to stare again, but she couldn’t bring herself to care.

The phone in her purse rang, slowly sucking the joy out of the moment. Swiping away the moisture from her eyes with one hand, she reached for her purse with the other.

“You don’t have to answer that,” Beau said.

When she glanced at the screen, the name facing her made her blood run cold. “It’s my mom.”

Beau was back to his intensely interesting menu, but he wasn't so engrossed that he ignored her. "You still don't have to answer it."

But the pull to do as she'd always done was more than she could bear. She'd never ignored her parents. She'd never disobeyed.

The crushing truth crashed down on her. Even all of her loyalty and responsibility hadn't been enough to make them loosen the chains. Anna was twenty-eight years old, and her mother still told her what to do and demanded obedience.

She'd also never made them proud. Graduating with honors, working as an associate in the family law firm, winning cases—none of it was enough.

Despite her best efforts, her mother was probably livid and ready to burst on the other side of the phone call.

"Want me to do something about that?" Beau asked.

Anna glanced from the phone as it silenced and immediately began ringing again.

The muscles in Beau's jaw bunched as he eyed her phone. "Is she going to keep calling?"

Anna nodded. Of course her mother would keep calling. Catherine Harris would not be ignored by Anna or anyone else. She was born with an air of superiority that Anna didn't understand.

The ringing stopped, then started again. Beau

was still staring at her with his copper eyes, waiting for her cue.

The grip in her chest broke as she handed the phone to Beau. His rough fingers brushed lightly against her hand as he took it. He simply turned it off and rested it screen-side down on the table beside his silverware before leaning back in his seat.

That was it. She could have done that. Or could she? She'd never done it before. She'd never screened calls. Ever. Not from her parents, her friends, her clients, or anyone. She even answered Potential Spam in case it was a mistake.

"What if... what if there's an emergency?" Her voice shook along with her hands as she clasped them in her lap.

"Olivia will call me," Beau offered. "I'm nobody special, but I give you permission to take the night off."

The night off. It was a gift and a curse. She'd relish it now and pay for it later.

She studied Beau as he propped his arms on the table. He was much bigger than Dean. His arms were easily twice as thick as the man she'd spent the last year trying to please. Beau hadn't spent an hour prepping in the bathroom before they came to dinner, and he hadn't picked up his phone once since they left Blackwater.

A different waiter stopped beside their table, jerking Anna out of the ridiculous comparison she'd been making. The older man with graying black hair and weathered skin placed a glass of water in front of each of them before clasping the tray and his hands behind his back.

"Hello, I'm Joseph, and I'll be taking care of you this evening."

Anna requested a house salad and smothered chicken, while Beau ordered a steak and baked potato. When they handed the menus to the waiter, he gave them a departing nod and disappeared.

Once they were left alone, Anna leaned forward and asked, "Why did you agree to this?"

Beau tilted his head slightly. "Because I wanted a steak."

"No. Why did you agree to come on this trip with me?"

His attention shifted to the tablecloth. "Because Olivia told me to, and she scares me."

That wasn't the reason. It wasn't even half true. He wasn't scared of anyone. Sure, he'd do anything for his sister, but this? Coming on this trip with Anna was more than she'd expected Beau to do for Olivia.

"Beau."

The single word held a plea. He'd been helping her all day, but why? He didn't owe her anything. He'd never concerned himself with her problems before, and there had been plenty.

He laced his fingers together on the table and

looked at her. "There isn't an honorable reason. Stop looking for one. I'm here because you wanted to come on this trip, and your friend cares enough about you to clean my apartment for a month to get what she wants."

Okay. That was a good reason. At least there was something in it for him. She'd inconvenienced and let down enough people today.

"I appreciate it. When was the last time you took a vacation?"

Beau's attention moved from his hands to the restaurant around them, never landing on her. "The senior trip the summer after high school graduation."

That was a long time ago. Beau was in his early thirties. Olivia and Anna were a few years younger. Did she even remember much about him from school?

"Where did you go?"

"Camping."

Beau's senior trip wasn't unique. Most of their friends drove to a nearby winter sport resort, and a few wealthier friends flew to the Gulf Coast or Hawaii, sometimes San Diego or Las Vegas.

Anna hadn't gone on a senior trip. Her parents hadn't allowed it. Instead, she moved to Laramie and started her first semester of studies at the University of Wyoming, and Olivia had come with her.

Of course Beau would have gone camping with his friends. He'd always loved the outdoors and anything that involved getting his hands dirty.

Anna smiled softly. "And you haven't wanted a vacation since then?"

Beau let out a low huff. "Not really. I drank too much and woke up in a canoe about ten miles down the Snake River from where I started."

Gasping, Anna covered her mouth. "Ten miles?"

Two servers in black brought their dinner and placed the steaming plates in front of Beau and Anna. The warm scent drew a rumble from Anna's stomach.

Beau closed his eyes and bowed his head over the steak and potato he'd ordered. Of course he would pray before eating. He'd grown up in a Christian home and always prayed when their friends had meals at his garage.

Anna, on the other hand, had to pray discreetly when she was around her family. If her parents took notice of her prayers, they made a quick point to add their snarky comments. Worship of anyone higher than themselves was considered an offense.

Here, she could pray without judgment. Here, Beau would understand, and she didn't care what anyone else thought. Anna bowed her head and took stock of the long day. Just the act of praying reminded her to lean on God and the assurance of His love.

The meal was delicious. Beau practically scarfed down the food then relaxed in his chair, clearly satisfied.

Apparently, food was the answer to most problems because the unease and stress of the day melted out of her as she finished eating. They hadn't even picked up the conversation again when their waiter brought out a bowl with a thick slice of chocolate cake covered in chocolate syrup with whole strawberries on one side and a large scoop of vanilla ice cream on the other.

Despite her full stomach, Anna's mouth watered. "Wow. That looks delicious."

The waiter placed a spoon next to each of them and bowed. "Congratulations. Enjoy."

"I forgot I mentioned it was my wedding day while making the reservations," Anna whispered as soon as the waiter disappeared.

She picked up the spoon and scooped up a small bite of the cake. When Beau didn't reach for his, she gestured to his spoon with hers.

He shook his head. "That's all you."

"You don't like chocolate cake?"

"I didn't say that."

"I can't eat this by myself. I need you to help me."

After a few thoughtful seconds, Beau picked up the spoon and dug out a heaping chunk of the cake.

Somehow, he swallowed the bite without looking like a greedy chipmunk.

When he reached for his second bite, Anna chuckled. “What do you think?”

“It’s amazing, and you know it,” he mumbled before inhaling another spoonful of cake and ice cream.

Her lips spread into a smile as Beau enjoyed the dessert. “I hardly ever see you eat sweets.”

Beau paused and held his spoon above the plate. “Not much use for them when work is waiting.”

Anna dragged the tip of her spoon through the syrup. “You don’t hear about a lot of workaholic mechanics.”

“What else am I going to do?” Beau helped himself to a strawberry.

“So, you don’t love your job?”

“I do, but I don’t want to just sit in my apartment if I don’t have anything else to do.”

Dean worked a lot, but he also hated his job. Most of their relationship consisted of his travels and complaints about work. Now that she knew about his secret relationship, how much of what he’d said had been true?

The waiter appeared next to their table just as Anna scraped the bottom of the bowl.

“Can I interest you in coffee?” the waiter asked.

Beau quickly wiped his mouth with the white napkin. “Actually, can we get one of these to go?”

"Certainly."

Anna fought against a smile. "You really liked it?"

"Loved it. Are you going to help me eat it when we get back to the room?" he asked.

The room. Of course they were sharing a room. Dinner had eased some of the tension between them, but the thought of returning to their quiet room sparked new nerves within her.

Maybe sharing dessert with Beau would prepare her to share a room with him. After all, they had seven more nights to spend together.

CHAPTER 8
BEAU

A good steak could make even the worst situations bearable. If nothing else, he'd eat like a king for the next week.

Was food the way to Beau's heart? Probably. He just wasn't going to announce it to his present company.

Anna strode into the room with her shoulders pulled back and her head held high. An hour without her phone ringing or talking about Dean had done wonders for her mood.

"Oh! Do you want to check out the hot tub?" she asked, rounding on him with wide eyes and a bright smile.

No wonder Anna got everything she wanted. It wasn't easy to say no when she lit up like a sky full of fireworks when she was happy.

But the hot tub? No way. Anna was a knockout.

That was a fact, not an opinion. The less he saw of her, the better.

He put the dessert on the counter and headed for his bag. “Nope. I’ll be at the gym if you need me.”

He brushed past Anna without glancing her way, but her delicate fingers wrapped around his arm, stopping him in his tracks.

“Hey,” she whispered.

Every muscle in his body tensed. Why did Anna feel like a threat when she was this close?

Slowly, he turned. Her light-blue eyes searched him with a dangerous brightness.

Her words were soft, but they held plenty of weight as she whispered, “Thank you for coming.”

With a nod, he stepped out of her grip. Her fingers trailed across his bicep as he disappeared into the bathroom to change. When he stepped back into the room to grab the key card, Anna was wrapping a towel around her body.

More coverage was all for the best, but not when her top was strapless. He’d never found bare shoulders to be a problem, but she was hard to ignore when they were the only two in the room.

Beau grabbed the card from the counter and turned his attention toward the wall. “I’ll be back in an hour.”

After all but jogging to the elevator, Beau pressed the button for the first floor and leaned back against the wall. Threading his hands into his hair, he closed his eyes and sucked in deep breaths.

She needed to get one thing straight. He wasn't honorable or perfect, and he wasn't here for her.

He'd run away as many times as it took to get the message across. While she was doing romantic things like lounging in the hot tub, he would be as far away as possible.

Would distance keep his thoughts in check when he knew what she was doing? Probably not.

An hour in the gym with rock music blasting in his ears was enough to get his mindset under control. Anna who? She didn't exist in his world. If she did, thoughts of her were carefully filed away under "Not Beau's business."

The room was quiet when he returned. It wasn't that Anna was a loud person. She just had a way of screaming her presence whenever she was near.

Grabbing his sleep clothes, he slipped into the bathroom. Tile covered the floor and walls, and a granite countertop ran the length of one wall. The double shower was outrageously large, and the whirlpool tub was equally extravagant. This bathroom was bigger than his bedroom at home.

So what if he took an extra five minutes in the shower? The heat and water pressure soothed his aching shoulders after an unnecessarily tough workout.

Clear-headed and ready for bed, Beau tiptoed

out of the bathroom. The lights were still on, but there was no sign of Anna.

Good. She'd probably gone to bed already, and he could grab a pillow, hit the couch, and go straight to sleep.

He'd barely taken two steps into the common room before the balcony door slid open and Anna stepped inside. One hand gripped the towel at her chest, and the other shook as she closed the door behind her.

When her gaze met his, the color drained from her face, leaving dark circles under her eyes and pale lips. She'd been glowing when he left an hour ago.

"Anna?" Beau asked, taking a quick step toward her.

She melted just as he reached her, grabbing her body as her eyes rolled back and she went lifeless in his arms.

Gathering her to his chest, he knelt and brushed the wet hair away from her face. "Anna. Anna!"

Her eyes opened, and she blinked rapidly, grabbing for his shoulders. "What?"

Her skin burned against him, seeping through his clothes. "You're burning up. Have you been out there all this time?"

"Um, yeah," she said groggily.

Adrenaline surged through him as he wrapped her up and stood, cradling her in his arms. Gently, he rested her on the couch and pulled his phone from the pocket of his sweatpants.

"I'm fine," she whispered, pressing her shaking hands to her temples.

No, she was not fine. As a matter of fact, Beau wasn't fine either. His pulse raced harder than it had during his workout.

Travis answered quickly with a friendly, "Hey, man."

"I'm here with Anna, and she just spent an hour in the hot tub and passed out. What do I do?"

Travis's casual tone died, quickly changing to all business. "Is she conscious now?"

"Yeah."

"How long was she out?"

"A few seconds." A few seconds felt like hours when his chest seized, waiting that long moment for her to come back to him.

"Is she nauseated?" Travis asked.

"Are you nauseated?" Beau repeated for Anna.

She slowly shook her head. "No."

"She probably got too hot. Try putting her in a lukewarm bath for a few minutes and have her drink lots of water. Eating would probably help too."

The crushing fear began to ease as Travis's calm tone gave logical direction. "Thanks, man. I'll try that."

"Call me back with an update," Travis said.

Beau ended the call, putting the phone to the

side and scooted closer to the couch where Anna lay. "How are you feeling?"

"A little better. I didn't realize I was out there that long until it was too late."

"Travis said you need to sit in a lukewarm bath for a little bit. I'm going to run the water, and I'll be back to get you."

She gave him a tiny nod as her eyes drifted closed. She wasn't bouncing back as quickly as Beau hoped, but maybe the bath would do it.

When the water was running, he went back to get Anna. She opened her eyes when he knelt beside her.

"Are you ready to move?" he asked.

She nodded, and he took that as his cue. Sliding his arms behind her back and knees, he gently lifted her to his chest, leaving the wet towel on the couch. Her arms wound around his shoulders, and her head rested against his shoulder.

In the bathroom, he lowered her into the water, careful to set her down easily. Once she was settled, Beau quickly pulled his arms away. Being close to Anna, touching her, worrying about her—the closeness tangled his thoughts into an anxious knot.

"You okay?" he asked, stepping away from the tub where Anna wore nothing but a tiny, hot-pink bikini.

"Yeah. I'm feeling a lot better," she whispered,

raising her knees until they propped up out of the water.

"I'll be right back." Beau quickly jogged to the minibar and grabbed a bottle of water. Remembering Travis's suggestion to eat, he picked up the room service menu before heading back to the bathroom.

The color was returning to Anna's cheeks, and she gave him a soft smile as he handed over the water.

"Thanks. Sorry I caused so much trouble."

She had caused trouble, just not the kind she thought. "You scared the life out of me," He sank to the floor, resting his back against the wall beside the tub.

Anna swiped her hands over her face, leaving water droplets racing down her skin and dripping from her chin. "Sorry again."

Beau held up the menu and opened it. "What do you want to eat?"

"We just ate," she reminded him.

"Yeah, but Travis said you need food."

"What about the dessert?" she asked.

"I don't think that's the kind of food that's going to help you recover from overheating."

"But it's the kind of food that'll taste good," she pointed out.

Beau pushed to his feet. "Fine. We can start with dessert."

He grabbed the bag from the counter and took it into the bathroom. He opened the container with the cake, then the separate bowl with a lid on it.

"The ice cream is melted, but the cake looks good," he said as he handed her the spoon.

She slid the spoon through the soft cake and lifted the bite to her mouth. Her eyes drifted closed as she chewed.

The skin on Beau's neck heated. How did she make something as simple as eating seem attractive?

"Where's yours?" she asked.

"My what?"

"Spoon. You're eating this with me," she said firmly.

Beau shook his head and sat down beside the tub. "Nope. That's all you."

"You promised."

Her soothing voice had a way of turning off the rational part of his brain. How did she do that? Whatever she said seemed to make sense. It was as if she turned the volume down on his logic.

When he didn't move to get another spoon, she scooped up another bit of cake and held it out to him.

"Nope. I'm good."

She waved the spoon in front of his face. "You'll be better after eating this bite of cake."

She wasn't going to give it up, was she? Against

his better judgment, he took the spoon from her and slid the cake into his mouth.

Shoot, it was just as good now as earlier. He never ate desserts at home. Why had he been skipping the best part of the meal?

He loaded up the spoon with another bite and held it out toward Anna. “Happy now?”

Instead of reaching for the spoon, she leaned forward and took the bite.

And that was how Beau ended up feeding Anna cake in the bathtub on her wedding night.

CHAPTER 9
ANNA

Anna laid the spoon beside the few remaining bits of chocolate happiness and sighed. "That was the best medicine."

"Now I need to go back to the gym," Beau said, closing the container.

Anna rolled her eyes as she leaned back in the cool water. "I think you can afford to skip this one."

She'd seen more of Beau's well-defined muscles in the last three hours than ever before. The fitted T-shirt he wore pulled tight across his shoulders and around his arms, guaranteeing she noticed.

Aside from his physique, it was the silent worry in his eyes that captivated her attention. He'd jumped into action when she didn't feel well and brought her everything she needed.

"You don't have to sit in here with me," she said as she stretched out in the spacious tub.

He leaned against the wall, propping his thick arm on his knee. “I’d better keep my eye on you. I’d hate for you to pass out in the tub and drown.”

Anna rolled her eyes. “I’m feeling one hundred percent better. I got too hot. That’s all.”

“Can’t chance it. Olivia would kill me if I didn’t make sure you were okay.”

What did it say that his kindness made her chest swell with a warm happiness? Even if he was just looking out for her because he wanted to make his sister happy, that was an honorable reason, and she admired his devotion.

What did she really know about Beau? He was her best friend’s brother. He worked hard. He owned a business that he built from scratch. He cared about his family and would do anything for them. He went to church weekly and worshiped God instead of merely claiming to like Dean did.

And he was handsome. There was absolutely no denying it. His dark hair swept to one side, and he kept his beard short and neat.

He looked up at her, and their gazes met. His eyes were a light copper with flecks of gold. Had she ever made eye contact with him before today? Surely, she would have remembered the beautiful uniqueness of his eyes.

Anna crossed her arms over her chest, suddenly aware of the tiny swimsuit she was wearing. She’d packed it assuming she’d be on her honeymoon, then it hadn't been an issue when she sat in the hot tub alone.

Now, it was difficult to forget how Beau had tossed the towel to the side and carried her tightly against him into the bathroom.

She sat forward, using her arms to cover as much of her front as possible. "I think I'm ready to get out of here."

Beau got to his feet and grabbed a towel. "Are you sure you're okay?" he asked.

She stood slowly as the water slid off her bare skin. "I'm fine."

He handed her the towel and stepped out of the bathroom, closing the door behind him.

Anna hugged the towel to her chest. Beau had been so sweet to her all day. His behavior was completely at odds with the stern, silent man she thought she knew. She'd always respected him, but she didn't really know him.

Amazingly, she hadn't thought of Dean and the wedding much since dinner. Turning off her phone had done wonders for her mood.

She owed a thanks to Beau for that. If he hadn't said something, she would have let the calls, messages, and emails overrun her night.

After taking her time drying off and brushing through her tangled hair, she stepped out of the bathroom with the towel wrapped around her.

Beau sat at the table with his phone to his ear.

"Yeah, I think she's fine now. Thanks for your help."

Beau turned to her and let his gaze roam from her head to her toes and back up again.

He was checking on her, not checking her out. If that was all it was, why did her skin burn in the wake of his gaze?

"I'll call you later." Beau rested his phone on the table and stood. "You okay?"

She pressed her lips together and nodded. "I'm fine." She needed half a dozen deep breaths to steady her racing heart, but she was fine.

Beau pointed toward the bathroom. "Is there another towel in there? The couch is soaking wet."

Anna pressed a hand to her cheek. "Oh no. I'm sorry. I got out of the hot tub in a hurry and didn't dry off well."

"It's fine. I'll let the cushions dry and pull out the bed."

Anna's nose scrunched. "Sorry. It's probably not a pull-out bed."

Beau's shoulders sank. "What? Why not?"

"Those aren't standard in higher end rooms."

Beau's eyes closed, and he took a deep breath. "Right. It's fine. I'll just call and see if they can bring me a cot."

Anna rolled her eyes. "You don't have to sleep on an uncomfortable cot. The bed is king size. You can sleep on one side, and I'll sleep on the other. We don't have to even get close to each other."

Beau's attention shifted to her towel before quickly jerking back up again. "You should get dressed. It's cold out here."

She still had on her skimpy bikini, but Beau couldn't tell with the towel wrapped around her. Suddenly, the room wasn't cool anymore. Her face grew warm as she tightened the towel around her.

"Right. I'll go do that." She slipped into the bedroom and closed the door behind her.

What was she doing? Parading around in front of Beau wearing little to nothing? She'd never been particularly shy about her body, but she tended to favor modest clothing. The little bit she wore now was the opposite of modest, and she'd been pressed up against Beau's chest tonight.

Pinching the bridge of her nose, she closed her eyes and took a deep breath. Beau was a friend. He was the brother of her friend.

But he was being nice, and she was noticing him, and her thoughts were getting all twisted. Not to mention her body's unwelcome reactions whenever he was around.

She could blame it on the stress of the day, right? She'd found out about her fiancé's affair on their wedding day. That was plenty of cause for momentary lapse in judgment.

Shaking her head and pushing wayward feelings

to the side, Anna dressed in a silky pink tank top and shorts set. Everything else she'd brought to wear to bed was wildly inappropriate for a night spent with Beau in the same room.

Running her fingers through her hair, she stepped out of the bedroom. Beau had covered the couch in a few towels and stood by the window with his arms crossed over his broad chest, looking out at the snowy darkness. The expression he wore said he was tired until he turned to her.

He brushed a hand through his hair. "Everything okay?"

"Yeah. You look tired," she said low as the late hour wrapped around her like a heavy cloak.

He jerked his thumb to the couch. "Still wet. I think I'll wait for it to dry a little more and just sleep on it."

"That's ridiculous. Let's just go to bed. I'm exhausted, and so are you."

Beau rubbed a hand down his face and around the back of his neck. He did look tired, and she'd never seen the slow, sleepy side of him.

"Fine, but you can't tell Olivia about this. She'd think too much."

Anna chuckled. Olivia was funny and honest to a fault, so she'd probably draw all kinds of wild conclusions if she found out Anna was sleeping in the same bed as Beau. "My lips are sealed."

He stepped beside her, stopping only a few

inches away, and pointed his finger at her. "Mine are too. Don't get any ideas about taking advantage of me in the night."

She pressed her lips together to hold back the chuckle, but it bubbled out of her anyway. "Okay. I'll be a good girl."

Beau's eyes widened, and he dropped his hand. "Actually, I think I should sleep on the couch."

Anna rolled her eyes and pointed toward the bedroom. "Get in there. We're adults, and we can keep our hands to ourselves," she bossed.

He took his sweet, precious time eyeing the couch before making up his mind and marching past her into the bedroom.

Everything would be fine. They would sleep on opposite sides of the massive bed with plenty of free space for Jesus between them.

After all, this was Beau, and if he'd proven anything to her today, it was that he was one of the good ones—an important fact she hadn't noticed before he agreed to put his life aside for a week to come on her honeymoon with her.

CHAPTER 10
ANNA

The morning sun streamed through the window as Anna rolled over in bed. With the blanket and sheets pulled snugly under her chin, she sank into the comfortable mattress for half a second before blinking her eyes open. It took a moment for the events of yesterday to hit her like a freight train.

The wedding. Dean and Misty.

Beau.

The last thought allowed her to roll onto her back and stretch her arms over her head. By the time she crawled into bed next to Beau last night, she'd been halfway to the best sleep of her life.

Dear goodness, she'd slept next to Beau Lawrence. Popping up like a Jack-in-the-box, she looked to the other side of the bed to find it empty.

Had she dreamed it? But how did she explain

that she was indeed in the honeymoon suite at a luxury ski resort?

Pushing her fingers through her hair, she tossed back the blanket and got out of bed. Whatever waited for her, she needed to face it head-on.

Anna stepped into the common area of the suite where Beau sat at the dining table with one hand wrapped around a mug of steaming coffee and a Bible open in front of him.

He glanced up at her, but his expression was unreadable. “Morning. Breakfast is ready.”

The warm smell of cooked meat hit her at that moment. The table was covered in all kinds of breakfast foods from bacon and eggs to fruit and yogurt.

The sight was enough to make her mouth water and conjure a lump in her throat at the same time. Beau had gotten up early to read the Bible and order room service.

Yep. The tears were coming, and she had precious seconds before they made their appearance. “Thanks. I’ll be right back.”

Slipping off to the bathroom, she splashed water on her face and dried the tears along with the rest. It was a shock. That was all. Would Dean have gotten up early to read the Bible? No. Would he have ordered room service before she woke up? Probably not.

That was all she needed to see the events of yesterday for exactly what they were—a blessing.

With dry eyes and clean teeth, her shoulders lifted easier. Who cared if Dean had betrayed her? Who cared if he left her with a mess to clean up? It was best to move on and call it a lesson.

Beau stood in the kitchen pouring more coffee from a carafe into his mug when she stepped out of the bathroom. It was amazing what a splash in the face could do for her mood.

"Morning," she said, allowing the genuine smile to have its way.

Beau rested his back against the counter. "I asked Olivia what you'd want, but I ordered a little of everything. I'll eat whatever you don't want."

Anna rolled her eyes. "There is no way I could even make a dent in that spread. You're eating with me."

Beau lowered the mug from his lips and pinned her with an intense stare. "Someone is bossy first thing in the morning."

Her lips pressed together to mask her grin. She'd never seen this side of him. Early morning Beau with tousled hair didn't hold the same intimidating air as regular grumpy Beau. "Let's just eat so we can get on the road."

"What are your plans for me today?" he asked as he followed her to the table.

"Well, I'm planning a three-hour drive to Freedom, then ice skating before the Tree Lighting Ceremony in town."

Beau took his seat and bowed his head, saying a silent prayer before reaching for the plates and handing one to her.

"Are you okay with that?" she asked.

"I'm not really an ice skating kinda guy. Do I have to do it?"

Anna scooped eggs onto her plate, suddenly starving. "No, but I'm going to do it. It's on my bucket list."

"Your what?" Beau asked.

"My bucket list. Things I want to do before I—"

"I know what a bucket list is. I just didn't expect you to have one."

Her back straightened as she reached for an apple. "Why not?"

"I just assumed you'd already done anything you wanted to do."

"Why? Because I have money?"

It was a valid question. People assumed that money bought everything. To an extent, the thought was correct. In reality, money only caused problems. She'd watched her family blow through money like it meant nothing her entire life. Now, she made sure to save, invest, and spend her money wisely.

Aside from a lavish wedding. Most of that had been planned back when she was a pre-teen and hoping Justin Bieber would ride her off into the sunset in a pink convertible.

Thank the Lord for unanswered prayers.

Beau shrugged as he tore a bite of bacon. “You’re an adult. You can do anything you want to do. Why wait until now to ice skate?”

Oof. She’d never thought of it that way. She could have easily checked things off her bucket list for years. The truth was, she’d been too scared to do anything. She cared too much about what her parents thought, and she’d been too wrapped up in her work responsibilities to think about doing anything for herself.

Anna rolled the apple over in her hand. “I don’t know. I guess I just thought marriage meant freedom.”

Beau scoffed, almost choking on his coffee.

Anna’s chin lifted. “What’s so funny?”

“I have the opposite view of marriage. Once you’re tied to someone, your life isn’t yours anymore.”

Rolling her eyes, she put the apple down and dipped yogurt into a bowl. “Why do men think being married is the equivalent of death? Sharing your life with someone should be fun and amazing.”

“I didn’t say it wasn’t those things. I said you’re tied to someone else. That means you make decisions together. If *you* want to do something for *you*,

you might as well go ahead and do it before you settle down and have to involve someone else."

"I guess that makes sense." Maybe Beau was on the right track. At least he viewed marriage as a partnership and not a prison sentence.

"What kind of things are on this list?" he asked.

Shoot. She hadn't thought he'd care to know the details. Why was she nervous to tell him? It wasn't as if any of the things she wanted to do were a secret. They'd be checking off a bunch of them on this trip.

Well, item number one had always been "get married." It didn't look like that one was happening anytime soon.

"Things like snowboarding, ice skating, seeing the northern lights, and flying in a hot air balloon."

"Those are kinda boring," Beau said as he took another bite of bacon.

"Ugh. Rude," Anna spat. "How dare you judge my list."

"Just saying. Seeing the Northern Lights sounds fun, but if we're going to do some once-in-a-lifetime stuff, at least make it a little crazy."

"What's on your bucket list?" Anna asked quickly.

"I don't have a bucket list. I do what I want when I want."

Rolling her eyes, she dragged her spoon through

the yogurt. "Okay, well then what's something you think we should do?"

Beau shrugged. "Do you have a tattoo?" he asked.

Anna's eyes widened. "No! Of course not."

"Ever thought about it?"

"No. I have a corporate job."

"Hide it," Beau retorted quickly.

Anna stared at Beau with her mouth hanging open as he stuffed his face with scrambled eggs and hashbrowns. How could he talk about getting a tattoo like it was something someone might do on a regular Tuesday?

Her mouth closed after a few seconds. Would it be so bad to get a tattoo? Beau had plenty of them. She'd noticed a few on his arms whenever he wore T-shirts but hadn't gotten close enough to see what they were.

Because she had no business getting that close to Beau. He kept everyone at a distance.

"You thinking about that tattoo?" Beau asked without looking up.

"No, I'm not," Anna quipped.

They finished breakfast without more conversation, but she *was* thinking about the tattoo. Or rather, she was thinking about what Beau said about her bucket list. The things on her list *were* boring in a way. None of them would push her out of her comfort zone.

After breakfast, they packed and checked out of the hotel. With a long drive ahead, Anna opened her laptop and checked in with work while Beau drove farther into the Rocky Mountains.

She made a point to only open her work email. There wouldn't be any disasters waiting there. Well, no disasters that were hers. Solving problems for clients actually did wonders for her mood.

After an hour of staring at the screen, Anna stretched her arms above her head. Snow blanketed the mountains in a glistening white as the sun cast its rays on them.

Beau's phone rang, slicing through the peaceful silence she'd gotten lost in all morning.

He answered the call and raised the phone to his ear. "What?"

Anna pressed a hand to her lips to hide her smile. It had to be Olivia.

"That's dumb. I'm not doing that." He was silent for another moment before he said, "No. Don't ask again."

It was difficult to look engrossed in the scenery when she was enjoying the back-and-forth between Beau and Olivia. The Lawrence siblings couldn't have been more different, but they'd somehow found an odd way to communicate and co-exist in each other's worlds.

"Don't call me to talk smack about people, especially that loser. I don't want to hear his name ever again."

Great. Olivia had something to say about Dean. Whatever it was, it probably wasn't good. Thankfully, Anna was also of the opinion that if she never heard Dean's name again, it would be too soon.

"Here. Talk to Anna." Beau held out the phone to her without taking his gaze off the road ahead.

"Hey, Liv."

"Good morning, sunshine. How is Beau treating you?"

Anna glanced at the man in question, driving stoically through the mountain passes. "Great actually."

"Good. Make him behave. If he gets unruly, put him in timeout for half an hour. That usually does the trick."

"I'll keep that in mind." Truthfully, she hadn't wanted to distance herself from Beau yet. The feeling might not be reciprocated, but his grumpiness had been on the low side of the scale since they left Blackwater.

"Also, do you want me to log in and respond to messages on your social media accounts? I don't mind taking care of that if it'll help you to step away from it for a while."

Olivia was truly a gift from the Lord, but she had no idea how many messages the fashion vlog received in a day. "Thanks, but I'll take care of it. I have to decide on a course of action before I do anything."

Anna glanced up as a cute little cabin-style store came into view. When the sign out front was close enough to read, she gasped and pointed. "Beau!"

The car swerved into the other lane before he reined it in. "What?"

"That bookstore looks so cute! Let's stop there!"

Beau let out a sharp huff. "You scared the life out of me! You could have gotten us killed!"

"Don't be scared. It's just a bookstore," Anna said before biting her lips together. Maybe she'd overreacted a tiny bit.

Beau slowed the car and turned into the small, gravel lot. "It's not the bookstore I'm afraid of," he mumbled.

"Tell him to shut up and drive," Olivia said. "He's such a drama llama."

"I know. He almost drove us into a ditch because of a bookstore," Anna said, glancing over at Beau to gauge his reaction.

He parked in front of the cabin and turned off the car. Reclining the seat, he pulled his ball cap over his face and crossed his arms. "I'll be waiting right here."

"Oh, come on. You're not going with me?" Anna asked.

"I'm going to let you handle things there. Remind him that he's a stick in the mud and this is his one chance to become moderately cultured," Olivia said.

Anna took in the surly man leaned back in the driver's seat of her car. "I don't think he cares about being cultured."

A muffled "Oink" came from behind his cap.

"He claimed men are pigs and he warned me," Anna said to Olivia.

"True story. I gotta run. Have fun. Love you."

"Love you too."

Anna stuffed the phone into her purse. "Come on, Beau. Please just go inside with me. I feel like I'm a teenager getting dropped off at the mall by my parents."

"Do people do that anymore?" he asked from behind his hat.

"I hope not. It was weird. Anyway, how about you go book shopping with me and we forget about ice skating?"

Beau lifted the hat from his face. "Really?"

"Really. I don't think I'd like ice skating anyway. I just wanted to try it to see if I would like it."

"That's actually a good reason to have something on your bucket list," Beau said.

"Yeah, but you got me thinking about how life is short and maybe I shouldn't do things I doubt I'm going to like."

"Fine, but I don't read books."

Anna rolled her eyes. Men and books. "Why? Are you afraid you'll learn something?"

"Actually, I read manuals all the time, and I have no reason to read if it doesn't teach me something."

Wow. So this was what it felt like to be speechless. He'd put her in her place, and her lips bloomed into a grin. "I love that. Good for you."

"I don't need a gold star," Beau said, completely bored with the idea of being rewarded for something that was expected of him as a business owner.

Anna turned in her seat to fully face him. "I have an idea."

"An idea like the one that got me on this trip? I'll pass."

"Stop acting like you're not having fun. How about you pick out a book for me, and I'll pick out a book for you?"

Beau pointed to the shop entrance. "I guarantee there isn't a single book in that place I'll like. You're setting yourself up for failure. Plus, why would you trust me to pick out a decent book for you? I don't even know you that well."

"What's my favorite color?" Anna quickly asked.

"Pink," Beau answered immediately. "That's not fair. You're kinda loud about it."

Ignoring his pessimism, Anna continued. "What are three things I love?"

"Fashion, love, and God."

Anna stared at him as the accuracy of his answer

sank in. Those were the exact things she would have listed as her top three, though, not in that order.

When she didn't speak, Beau shifted in his seat. "Those were easy questions. I don't know anything else about you."

There was a single, tiny, brave bone somewhere in her body that wanted to call him out. Beau didn't always speak, but he heard everything. How many things had he learned about her over the years and catalogued away?

"Okay. So are you going to buy me a book? If you do, you can decide what we do today besides ice skating," she offered. A tiny thrill shot up her spine. Letting Beau make the plans could either be fun or terrifying.

Beau slid his hat back onto his head and leaned the seat up. "Let's go find some books."

CHAPTER II
BEAU

This whole trip was full of firsts. Stepping into a bookstore wasn't on Beau's bucket list, but here he was, brushing shoulders with smelly literature.

Anna, on the other hand, lit up like a Christmas tree when she stepped into the cabin that had once been a home. "You've got to be kidding me," she whispered. "Look at this place!"

"This is not a joke. This is a nightmare," Beau said.

Anna bumped his shoulder. Well, her shoulder bumped against his arm because of the height difference. "Stop being dramatic. Go find my book."

Beau inhaled a deep breath and immediately regretted it. The musty smell of decaying words lodged in his nose. "Let's get this over with."

Shelves lined the walls, and freestanding shelves

were positioned in the middle of each tiny room. Labels were taped to the tops of the shelves, and he scanned the ones in the first room.

How were there this many books?

Think. What would Anna like?

He scanned the labels as he passed.

True crime? No.

Biography? No.

New Age? What did that even mean?

He wandered through a few rooms before seeing the first sign for romance.

Great. It was the largest room in the house. The wall shelves were covered from floor to ceiling, two tall shelves ran parallel in the center of the room with books lining both sides, and stacks of smaller books balanced in piles.

Anna's book was definitely in this room, but where to start? Something cavity-inducingly sweet. Something with a happily-ever-after. Something absolutely unbelievable.

He stopped at the first stack of books and picked up the one on top.

Ravaged by the Viking? Not it.

Claimed by the Highlander? Pass.

The Sheik's Hired Mistress? Nope.

Good grief. All of these sported shirtless men with long hair cradling women in flowy dresses showing way too much chest. Were these the books women read?

Hmm, maybe Anna's book wasn't in here. After walking around the room scanning the shelves, he searched for another idea.

Anna peeked her head into the room. "Find anything?"

"Uh, not yet." Heat crept up the back of his neck. Why were there so many shirtless men on these book covers?

Her brows lifted tauntingly. "You've been in here for half an hour. I was just checking to make sure you weren't lost."

Half an hour? Shoot. Why was this taking so long? They should have been back on the road by now. "Give me a few more minutes."

Anna smiled. "Okay. I'm going to purchase your book. I'll be waiting at the front."

Seriously? How could she have found a book for him in this place? He never agreed to read whatever she picked out. He'd toss it in his bag and donate it to the secondhand store when they got home.

A small table by the door leading out of the romance room caught his eye. A sign taped to the wall behind it read "Christian fiction."

That was what Anna would like. He picked through the books looking for something sweet. Most of them had couples hugging or kissing on the covers, but one had a grinning man with a snowy background on the front. He flipped it over and read the description about an attorney who would most likely fall in love with some guy she dated a long time ago. Coincidentally, the love story happened in Colorado at Christmastime.

Perfect. Beau headed for the register where a white-haired woman greeted him with a friendly smile.

"Did you find everything okay?" she asked.

Beau handed over the book with a man on the cover. How in the world did he end up here? If someone told him he'd one day buy a romance book for his sister's best friend while on her honeymoon, he would have laughed in their face. "Um, yeah. I think so."

The woman hugged the book to her chest. "Oh, this one is good! I read it the Christmas before last."

Beau scanned the room, but Anna was nowhere to be found. "It's for my friend."

"She told me all about you. From what I hear, you're going to like the one she picked for you too."

Doubtful.

The woman bagged up the book and handed it to him, smiling like she was the keeper of a really juicy secret. "Have a good day."

He wandered toward what he hoped was the exit and found Anna brushing her delicate fingertips lightly over the spines on one shelf. The wonder in her eyes seemed completely out of place in a house filled with dusty books.

Beau filed that away under things he'd never understand about Anna.

The groan and creak of his boots against the wooden floor alerted her to his presence. Anna turned slowly, glancing between him and the bag in his hand. "Finally. I was thinking I'd have to drag you out of here."

Beau shoved the bag at her. "Here's your book. Let's go."

She took the bag and handed one back to him. "Tradesies!"

"No, not tradesies. This is a very official business transaction. I just bought us some freedom from your boring bucket list."

Anna gasped, eyes wide and staring at him. "You take that back!"

Beau shook his head and held the door open for Anna to exit. "I said what I said."

Instead of forging a path to the car, she hung back by his side. "What are we doing instead of ice skating?"

"I need to make sure I can make it happen before I say anything."

He opened the passenger door for her, and she made a show of rolling her eyes before sliding into the seat. "Fine."

When he rounded to the driver's side, Anna was already staring at him. "What?"

"Open the bag," Anna demanded.

He pulled the book out and read the title. "How to Win Friends and Influence People?"

"Yep. It's a good one. I read it for the first time in high school, and I try to re-read it every year. Every business owner should read it at least once in their life."

Beau eyed her warily. "I don't need friends."

"Forget about the friends part. Read it as an entrepreneur," she said.

"Whatever." He scanned the cover again. The text was plain, and nothing about it was fancy. "This says it's the best self-help book of the twentieth century. Not only did you get me an old book, but you got me a self-help book. Are you serious?"

"It was written almost a hundred years ago, but it's still great advice. Just trust me."

Beau shoved the book back into the bag and tossed it into the back seat. "Fine. Look at yours."

Anna tore open the bag like a kid ripping into birthday presents. She held the book in both hands and read the title. "*Amending the Christmas Contract.*"

Beau started the car and shifted into reverse. "It said Christian, and it was in the romance section."

Anna read the summary on the back. "She's an attorney, and it's set in Colorado. At Christmas!"

Great. She was getting all high-pitched and excited again. It was just a book.

"This looks amazing." She pressed the book to her chest and looked at Beau. "Thank you."

"Don't mention it. Ever."

"Okay. I'll tell you all about it when I read it." She tucked the book into the bag at her feet and pulled out her laptop. "I'm going to try to get some work done."

Anna sure did a lot of work for someone on vacation. At least she could work wherever. He couldn't really fix vehicles from hundreds of miles away.

A soft hum came from Anna a few minutes later. "Listen to this. 'Your vlog post with Camille Harding inspired me to start up a clothes closet at my church. We've already had tons of clothing donations, and I can't wait to help the people in my community. Thank you for being an inspiration to women.'"

"You really get fan mail?"

"It's not fan mail, but a lot of women struggle with confidence. I love fashion, and I want everyone to feel comfortable in their own body. If my advice helps them feel empowered, then it's a win."

Beau would not engage. Talking about clothes would lull him to sleep, and he needed to stay alert for the rest of the drive.

"But I also want women to know that their worth isn't tied up in beauty or appearance. So I try to make sure my audience knows they're perfect and loved just the way they are."

When Anna was quiet for a moment, Beau glanced over at her to find her looking back at him. "What?"

"Nothing. Just wondering what you're thinking."

"Not much. Just that I wear the same T-shirt and jeans every day, and I'm pretty happy about it."

"Hmm. See, most women don't have that confidence. You're so sure of yourself, but lots of people struggle with it."

"Do you?" he asked. It would be a stretch to think the gorgeous Anna Harris was secretly self-conscious about her body.

"No," she said simply.

"Then why do you spend so much time doing this?"

"Because... I don't know. It matters to me."

"Strangers matter to you?" Beau asked.

"Yeah. Is that so unbelievable?"

Kinda. What was in it for her? She was serious about whatever fashion stuff she did online. It was tough to connect the dots when she didn't have skin in the game.

Beau shrugged, and Anna turned back to her laptop.

"Here's a message from one of my online friends. 'Hey, Anna. I know you're on your honeymoon, and I hope you're having a good time. Let me know when you make it to Colorado safely.'"

Beau's brows immediately pinched together. "She knows where you're going on your honeymoon? How well do you know her?"

"We've been friends for years. We met through

the vlog, and now we talk every day. Her name is Brittany, and she's from California. She hopes to open her own boutique one day. We've been talking about meeting in person someday, but since I'm afraid to fly, that's kind of a far-off dream."

"What if Brittany is really Brandon, and you're being catfished?"

Anna laughed. "Brittany is definitely Brittany. We've had plenty of video chats."

Beau turned his attention back to the road. He wasn't a woman, but he had a sister. Even though he didn't worry about getting jumped in parking lots, he did enough worrying about Olivia to make up for it. "Just be careful."

"I will." She typed furiously for a few moments before stopping. "Oh, great. People finally found out that Dean and I didn't get married."

The lack of emotion in her voice had Beau glancing over to check and make sure it was really Anna. "Is that bad?"

She scoffed. "Well, this woman is pretty excited that Dean is up for grabs now."

Beau's nose scrunched as he checked to make sure Anna wasn't joking. "Are you serious? That guy is a loser."

"How can you say that?" Anna spat. "You don't even know him."

As soon as the last word was out, she gasped and covered her mouth with both hands.

Beau gripped the wheel tight enough to strangle the life out of any living thing. "Are you serious?"

"I'm so sorry. I—I'm just so used to defending him. It just slipped out." Her hands slid up to cover her whole face. "I'm such an idiot."

"No, he's the idiot."

Why was he talking so loud? Why did it bother him that Anna had felt the need to ever defend Dean when he'd treated her like dirt?

Anna made a cracked, sobbing sound just before the waterworks started. Beau shifted in his seat. He was trapped in a car with a crying female on a winding mountain road. There wasn't even a place to pull over so he could make a run for it.

A second later, Anna was leaning on his shoulder, gripping the arm he'd so innocently rested on the console between them. The muscles in Beau's neck tightened as she wiped her eyes on his shirt.

No, no. He wasn't a shoulder to cry on. He didn't have any body parts made for soaking up tears.

What was he supposed to do with this? He did not do tears. In fact, he avoided them at all costs.

After a little bit more crying and sniffling, Beau held onto the wheel with the hand connected to the arm she had a death grip on and tentatively reached out and patted her shoulder with the other hand. Two tiny pats, just in case the leaking was contagious or something.

"It's okay. Maybe he fell off a cliff after the

wedding and you'll never have to see him again," Beau offered.

Anna's chin snapped up, and she stared at him for a few tense seconds.

Was that it? Was it all over now?

She let out a choked sound, then another that quickly flowed into more.

Was she laughing or crying? This was all kinds of confusing.

Anna released her choke hold on his arm and wiped her eyes with her fingers before reaching into the glove compartment and pulling out a pack of tissues. The chuckling continued until she'd dried her entire face and blown out a gallon of snot.

"Better?" Beau asked, hoping they were out of the woods.

She shook her head and lifted her chin. "I didn't want to say anything because it sounded stupid, even to me."

"What are you talking about?"

"I didn't want to say I was unhappy. I mean, I have a great job, a nice house, a successful fashion vlog, and I had a man who wanted to marry me."

Beau held up a finger. "Just because he wanted to marry you doesn't mean he should get to."

"Right, but why wouldn't I have wanted to marry him? He was successful, handsome, hard-working—"

"Because he was a loser," Beau supplied. "That was his first strike."

Anna laughed. "What were the others?"

"He wasn't good to you, and he cheated on you. He's out."

She fidgeted with the tissue in her hands. "You're right, but I was too blind to see it. I felt like I should be happy, so I pretended I was. I mean, who would believe me if I said I wasn't? I couldn't sit in my beautiful house with my successful career and seemingly perfect fiancé and complain about my lot in life."

"Um, last I checked you and everyone else in the world is allowed to feel the way they feel regardless of how much sense it makes," Beau said.

Wasn't it that easy? Why did she care so much about what other people thought, especially if it cost her her own happiness?

"I wish it were that simple," Anna whispered, turning to look out the window.

"What if we make a rule for this trip? You get to say what you want, feel how you want, and have fun without worrying about anyone else's expectations. It's not like you have anything to prove to me."

Anna slowly turned toward him. "Like I said, I wish it were that simple."

"Why can't it be? I'd much rather you be genuine than acting a certain way just because you think it's expected. You might like being yourself if you tried it."

She was quiet for a moment before whispering, "It would be too good to be true."

"Come on. Just forget about the problems for a little bit. Say what you want to say. Laugh if you want to. You can even cry, but be warned that crying makes me uncomfortable, so I have no idea what to do when you do that."

She chuckled and wiped her eyes again. "So I just get to be my unfiltered self with you for a week?"

"Yeah. Give it a try. I know you're always talking about finding love and living happily ever after, but you might find out that you're happy on your own."

"Are you going to be your true self on this trip too? It's only fair that if I do it that you do too."

Beau shrugged. "Sure. Don't expect anything nice."

She chuckled. "You mean you're not a secret teddy bear on the inside?"

He leveled her with a quick stare before turning back to the road. He had one word for her that would sum up his whole personality. He'd already warned her. "Oink."

Anna smiled and took a deep breath. "And when we get home, our lives go back to normal?"

"Only if you want to. You might get used to

being the real you and want to be yourself all the time," Beau offered.

Anna nodded and straightened in her seat. "Okay. It's a deal, but I have one rule."

"Fine. What is it?"

"What happens in Colorado stays in Colorado."

"I thought we already established that," Beau said.

"Yeah, but it's a rule now. It's official."

"Fine. If you have a rule, I have one too."

"Another one?" Anna tilted her head slightly as she studied him. "Go on."

"You can't use the fake smile with me," Beau said.

Anna's eyes narrowed. She actually had the nerve to look surprised. "What fake smile?"

"The one you wear all the time when you're trying to make people think you're happy. It's just me. There isn't anyone to impress here, and whatever happens this week is about you. Don't be fake."

Anna swallowed hard and took her precious time deciding if she'd take him up on the pact. Once she decided, she extended her delicate hand out beside him. "It's a deal."

They shook on it, and Beau focused on driving through the mountains. The trip would be ten times better if Anna could loosen up and have fun.

CHAPTER 12
ANNA

Bundled in no less than five layers of winter weather gear, Anna wrapped her arms around Beau's torso from behind.

"Ready?" he shouted to be heard through the helmets and screaming wind.

She'd trusted Beau when he whisked her away from her wedding disaster on his motorcycle. Why were her thighs shaking against his now?

"We don't have to do this if you don't want to," he reminded her.

It wasn't that. She wanted to ride a snowmobile, but her central nervous system was sending out all kinds of danger signals. "I'm ready."

"You sure?" he asked.

Bless his soul. He really wanted her to be comfortable, but he was giving her way too many chances to back out. If he didn't step on it soon, she'd get cold feet.

"No," she shouted above the engine noise.

"Hang on," Beau said as he turned to face ahead.

Anna tightened her hold as Beau took off. Closing her eyes and pressing the front of her helmet against his back was the most she could do at first. After a few minutes of steady riding, her tight muscles loosened.

What did it say about her that her fear faded in dangerous situations simply because Beau was around?

What did it say about him?

She'd promised he could choose what they did today, but even after he told her about the snowmobile idea, he'd asked if she wanted to do it.

That tiny freedom had made her think twice about doing something that had initially sounded terrifying. Beau wouldn't have suggested it if he thought it was unsafe.

It wasn't long before she could lift her head and look around. The terrain was unreal. Mountains surrounded them on all sides topped with beautiful, white snow. A blanket of blue spread across the cloudless sky.

Now that she wasn't breathing like a runner, the ride was actually nice. They weren't going as fast as she initially thought.

They drove along trails through wooded areas and open spaces that were breathtakingly beautiful.

Beau tapped her hands linked around his chest and pointed toward the woods. A moose stood in the forest chewing on what looked like leaves, seeming unbothered that she and Beau were passing through.

Beau gradually increased their speed until Anna's heart began to race for a new and exciting reason—freedom.

That's what this was. It's what she'd been missing all along. Now that she'd experienced it, would she ever be able to go back?

She didn't want to, but life and all of its pressures would slowly creep back in once they returned to Blackwater. She'd always loved her home, but lately, it had all of the makings of a prison in disguise.

The sun burned a warm orange as it touched the mountain peaks to the west, and she rested the side of her helmet against Beau's back. Everything about the day had been perfect.

Eventually, Beau turned to look over his shoulder. "You tired?"

She wasn't finished with her newfound freedom, but the muscles in her arms and thighs were starting to ache. The adrenaline hadn't allowed her to fully relax for hours. "Yeah."

Beau drove them back to the rental headquarters

where they returned their gear and walked out into the twilight. The smile on his face was brighter than she'd ever seen it.

"See? Maybe that should have been on your bucket list," Beau said as he opened the passenger door for her.

"It definitely should have. I loved it!"

Beau rounded the car and settled behind the wheel. The casual air he carried with him was something she desperately wanted. He was so sure of himself and content in his own skin.

But there was something she wanted more than his confidence. She wanted her arms around him again. Pressed against him, she'd found comfort like she'd never known. That was the source of the freedom that she'd been reveling in all afternoon. He'd broken down walls and torn off locks she'd used to protect herself for years.

She didn't want that cage anymore. This liberation was spreading within her, and it all started with Beau Lawrence.

He turned and looked over his shoulder to back out, but he paused when he caught her staring at him.

"What?" he asked softly.

"Nothing. Just... thanks for making me do that."

It was more than the push. It was his solid belief that she would feel better if she broke free of some of the bonds that held her down.

"I didn't make you do anything," he corrected.

"I know. I guess I meant to say thanks for showing me something new."

A slow smile bloomed on his lips as he backed the car out of the parking spot. "I knew you'd like it."

Anna hummed low in her throat. "How did you know?"

"Because I suspect you need to get off the beaten path more often."

A wild and unruly flock of butterflies swirled in her middle. His response sounded like a cop-out even to her.

Beau knew her. He watched and listened, and he knew things about her that she was afraid to admit. Maybe if she followed his lead, she'd figure out how to tap into that happiness he kept mentioning.

An hour later, Anna brushed a hand down the side of her jeans as she stepped out of the bathroom. Beau lay on his back, sprawled across the short couch. With one knee up and one arm draped over his eyes, he was the perfect illustration of relaxation.

"Are you ready to see some Christmas lights?" she asked.

Beau lifted the arm from over his eyes and looked her up and down. "If you are."

What was it about his appraisals that set her skin on fire? His casual looks made her want to shed a layer of clothing to get rid of some of the heat.

"I've heard this is a huge deal here. They turn on

the lights to all of the trees throughout the town square at the same time."

Beau didn't say anything as he pulled on his boots. There was a good chance he didn't care one bit about Christmas lights, but she'd been excited about the ceremony since finding out it would be happening while she was in town.

Freedom, Colorado was known for its small town charm and Christmas celebrations. Tourists flocked to the ski town from all over the world, but the place still had a peaceful air about it.

Before they'd even reached the square, big signs started popping up for event parking. When the lots they passed started to look crowded, Beau pulled into one that sported a vacancy sign.

Thick darkness covered everything as they followed directions from the lot's attendant toward the square. After walking only a few blocks, more and more people filled the sidewalks.

The square itself was bright and lively. Colorful shop signs lined the perimeter, cottage-like vendor stations were set up at intervals, and a temporary stage sat on one side of the open area.

Beau leaned closer to be heard above the chatter. "This place is packed."

"I told you it was a big deal." Anna checked her watch. "The lighting doesn't begin for an hour or so. Want to check out some shops first?"

"If that's what you want," Beau said, scanning

the crowd warily as if a monster might jump out at any moment.

Anna pointed to a sign on the far side of the square. "Stories and Scones sounds good. The sign says they have the best coffee around."

Beau glanced down and grabbed her hand in his. "Stay with me."

Her grip tightened around his hand instantly, and Beau led the way, creating a path through the hoard of people with ease.

Anna pulled her coat tight around her neck. Holding hands was practical. It had a purpose. Why did her entire arm tingle with the contact?

As soon as they reached Stories and Scones, Beau dropped her hand and opened the door for her to enter. Even after he released the link holding them together, the warmth in her chest lingered as she stepped into the shop.

A cheery bell above the door chimed as the warm scent of cinnamon and spices greeted her. Shelves of used books lined one wall, and small tables were dotted to the right of the entrance. Across from the bookshelves, a pastry case was filled with everything from croissants and muffins to cupcakes and pies.

An older couple worked at the counter, but a few younger girls filed out of the back room to refill the desserts in the case. Two men zipped around the espresso machine constantly making specialty drinks.

They stepped into the line, and she leaned close to Beau. "What are you getting?"

"Coffee," he said, crossing his arms over his chest.

"That's it? What kind of coffee?"

Beau shrugged. "Black."

Anna chuckled and pointed to a sign. "Their specialty drink is snickerdoodle latte."

Beau scrunched his nose. "Sounds complicated."

"I'm going to try it. I'll let you know how *complicated* it is."

She stepped closer, brushing her arm against his. "Wow. You're so warm."

He glanced at her with a smirk that lifted one side of his mouth. "I run hot."

Whoa. Her stomach did an intricate flip that stole her breath.

Yep. Hot was the correct way to describe Beau. How had she never noticed? The dark hair and copper eyes shadowed his masculine features, and the beard covering the lower half of his face gave him a mysterious air. Aside from his physical appearance, he walked and stood with a commanding presence that radiated power.

Maybe it was the grin. Had she ever seen him happy before this trip? He always just kind of existed, going through the motions and occasionally reminding everyone about how little he cared about everything.

When they reached the counter, Beau placed a hand gently on her back, moving so she could stand almost in front of him. He turned to her, waiting for her to order first.

Couldn't she get a minute to catch her breath from Beau's seemingly innocent touch?

When she didn't speak, Beau cleared his throat. "Um, can I get a snickerdoodle latte and a blueberry scone?" He asked the middle-aged woman at the register.

"Sure! That's a crowd favorite."

"What else?" Beau asked.

Anna tilted her head, looking up at him as if she were seeing him for the first time. "Is that not enough?"

"You might want something later." He pointed to the pastry case. "Get another dessert."

When Anna turned to the register, the woman waiting was practically beaming. "You two are just adorable. Are you on your honeymoon? You definitely have that young love look about you."

"Something like that," Beau said.

Oh, that was an interesting answer, considering that they most definitely were not on *their* honeymoon.

The woman clapped her hands to her chest. "I

wish you both the best. What can I get for you, young man?"

"Coffee. Black, please."

The woman turned to the older man behind her and whispered loudly, "Give them the lovers special."

The man winked at her and disappeared into the back room. A minute later, he returned with a white bag and handed it to Anna. "On the house."

"Thank you so much. I'm sure we'll be back for more. Everything looks delicious," Anna said. She removed her gloves and stuffed them in her pockets to let the warm cup heat her hands.

"I'd love to see you two again. I'm Jan, so ask for me if I'm not out here at the register next time."

With coffee and warm baked goods in hand, they moved slowly through the throng of people in the shop and out onto the sidewalk. More people had arrived in the short time they'd been in the store, and it was difficult to move around.

"It looks like people are finding their spots for the ceremony," Anna said as they passed a few families who sat on the edge of the sidewalks.

Beau pointed away from the stage. "There's a clear spot over there. Maybe everyone wants to be closer to the action. Is that too far away?"

"It'll be fine. Hopefully, we'll be able to see from anywhere."

Beau tucked the bag of desserts under his arm

and grabbed her hand before leading her through the mass of people. His skin was warm from the coffee, and the sensations she'd felt when he held her hand earlier were magnified.

She'd expected him to balk at her request to go to the tree lighting ceremony. She'd expected complaints or excuses. Instead, Beau indulged her completely without any friction.

When they reached the clearing, there were only a few other people, mostly couples, hanging around beneath a large oak tree.

Beau leaned one shoulder against the trunk of the tree and held up the bag. "Want a treat?"

Anna checked the time. "Sure. It should be starting soon."

He opened the bag and pulled out the smaller white bag containing the "lovers special."

"What do you think it is?" she asked.

He held it out to her. "You open it."

She peered into the small bag. Two large chocolate-covered strawberries sat at the bottom. Anna pulled one out and handed it to him. "Looks good. One for you and one for me."

Beau took his strawberry, but he continued to watch her closely as she bit into hers.

"What?" she asked when he didn't make a move to try his.

"Nothing."

"You don't like chocolate-covered strawberries?"

"I do, but you can have mine if you want."

If he liked it and wanted it, why was he offering it to her? After taking her time chewing, she found the courage to ask the question that had been burning in her mind since they left the bakery. "Why didn't you correct Jan when she asked if we were on our honeymoon?"

Beau turned his attention toward the stage. "It's kind of a long story. Explaining it while we were in line would have been weird."

Okay, so he had a point. They would have gotten some odd looks after explaining she was on her honeymoon with a man who wasn't her husband.

Anna didn't have a husband. She'd spent months preparing herself to be a wife both mentally and spiritually. She'd prayed and planned, but now she was single again—starting over from square one.

She'd been thinking less and less about Dean. The sting of his betrayal had waned as if more than two days had passed.

In fact, her life with Dean held a dream-like quality. It played like a movie in her head, but the woman in the vision wasn't Anna. She was watching the show from the sidelines.

Maybe it had all happened without her. The past almost seemed calculated for her—absent of her will. Had she slept through the entire thing?

Yet, the past forty-eight hours were burned into

her memory. She'd stepped into a world of color after a lifetime of black and white.

The soft Christmas music playing through the square changed to an upbeat tune as the mayor of Freedom took the stage. The man was younger than she'd imagined the mayor would be, but he held the audience's attention with ease.

"Welcome to Freedom's annual Tree Lighting Ceremony. Christmas is our time to shine here in Freedom. I've lived here my whole life, and this small town is more than lights and skiing. It's filled with hope, love, and community.

"I've always thought the tree lighting ceremony was more than pretty Christmas decorations. It symbolizes God's love for us. It lights up the whole world, and I'm always happy to be reminded of the gift of Jesus and his sacrifice for us."

Anna glanced at Beau who listened intently to the mayor. She needed the reminder of God's love. Dean might have hurt her, but that slight was nothing compared to the hope she had in Christ.

Everything was going to be okay. She was going to go on with her life, and her goal was to be stronger than ever.

Suddenly, the trees and light posts around the square flickered on, illuminating the dark sky amidst gasps and awes. The crowd erupted into cheers as the town transformed. Dozens of trees were wrapped in various colored lights, garland sparkled on every shop sign, and everything from snowflakes to doves hung on light poles as far as the eye could see.

The breath Anna inhaled tingled in her chest as "Joy to the World" filled the air. When the buzz of the crowd overtook the song, she turned to look at Beau with wide eyes. He wore a mischievous grin, but his gaze darted down.

Oh, she was holding onto his arm. When had that happened?

She let her hand fall away and wrapped it around her cup with the other one. "Sorry," she said, loud enough to be heard above the roaring of the crowd.

"It's fine," he whispered before turning to scan the scene.

Heat crept up her neck and cheeks despite the blistering cold. Beau kept his distance from everyone. She'd known him to be that way in all the years she'd known him.

But she'd never known him like this. Alone, relaxed, and just enjoying life.

Soon, the throngs of people on the sidewalks thinned and the lines in stores shortened. They visited each shop and vendor as she asked Beau repeatedly if he was ready to leave, but he never said yes. Instead, he carried the bags as they bought Christmas gifts for their families and friends.

Christmas shopping with Beau wasn't something she would have ever expected to experience in her life, but it should have been on her bucket list.

They drove back to the lodge in silence. With her head resting against the seat, she didn't feel the need to talk. Beau had been right beside her the entire day, and every minute of it had been perfect.

Back in the room, Beau took the bathroom first, changing into his pajamas and getting ready for bed. When it was Anna's turn, she took her time basking in a hot shower.

When she looked in the mirror, the woman staring at her was glowing. Not from the heat of the water but from the excitement of the day that still lingered.

The room was quiet when she stepped out of the bathroom. Unlike their room from the night before, this one had the bed, couch, TV, and a small table all together in one area. It still featured all of the opulence of a luxury honeymoon suite, but the atmosphere was cozier than the other place they stayed.

Beau lay sprawled on the couch asleep with one leg hanging off the side. He was much too big for the small piece of furniture, but he'd absolutely shut down her offer to share the bed.

It was probably for the best. She'd never slept in the same bed as a man until last night, and she didn't intend to make a habit of it. Even so, Beau was probably the only man she'd agree to sleep next to. Come to think of it, she trusted him more than any other man she knew.

She trusted too easily. That's what got her into the situation with Dean in the first place. Thinking the best of people sounded like a good thing until the people she loved and trusted started stomping all over her while she walked on eggshells.

Looking at Beau, it was difficult to keep her distance. Her heart made decisions, and her brain rarely got a say.

Had she wanted to be loved so badly that she'd been blind to Dean's affair? All she was left with was a taunting voice in her head saying "I told you so."

But what she was feeling for Beau was more than appreciation. It wasn't infatuation either. She wasn't in love, but it went against her instincts to push away from him when he was so kind and patient with her. He'd made it his mission to build her up and make her happy with herself, but he was drawing her to him.

Yeah, rushing into relationships only left her heartbroken. Besides, Beau wasn't interested in her. At least not in a romantic way. He'd only agreed to come with her to make his sister happy.

Anna's phone rang, and she quickly silenced it. Every time the noise pierced the air, her body froze as an unseen fear wrapped its claws around her neck.

But it wasn't her mother's name on the screen. It was Tiffany, Anna's legal assistant at the firm.

Anna slipped into the bathroom and closed the door. "Hello."

"Hey, I'm so sorry to call you this late, but we have a problem."

At least Tiffany didn't beat around the bush. "What's wrong?"

"Your parents are absolutely losing their minds. I mean, Catherine makes me want to melt into the floor on a regular day, but she's been furious all day. I have plenty to do to take care of your cases this week, but she's been loading me up with tasks for her cases too. I'm not talking about sending update letters or returning calls. She's had me drafting motions and proposed orders. She even asked me to draft a brief."

Anna placed her hand on the cool granite counter next to the sink. Of course her mother was unhappy with her. She hadn't answered a single call or text since she ran off from her wedding. It hadn't crossed her mind that her mother would take it out on Tiffany.

"I'm so sorry. First, she shouldn't have asked you to draft a brief. That's not your job."

"I know!"

"And I'm sorry this is coming down on you. She's mad at me."

Tiffany let out a deep, soulful sigh. "I'm really

sorry about the wedding. I couldn't believe it when I heard."

"It's okay. I'll be fine. I—"

Anna trusted Tiffany, but she didn't want word getting back to her mom about where she was. It wasn't out of the realm of possibility for her mom to do something drastic, like show up at the hotel.

"I'm taking care of the messes from the wedding, so hopefully, she won't have a reason to be mad at me when I get back."

It wouldn't be enough. Anna knew it. Her mom wouldn't let this go easily. There was no doubt in her mind that Catherine Harris would have demanded she go through with the wedding, mistress or not. That was one of the reasons why she hadn't gathered the courage to talk to her mother yet.

"This is going to be the longest week ever. No offense to you. He did you wrong. But your mom is on a warpath, and she's out for blood."

"I have no doubt," Anna whispered. Her mother was the last person she wanted to talk to when she was upset. Catherine didn't understand invisible things like feelings or emotions. Everything needed a direct path to reality, and Anna's obsession with true love and living happily ever after was ridiculous to her. Success was only measured in dollar signs for Catherine.

Anna, on the other hand, didn't care how much money she had. Enough was plenty.

"I'm really sorry you're dealing with this. Send me the things I left for you to do, and I'll take care of them so you won't be overloaded doing the things Catherine is giving you too."

Tiffany groaned. "This stinks. I don't like working for her. I like working for you."

"The feeling is mutual, girl. I don't know what I'd do without you. Also, don't write the brief. I'll do it when I get back."

"Thank you! And I'm not sending you this work. I hope you're hundreds of miles away from her fury."

"I'll call you tomorrow, but keep me posted if you need anything," Anna said.

"Have a good trip."

Anna ended the call and tiptoed out of the bathroom. Beau now had a blanket draped over his lower half while he tapped on his phone.

"Everything okay?" he asked.

"Yep. Just going to sleep."

Beau turned off his phone and put it on the back of the couch. "Good night."

"Good night."

Once she snuggled beneath the covers, she turned to look out the big window at the dark, starry night. Despite everything Tiffany had mentioned about Catherine's behavior, the fear Anna always carried around her mother started to drift away as if it had always been connected to her by a slip knot.

CHAPTER 13
BEAU

"Absolutely not."

"Absolutely yes," Anna countered.

She might be cute and bossy, but she was not getting away with this one. He was in his thirties, and he wouldn't cave to peer pressure.

Beau crossed his arms over his chest, settling into a stance that said he was putting his foot down. "I'm not doing it."

"Then I'll just drag you around like a doll. This is my dream. My dream," Anna repeated with all the seriousness of a tiger cub.

Okay, serious Anna was kinda hot. If he didn't get a grip on himself soon, she'd overpower him. "Why do your dreams have to include close proximity to another person?"

"Because I grew up making Barbie and Ken kiss a

lot," Anna said as if her childhood role-playing had anything to do with the current subject.

Stand your ground, man. "How did I get involved in this Barbie-Ken drama?"

"You didn't. You got involved with my drama, and now you're seeing the pleasantly bright side of me you never knew about," Anna said, propping a hand on her hip.

Why did she have to draw attention to her body? It was a weapon, and she was wielding it like a sword.

Beau rubbed a hand over his face. Why wouldn't she just give it up? "I don't want to dance."

"But dancing with me is going to be fun. I promise we can laugh about it later."

"Oh, there would be plenty of laughter. At my expense. And you don't even care!"

Anna stepped closer and rested her hands on his crossed arms, lodging a breath in Beau's throat.

Shoot. Now she was touching him. The alarms in his head were screaming "Mayday!"

"I do care," she said, softly and tenderly, just inches away from him. "I also know you'll overcome this struggle and come out stronger on the other side."

Beau's shoulders fell. "You're acting like we're going to battle or something."

"Well, that's how you're acting too. This isn't a big deal. One dance class. It's two hours."

"Two hours! That's a lot of dancing."

"No, it's not," Anna said with a wave of her hand, dismissing his fears like she was swatting away a mosquito. "Time flies when you're having fun."

"Oh, so it'll seem like ten minutes to you and an eternity to me."

Anna rolled her eyes, but a pleased grin bloomed on her shiny lips.

Don't look at her lips! Those are completely off-limits.

She rubbed her hands up his arms to rest on his biceps. His skin tingled in the wake of her touch, making it hard to concentrate on her words.

"Listen, I know I'm a lot. I know I ask for too much, and I get way too excited about everything. I'm only asking you to show up and go through the motions. You don't have to do a lift or shake your behind."

"That's good news. You've erased of all my fears," Beau deadpanned.

Her shoulders lifted, and that tentative grin spread to a full-blown megawatt smile. "Good. I aim to please. Now, let's go dancing."

Grabbing his arms, she uncrossed them and took his hand in hers, dragging him to the door of their hotel room and out into the hallway.

"I didn't say yes," Beau protested.

"You didn't say no either. Stop talking and start walking."

She slid into the elevator and rounded on him as soon as the doors closed them inside—alone.

Her hands were immediately on him. Brushing over his arms, gripping the tops of his shoulders, massaging the tight muscles. "You need to relax before we get there."

"How am I supposed to relax when you're touching me?" It was a legitimate question. Every nerve ending in his body fired at once when she touched him. If she didn't get her hands off him soon, he was going to spontaneously combust.

"Why are you breathing so hard?" she asked.

"Because you're touching me!"

Anna lifted her hands and held them up, showing her innocence. "Okay. I'll stop. Just trying to help."

Anna was definitely not helping. In fact, she was the subject of all his problems. His life would be one hundred times easier if he didn't have to pretend he wasn't entirely too affected by her mere presence.

Fifteen minutes later, he was resting his hands on Anna's waist and contemplating all his life choices.

"Dancing is a team performance, but you're not putting on a show for anyone else. You're dancing for yourselves."

The petite woman leading the class was probably in her late fifties with graying hair pulled up into a high, bouncy ponytail, and she radiated the same level of pep as a college cheerleader.

"I am not dancing for myself," Beau whispered.

"You're dancing for me. It's very noble of you," Anna whispered back.

Good grief, she was misinterpreting everything.

"The art of intimate dance is instinctual, but some can be taught. You must give in to your base desires."

Beau's grip tightened on Anna's waist. "What did she say? What kind of dance is this?"

Anna's eyes widened, and her nostrils flared slightly as her breaths picked up speed. "Um, I forgot about that. I just remembered it was a dance class that sounded fun."

"Fun for a couple on their honeymoon!" Beau whisper-screamed.

Anna's nose scrunched, and her eyes narrowed as she mouthed, "Sorry."

Sorry? That was all she had to say for herself? He was a circus monkey being made to dance, and she was *sorry*.

"Men, keep your hands on your queen's hips and pull her to you until you are touching each other from chest to thighs."

"I can't do this," Beau said, frantic as the studio door moved farther and farther away. "I'm not doing that."

Anna stepped closer, leaving less than an inch of space between them. “Relax. We can fake it.”

“What is this?” the instructor asked at their side.

Beau glanced from the instructor to Anna. What was the question? His brain was in the process of a malfunction, and nothing made sense.

Anna rested a hand on Beau’s chest. “We’re first-time dancers, and he’s shy.”

Shy, scared, terrified—something like that.

The woman poked her slender finger at his shoulder and pinned him with her unwavering stare. “Hold her like you love her!”

No. No, no, no, no. Was it too late to make a run for it?

“It’s okay. Just give him a minute to get used to this,” Anna said in a sweet, neutral voice that would have made even him obey.

The instructor’s gaze could have pinned him to the wall. “I need you to get into it soon. We’re moving through these steps quickly.”

Beau stretched his neck from one side to the other, still holding Anna’s waist. “You don’t have to defend me.”

The instructor clapped her hands and shouted to be heard throughout the room. “Now, let’s get comfortable. I want you to slowly sway with your partner. Move as one from side to side, getting closer as you go.”

Great. Getting closer to Anna was as dangerous

as getting closer to the sun. Beau closed his eyes and focused on evening his breaths.

Anna slid her arms from his chest over his shoulders to his back and her hips moved slowly beneath his hands.

"Is this okay?" she whispered against his ear.

"You better not tell anyone about this," he said slowly.

She chuckled softly. "What happens in Freedom stays in Freedom."

"No one would believe you," Beau added.

"That's one hundred percent true."

Beau opened his eyes and promptly closed them after catching sight of the couple next to them rubbing against each other in wild movements. "We are not doing any of that."

Anna laughed low in her throat and rested her forehead against his chest. She was doing a good job of making their movements casual instead of "intimate."

"Just keep moving together," the instructor said. "You're becoming one."

"I'm becoming nauseated," Beau whispered.

Another laugh from Anna, and a new idea took shape. Maybe they could laugh through this like Anna had said earlier, instead of taking it seriously.

The music lowered as the instructor said, "Now, I want you to whisper sweet things into your partner's ear."

Beau leaned down to press his lips against Anna's ear and turned on the deepest, sexiest voice he could muster as he whispered, "Fruity Pebbles."

Anna's laugh was instant, gaining them looks from the nearby couples.

"Shh. You're making a scene," he whispered, holding her closer. Man, her hair smelled amazing. The soft vanilla scent tingled in his nose.

When her laughter died, he tensed his jaw and leaned in again, brushing his nose against her temple, breathing in her intoxicating presence. Her breath hitched as he slowly whispered, "Belgian waffles."

There it was again, her larger-than-life laughter that vibrated throughout his entire body. She relaxed against him, and their swaying became more natural—more fluid as they moved together in sync with the music.

"What's so funny?" he asked, leaning back a fraction to look her in the eye. "She said to whisper sweet things."

Anna bit her bottom lip, but her smile refused to be stopped. Man, she had a radiance about her that lit up the entire room.

"You want to hear something even sweeter?" he asked, baiting her to take him up on this stupid game that was keeping him from losing control and pressing his lips to hers.

"What?" she asked, breathy and full of wonder as she stared up at him as if he were her hero.

Beau tilted his head down to her ear once again, taking his time, building the tension as her breath spilled hot and tingling on his neck.

"Brownie sundae," he whispered, low and rumbling against the shell of her ear.

Was he imagining things, or did she just shudder against him?

"That's very, very sweet," she whispered back, tilting her head up to press her soft cheek against the scruff of his jaw.

She fit perfectly in his arms now—somehow an extension of him as they swayed. How had he become so comfortable around her in so little time?

It wasn't the dance. It was everything. Eating meals together, picking movies, and deciding on things to do in between the activities she'd already planned.

It was easy—too easy. Being near her was like getting a tattoo—painful at first, then decidedly awesome.

They moved on to actual dance moves, but Beau stopped complaining. Once Anna started laughing, he was able to let go of the nervous energy and have a good time.

Well, a very moderate good time. He didn't touch her nearly as much as the instructor wanted, and despite the daggers she was trying to shoot at him from her eyeballs, he wasn't going to touch all over Anna without her consent, and especially with an audience.

With her consent and in private quarters, they'd both be in trouble.

Anna spun toward him again, brushing his chest with her hand as she landed against him and giving him a smile that hinted she knew exactly what she was doing to him.

Her stare was too hot—too bold and wanting. He had to do something before this went too far.

Well, too far in public. This wasn't the kind of relationship transformation that the world needed to witness. Maybe there wasn't anything happening at all. Hopefully, his brain would rewire itself as soon as his hands were off her, and he'd remember why he wasn't allowed to touch her.

When she leaned in, he whispered, "Cinnamon rolls."

She laughed again, and that sound would forever be the music behind the highlight reel of his life. "Are you hungry?" she asked, still chuckling and smiling like she'd never had this much fun in her life.

"Starving," Beau said as he spun her away from him.

When she twirled back toward him, he turned her and dipped her low, holding the dramatic pose just like the instructor showed them.

"We have just enough time to get a shower before our dinner reservations," she said while parallel to the floor in his arms.

"What are we having?" He pulled her up from the dip.

Anna kept up the dance, but her gaze didn't meet his.

Whatever it was, her avoidance said there was a good chance he wouldn't like it.

CHAPTER 14
ANNA

"Good grief, you said it wasn't that fancy," Beau said as a tall, lean man wearing an all black suit rounded in front of the car.

No amount of stalling was going to save her from revealing the truth about dinner to Beau.

"It's not." In truth, it wasn't formal dining—it was *romantic* dining. The Bite was well known, even outside of Freedom, for more than the price.

Beau got out and handed the key to the valet attendant before coming around to her side. It was nice that Beau always made a point to open her door, but she often beat him to it.

Not this time. Her legs were choked by temporary paralysis as ideas raced through her head.

If she told him before they went in—before the valet drove away with their car—he'd have a clean chance to back out.

If she waited until they were seated inside, there was a slight chance he'd cause a scene. Though, she'd never known Beau to be rude to strangers or make much of a fuss.

He opened her door, and she reached for his hand. Having that small link to him eased some of the anxiety crushing her chest.

Dim lighting bloomed inside the restaurant, and soft classical music filled the air. A petite woman with dark hair and eyes greeted them with a gentle smile.

"Hello, welcome to The Bite. What is the name on your reservation?"

"Lawrence," Anna said. Once again, Olivia saved them from an awkward encounter by changing the name on the reservation.

The woman clasped her hands in front of her and said, "I'll show you to your table."

When they entered the dining room, Anna's hands grew clammy. The ridiculously small tables were all set for two and far enough away from each other to provide plenty of privacy. Some couples were already enjoying their meals, and Anna dared a glance at Beau.

Oh no. The wheels in his head were turning like a race car on the track. His gaze darted from couple to couple before he glanced down at her with one brow raised.

The hostess gestured toward their table where

one menu rested in the center between two carefully folded napkins. The table itself was thin between the two seats and long on the sides—uniquely made for the modified eating style.

"Your server will be with you in a moment. Enjoy your evening at The Bite," the hostess said before leaving them alone.

Beau squirmed in his seat, shifting his legs beneath the table. "These tables are so small. There isn't anywhere I can move without touching you."

Heat crept up Anna's cheeks as Beau's knees brushed against hers. "I think that's the point. I'm sorry I didn't tell you about this."

"Tell me about what?" he asked, finally giving up on the leg situation and settling his thighs framing her knees.

Anna pointed to the swirling script at the top of the menu.

Beau leaned over to read it, and the fresh scent of his spicy soap tingled in her nose. Was it getting hotter?

Beau tilted his head slightly as he read, "The romantic evening will test your awareness of your partner. Instead of indulging in each of the eighteen courses of tonight's dinner on your own, you will choose which of our handcrafted creations you believe your partner would enjoy most and feed each other using your hands." He frowned at her, as if she were a traitor, then continued, deadpan.

"Anticipate your partner's needs and tap into a mindset that links the two of you together. A happy partner will, in turn, shower you with more affection, forging a greater bond with each bite."

Yep. It sounded even worse when he said it. Granted, Anna's explanation of the unique dinner would have been a lot simpler.

No spoons, forks, or knives, and they would be feeding each other.

No biggie for a newlywed couple.

Quite a personal experience for two people who weren't even dating.

Anna flattened her palms on the white tablecloth. "You don't have to feed me. We can just treat them like finger foods."

Beau's eyes widened, and his mouth opened to speak, but a tall man dressed in black appeared beside their tiny table.

"Good evening, Mr. and Mrs. Lawrence. It's an honor to have you dining with us at The Bite." He gestured toward the menu on the table. "We have two menu choices. The Light and Fresh menu features fruits and crisp flavors, while the Holiday menu offers cozy comfort foods and warm spices. Your meal will be revealed in sets of three, and you'll have plenty of time to taste and choose which of our special treats your partner would enjoy. When you're ready for another set, just turn this light on."

He touched a switch at the bottom of a small

lamp on the edge of the table, illuminating a small flame.

"What can I get you to drink?"

They each ordered water, and Beau wiped at his brow as soon as they were alone again.

"I'm sorry," Anna whispered, not needing to lean toward him to be heard.

"Feeding each other? Are you kidding me?"

"You don't have to do it. These people don't know us, and we won't see them again."

Beau shifted in his seat, brushing his legs against hers.

Okay, she'd made a mistake keeping the dinner from him. How could she have made him this uncomfortable?

He propped his arms on the table, then scooted them back toward him, trying and failing not to cross over to her side of the table. It was impossible. His arms were almost as wide as the surface.

Anna rested her hands on his arms. "I'm sorry. I should have told you."

Beau stared at his arms and her hands spread over them. Was her hope of calming his unease working?

"We can leave if you want," she quietly offered.

After a pause that felt like a lifetime, Beau lifted his chin and faced her, leaning the slightest bit closer to her. "It's fine. Sorry I overreacted."

Anna stared, unblinking. "I—I don't want you to do anything you don't want to."

Beau stared right back, steady and sure. "I don't do things I don't want to do."

Little flutters lifted in her middle. He'd indulged her so much already, but she believed him when he said he wasn't the type to be pressured into doing things he didn't want to.

Anna shifted in her seat a little, marginally moving her hands over Beau's forearms. He hadn't made a move to brush her off, and the crushing grip around her spine eased when he let her stay.

"You must be really hungry," Anna said, hoping to bring back the fun and bold Beau she'd danced with earlier.

Beau's lips lifted on one side in a slow, mischievous grin. "Something like that."

Oh, there was that rush again—the one that had consumed her during their dance lesson. It was equal parts thrilling and terrifying.

It was also completely new, and it only happened when Beau did or said sweet or selfless things.

Good grief, these were feelings. Intense romantic feelings for Beau Lawrence.

The when and how of it was still a blur, but somewhere along the way, sparks had kindled without her knowledge. She looked into his eyes as he gazed at her, unblinking. Sure, Beau was handsome—

Wait, handsome wasn't the word. He was tall, dark, and handsome. Broody and mysterious. Rugged and masculine with confidence to back it up.

The waiter arrived with her water just as she was beginning to panic. Her breaths were running off in their own marathon while she was trying her best to sit still and act as if she were unaffected by the man whose arms and legs touched hers.

"Have you decided which menu you would like to experience today?" the waiter asked.

Beau nodded to her, and she sucked in a restoring breath. "I'd like the Fresh menu, please."

"I'll take the Holiday menu," Beau said.

"Excellent. I will return with your first course momentarily. If you would like to wash your hands before the meal begins, the washrooms are just that way. I will bring damp cloths you may use between sets if you prefer."

And with a bow, he was gone again.

Anna pushed her chair away from the table. "I'll wash up."

"Me too," Beau said, following her to the washrooms.

Once she was alone inside the small room lined with sinks and mirrors, Anna closed her eyes and focused on calming her breathing. She could do this. She *wanted* to do this.

Oh, yeah. That was the scary part.

But this was *Beau*. She'd never been afraid of him before. Now, she couldn't look at him without feeling like she'd stuffed her stomach into a clothes dryer and turned it on.

She took another breath and shoved it out with a huff. No one would believe her, but Beau was fun, and he made her happy—truly happy.

There was another feeling rushing to the surface, ready to be named. Was it safety? Security?

Hope?

Beau had taken everything negative about her current situation and somehow drained the hurt and filled her with joy.

She'd always been careless with her heart, giving it to the first man who looked her way. Now that Beau was looking at her, the thought of losing him the way she'd lost Dean or any of the other men she'd dated seemed like a much greater risk.

Losing Dean had wounded her pride and damaged her self-esteem, but nothing else was injured.

If she allowed Beau to have the power over her that this kindling foreshadowed, he could do more damage than anyone else. She already trusted him way too much—so much that it seemed an extension of trusting herself.

Which, she'd recently found out, she should *not* do. Hence her decision to *almost* marry Dean Simmons.

Anna washed, rinsed, and dried her hands. Beau wasn't Dean, thankfully, and she wasn't going to let her ex hold any kind of sway over her future.

When she opened the door to step out of the washroom, Beau was leaning against the wall with his hands in the pockets of his charcoal slacks. The light-gray shirt he'd worn to dinner really popped against his dark skin and hair.

He straightened and offered her his arm before walking back to the table with her at his side.

Yep. She was completely caught up in Beau's gravity. Chances were high that she'd get her heart broken this time.

The waiter returned with two long, narrow plates just as they sat down. He pulled a small flashlight from his pocket and pointed the light at each small bit of food as he introduced each concoction.

Then he was gone again with a polite, "Enjoy."

Of course, Anna's choices were in front of Beau, and his choices were in front of her. They'd have to make a smooth switch.

"It looks good. Which one do you think I'll choose first?"

Beau picked up a tomato, mango, and basil bruschetta on a tiny slice of toasted sourdough and lifted it between them. "This one."

Anna bit her lips between her teeth before shrugging one shoulder. "Maybe."

"It is, isn't it?" he asked, pinning her with a stare that dared her to admit it.

Huffing in defeat, she whispered, "Okay. It is."

Beau gave a small nod with his chin. "Open."

The air, her skin—everything warmed in the second she hesitated. When Beau didn't back down, she leaned forward an inch and opened her mouth. He placed the small bite on her tongue, brushing the pad of his thumb over her bottom lip. It was the briefest of touches—so fleeting she could have imagined it.

But she didn't. Her lip tingled where his rough thumb had touched.

Fighting to breathe while the adrenaline surged through her body, she closed her mouth to chew. The tomato and mango burst over her senses, and her eyes widened.

"How is it?" Beau asked, entirely focused on her—hanging on her every word.

She swallowed the bite and wiped her mouth. "Amazing. So good."

Beau's gaze darted to the plate in front of Anna. "Which one am I choosing?"

She looked down at the offerings. A cranberry brie bite, a slice of spiced apple sprinkled with cinnamon, and a pinwheel with thinly sliced ham in the center.

Deciding on the pinwheel, she lifted it between them and raised her brows in question.

Beau nodded and leaned forward, opening his mouth for the bite. When his lips brushed her fingertips, the tingle shot all the way up her arm.

Ha! She was not only having dinner with Beau Lawrence, but he actually seemed to be enjoying it. How did they get here, and why did she love it so much?

Beau's expression was unreadable as he chewed, and it was impossible for Anna to tear her attention from him as she waited. "Well?"

He swallowed and squinted one eye. "It's really good."

"You sound surprised."

"I expected it to be kinda bland, but whatever that white stuff is in the middle is good."

"Horseradish." She recalled reading it on the menu.

Beau was surprised by horseradish, and Anna was surprised by him. That was an accurate description of one of her biggest flaws. She read too much into everything. Was she doing that now? Had the realization of her budding feelings for Beau already spiraled out of control?

There was only one way to find out. Olivia Lawrence would be receiving a very important phone call as soon as Beau wasn't around.

CHAPTER 15
ANNA

Dinner at The Bite would proudly be sitting at the top of Anna's all-time favorites list until the end of time. Everything from the delicious food to the amazing company made it memorable.

They'd gushed over the food and laughed entirely too much, and Anna was still riding the high when they returned to the hotel room.

"I can't believe you asked for a dozen of those steak kabobs to go," Anna said as she slid her jacket off.

Beau took it from her and hung it in the closet. "I might want a midnight snack."

Grabbing a hair tie off the nightstand, Anna swirled her hair into a high bun. "I think I'm going to check out the hot tub."

Beau stopped and crossed his arms, pulling his shirt way too tight over his broad chest. "Are you serious? You scared me to death when you fainted the other night."

"I won't stay that long this time."

Beau glared at her, accentuating his already fierce expression. "I don't like it."

Anna lifted her chin. She'd made a mistake, but she'd learned from it. There wasn't a reason to swear off hot tubs altogether. "Then come with me."

"I don't have a swimsuit," Beau countered.

"They sell them at the shop downstairs. I saw them earlier."

Beau stood frozen, studying her with way too much interest.

Anna clenched her teeth while she waited. He was thinking about it way too much, which meant he was going to give in.

Don't react. Don't react.

His arms fell from their cage around him, and he sighed. "Fine. I'll be right back."

As soon as the door closed behind Beau, Anna punched her fist into the air and whisper-screamed. Her cheeks strained with the intense smile.

Fumbling in her clutch, she pulled out her phone. Her heart plummeted in her chest. More missed calls and messages from both Dean and her mom.

Nope. Not going to focus on those rain clouds. She needed Olivia, her bright and optimistic friend.

She pressed the button to call while she jogged to the closet. It didn't take Olivia long to answer.

"Hey, traveler! How's Colorado?"

"Amazing, but that's not why I'm calling. Well, that is sort of why I'm calling. I have a problem."

"Uh-oh. Is it Dean? I can send Dawson or Gage to break some bones."

"Liv!"

"I meant like a pinky finger or something. Maybe a nose. Whatever."

Anna chuckled. "Dean isn't the problem. It's Beau."

Olivia sucked in an uncontrolled breath. "I will slaughter him!"

"No, no, no. It's not like that. He's been good. Really good. Too good, if you know what I mean."

Olivia scoffed. "No, I don't know what you mean. Did he hit his head?"

Anna glanced at the door as she shuffled through the swimsuits she'd packed. "Not that I know of, but I guess it's possible. Today, we took a two-hour intimate dance class, and we just got back from having dinner at The Bite."

"Time out. Did you say intimate dance class? And are you talking about that place where you feed each other?"

"Yes, and yes!"

"He danced with you?" Olivia shouted. "Did you film this? Pics or it didn't happen."

"It did happen, and we both laughed the entire time. I said I wouldn't tell anyone, but you're not everyone. So don't blab. Then he fed me. Liv, tell me I'm not dreaming."

"I—I don't understand. So, you're saying he's being sweet?"

"Extremely." Anna found the swimsuit she'd been looking for and closed her fist around it. "Liv, this has been the best trip. I've had so much fun, and he's always so nice. I'm scared."

"Well, I guess there's a chance he's having a psychotic break or he's been living a lie for the last thirty-two years."

"Yeah." Those two options were more likely than Anna's idea that he was starting to like her too.

"Wait, what are you saying? Do you like him? You like him!"

Oh no. Fear wrapped its claws around her throat. "I think I do. Liv, help me. It's only been three days."

Yep. Some things never changed. Anna's ability to develop feelings without notice was leading her toward heartache once again.

"Hold on. Give me a minute to process. You're catching feelings, but is he giving you any signals?"

"I'm not sure. That's why I'm calling. I thought you might be able to tell me if I'm imagining things."

"Okay, let me get my popcorn ready."

"Remember when I passed out that first night?"

"Yeah. Scared the life out of me. Thanks for that."

"He helped me get into a bath of lukewarm water and then brought me chocolate cake and sat with me until I felt better."

"Please tell me you were clothed," Olivia said.

"Swimsuit, of course. That would have been so awkward."

Memories of Beau carrying her that night floated to the surface. Nothing about being pressed up against his chest had been awkward.

"I'm glad he was there. I was really worried about you."

"I'm glad he was here too. Yesterday, he took me to a bookstore, and we bought books for each other. He got me a Christian romance set in Colorado at Christmas."

"That's cute."

"The woman in the book is an attorney."

"Oh, nice."

"It just sounds like he put a lot of thought into it."

"Rightly so. Carry on. I need more."

"Then he took me out on a snowmobile."

"Did you set that up? I don't remember you talking about it."

"No. He did! He heard about my bucket list and

decided I should add more things that take me out of my comfort zone. It was so much fun."

Olivia hummed. "So you two have been getting close. I still can't get over the dancing."

"Me either. Liv, I never saw this coming, but I like him. A lot."

"I don't even know what to think right now. Part of me wants to jump around and squeal and squeeze you until your ribs crack. The other part desperately hopes Beau feels the same way because I'm terrified you'll get your heart broken again."

Anna pressed the heel of her hand to her chest. "That's exactly what I'm feeling. Help me!"

"Calm down. That's my first suggestion. You went on this trip to have fun and relax after an incredibly stressful breakup. Remember that."

"Okay." The word came out shaky, but Olivia was right. Anna had been living in the moment and having the time of her life until she decided to over-analyze her feelings.

"Next, throw out your expectations. Out the window. You can have a great time on this trip with Beau without any strings attached. You might get home and find that the feelings were just temporary. You might find out that he snores and kicks the covers off his bed and decide he's a monster."

"He doesn't do either of those things," Anna whispered.

"How do you even know? Are you sneaking into his room?"

"Well, he slept next to me the first night. There was only one bed, and I kinda got the couch wet when I passed out as soon as I got out of the hot tub."

Olivia gasped. "You slept in the same bed?"

"It was only that first night, and he slept on top of the covers. As far as I know, there wasn't any kicking or snoring. Did you know he wakes up early and reads his Bible while he drinks coffee?"

"No, but that would explain why God hasn't smote him for his bad attitude yet," Olivia said.

"He has these moments when he resists, but then he gives in and we have the best time. He's so funny."

"Cheese and crackers, Anna! You sound like you're completely into him."

Anna swallowed hard and sat down on the edge of the bed. Resigned, she whispered, "I am."

Olivia sighed. "I love you. I love you so much. Please don't let him hurt you. I would kill him without a second thought."

"No, you wouldn't," Anna said low.

"I would. I would do anything for you. If he does anything that makes you sad, just let me know and I'll trash his apartment before he gets home."

There was a click at the door the second before it opened and Beau stepped inside.

"Gotta go. Love you," Anna said quickly before ending the call.

Beau pulled a pair of royal-blue swim shorts out of a plastic bag. "You didn't have to rush off the phone. I can leave if you need some privacy."

"It was just Olivia." Anna stood and held up the swimsuit still wadded up in her hand. "I'm going to change."

Anna slid into the piping hot water just before Beau stepped out onto the balcony. The dark night cast shadows over everything, but there was absolutely no way she could miss the sight of him walking toward the hot tub.

Beau worked out! And he'd been hiding beneath inconspicuous T-shirts this entire time.

Anna jerked her attention from Beau's chest to the very boring water. It wasn't nice to ogle him, especially when she'd purposely slipped into the hot tub early to hide her own body.

Not that she was embarrassed of the way she looked. She'd intentionally packed skimpy bikinis for the trip under the impression her new husband would be the only one to see so much of her.

Oh, and there was the tiny fact that she suddenly cared what Beau thought of her. She hadn't decided what to do about that yet, but she didn't want to win him over with her body. It was the most unimportant part of a relationship.

Looks came and went. Bodies changed. She repeated those truths often on her fashion vlog.

Beau sank into the warm water, sitting as far away from her as possible and taking up a whole lot of space. Despite the steaming water and the chill of the night air, Beau captivated all of her attention.

He picked up his phone from the side of the hot tub and tapped on the screen. "You have ten minutes."

"Ten minutes?" she asked.

"I looked it up. You shouldn't stay in a hot tub any longer than that."

Oh. He wasn't trying to be bossy. He was looking out for her.

Ugh. There was the tightening in her chest again —the tight squeeze that reminded her of Beau's unexpected sweetness.

"Let's play twenty questions," she said, desperate to be comfortable sitting this close to Beau.

"I reserve the right to decline any questions I don't want to answer. Same goes for you."

"Of course." He was right to suggest an out. She didn't want to pressure him to talk about anything he didn't want to, and it was nice to know she had the same option.

"You first," he said.

"How did you start your own business?" she asked.

He lifted his arms out of the water and stretched them out on the rim of the hot tub on either side of him. If he'd taken up space before, his area just doubled. "That's what you want to know?"

"Yeah. It's great that you saw something you wanted to do and went for it. You're in control of everything. It just seems so... freeing."

Beau shrugged. "It is. I didn't want to work for an idiot, and at the time, I was the only person I trusted to do things right."

Anna bit her lips between her teeth. It was such a Beau thing to say, and she loved it.

"Dad gave me a start-up loan. It took every penny both of us had, but I was determined to pay him back no matter what. I had the loan paid off by the third year. Now I need to hire more employees because we have more work than we can handle."

"That's amazing," she whispered. She'd spent plenty of time at Beau's garage. Despite his gruff demeanor, customers respected his honesty, and he had plenty of repeat business. She'd seen cars float in and out of the shop more than once over the years.

"What exactly do you do online with the fashion stuff?" Beau asked.

Oh yeah. It was his turn. "I share fashion tips and tricks for different body styles and trends.

Boutiques send me exclusive pieces to share and talk about. Usually, it's either to announce an upcoming line or gauge interest so they can anticipate trends."

"They send you clothes for free?"

That was a separate question, but she'd allow it. "Yes."

"Do you make money from it?"

Okay, he was running away with the questions. "My social channels are monetized, so I get paid whenever someone watches my videos. I also have affiliate links with many boutiques and companies, which means I get paid whenever someone purchases something after clicking on the link I shared."

Beau's eyes widened. "Wow. I had no idea."

"My turn," Anna said, shifting in the warm water. "What has been your favorite part of this trip so far?"

Silence settled around them as Beau considered his answer. Was it really this difficult to decide? She'd assumed snowmobiling would be the clear winner.

"Pass."

What? Why would he pass on that one?

"Okay. What's your favorite food?"

"Steak. Ribeye. Medium."

Anna chuckled. "So predictable."

"Who doesn't like steak?"

"It's not my favorite. I prefer baked or roasted chicken to any other meat."

"I mean, I don't have anything against chicken or really any other food. It's just hard to beat a good steak."

A gentle warning floated to the surface of her thoughts. Why had she asked about his favorite food?

Because she'd always been told—mostly by her mother—that a good wife always prepares her husband's favorite foods. Anna had spent over a year learning and perfecting Dean's favorite foods.

Was she programmed to repeat her mistakes? The urge to put aside anything she'd done with Dean was strong. Where had she gone wrong? How could she know what exactly drove him away?

"My turn?" Beau asked, interrupting her downward spiral.

Anna nodded, still reeling over her self-revelation.

"How many times has Dean called you since we left?"

Wow. Beau didn't pull punches. "Um, a lot."

"How many have you answered?"

Okay, Beau liked to double up on his turn every time. "None."

His expression didn't change. She'd been watching closely how the shadows fell over his features.

No reaction at all? It had taken all of her willpower not to answer calls, even if the calls were from Dean.

She brushed stray hairs from her ponytail away from her face. "Do you date?"

"That's a very general question," he said.

"I'll accept a very general answer. I just haven't seen you with anyone since maybe high school."

Beau rested his head back, completely relaxed despite the conversation topics. "Not really. It never lasts long."

"Why not?" If he could ask more than one question, she could too.

"I can tell pretty quickly if it's real, and then there isn't any point dragging it out."

"Are you super picky?" she asked.

"No. I'm just not going to devote my time to a relationship that won't last."

Anna sank another inch into the water. "I wish I'd known," she whispered.

Beau lifted his head. "What do you really love? Not who. What."

Thank goodness he was steering the questions back to safe territory. "I love my job. Well, parts of it. I love helping people, but I don't like bending the rules to fit an agenda for my client."

Yes, she'd initially become an attorney because it was all she'd ever known growing up with two of them. They were both cunning and fierce, and a part of her had hoped she could somehow learn how to be assertive and confident like them.

Too bad it hadn't happened for her. She wasn't cutthroat, and she didn't manipulate evidence or people to win.

"As far as the fashion vlog goes, I love building people up and giving them confidence. I want people to see themselves the way God sees them—beautiful and perfect as He intended."

Beau didn't respond. He just waited, which only gave her more time with her thoughts.

"What do you think I'm doing wrong?" she asked. "The truth. I can handle it."

He didn't ask for clarification, but he took his time staring into the night before he turned to her.

"Nothing. Wait, there's something. You're chasing after love, but real love won't make you chase it."

A pricking behind her eyes had her inhaling a deep breath through her nose. He was right. He was so right that it scared her, and there wasn't anything she could do to change it.

No one had truly loved her yet. That was obvious. No matter what she did or how hard she worked to make someone happy, she may never find someone who would love her back.

Why was she so worried about something she couldn't control?

Because she wanted it. She wanted a pure, real

love more than anything, but that life might not be God's plan for her. Could she accept it if that was the case?

"What are you afraid of?" Beau asked.

The answer was as clear as the night sky shining with hundreds of stars around them. "Not finding love," she whispered. Desperate to move on, she looked up and asked, "What are you afraid of?"

Beau pierced her with an intense stare as he lowered his arms and crossed them over his chest.

Of course he wasn't going to tell her what he was afraid of. Did Beau Lawrence even have fears? If he did, he didn't show it.

"What are you afraid of?" she repeated, determined to push him to answer this one because she'd already told him hers.

"You."

Anna sucked in a breath, but the air was too thick. Sweat dripped down the back of her neck and over her temples.

Her? But, why?

The alarm on Beau's phone pierced the air, jerking her out of the present.

Beau stood in a rush and turned off the alarm. "Time to get out."

"Beau."

"Time's up." He grabbed a towel and stepped out of the hot tub. "I'll get changed, then you can have the bathroom."

Who cared about the bathroom or changing clothes or anything when she had more questions?

But Beau was gone, dripping water behind him as he stepped into the room. Even if he'd stayed, he wouldn't have given her anything else.

Now, she wanted to amend her answer to his last question. She wasn't afraid of dying before she found love. She was afraid she'd already found it and he wouldn't love her back.

CHAPTER 16
BEAU

Beau downed the last bit of coffee in his mug and glanced toward the bathroom. He should have known it would take Anna an hour to get ready to go snowboarding. The woman could do literally nothing and still look good. All the time she spent getting ready to go out was unnecessary.

His phone on the table beside his Bible lit up, flashing his sister's name on the screen along with a smiling photo of her cuddling a fluffy brown chicken to her face.

He answered the call and sat on the couch that doubled as his bed. "What?"

"Good morning. How are you?" Olivia said in an oddly stern and professional tone.

Beau pulled the phone away from his ear. Yep. That was definitely his sister on the other end of the line. "I'm fine."

"Do you have to sound like the Beast from *Beauty and the Beast* when you say it?" she asked.

"What do you want?" Olivia wasn't calling to check on him. She had an ulterior motive, and he didn't like beating around the bush.

"I want to make sure you're being good to Anna. How is she?"

"Fine."

Happy.

Fun.

Annoyingly attractive.

Olivia paused before softening her tone. "She said you've been good to her."

"Did you think I'd leave her at a truck stop or something? I wouldn't be mean to her."

"I know. I'm just... surprised."

Shoot. Maybe he was a little on the rough side, but surely Liv didn't think he'd be mean to Anna on this trip. His sister and everyone else he spent time with on a regular basis understood he just wasn't the frills and bows kind.

Some called it abrasive. Some called it assertive. Some called him a grump or a jerk or other words that weren't polite to use in mixed company, but he'd never cared what anyone else thought of him.

Until now. Until Olivia thought he might hurt Anna after she'd just found out her stupid fiancé was cheating on her on the morning of her wedding.

"Why did you send me on this trip?" he asked. "Why'd you push for me to go?"

"Because I trust you, and despite what people say about you, you have a good heart."

Beau pushed a hand through his hair, but his movements were restricted by the layers he was wearing. "Please don't get sappy on me. I promised to protect her, and I'll do that."

"I know you will. But she could also use a friend."

"I'm not a shoulder to cry on, Liv."

"Just... be your usual, honest self. Okay? But be nice."

"I am being nice."

"What do you think about her?" Olivia asked.

Nope. Not going there. "I don't think about her."

Olivia hummed. "I think you're lying."

Whatever. He didn't care if she knew he was lying. This conversation wasn't happening. "I have to go."

"Please be good to her. I mean it."

"Yeah. You said that."

Anna stepped out of the bathroom wearing her cold-weather gear, and something kicked in his chest. How could she look so good even when she was covered from head to toe in puffy layers?

"Call me later," Olivia said before ending the call.

He shoved his phone and any thoughts about

the conversation with his sister into his pocket. "You ready?"

"As ready as I'll ever be. I don't know why this is on my bucket list. Actually, I do remember. I watched a documentary about a pro snowboarder when I was in high school, and he made it look easy."

"Fair warning, it's not easy," Beau said as he stood and grabbed the key card from the table.

Anna was quiet as they stepped into the elevator. The silence pricked at his skin as they descended to the main level.

"You okay?" he finally asked.

"Yeah. Just a little nervous."

She was more than a little nervous. If she didn't stop fidgeting, she was going to scrub the skin off her hands.

Beau reached for her clasped hands, and she stilled before glancing up at him.

"We don't have to do this," he reminded her. Stepping out of your comfort zone was all good and well, but watching Anna squirm like this had his own stomach winding into knots.

She cleared her throat, but his center of gravity had shifted to another place. She flipped one of her hands and threaded her fingers between his.

And he was done. Anna Harris stole his breath, his heart, and everything else he thought he owned. How did it even happen? She'd sneaked into his life like a ninja and destroyed him in just a few days.

He should let her go. He should pull his hand and his heart back and reclaim some small part of himself. She was going to go home, say she had a great time on this trip, and forget about him. Would he be able to do the same?

Then she smiled up at him and pinned him to the wall with an invisible dart. "Thanks. I would probably be backing out if you weren't here, but I think I'm okay."

Beau nodded once and swallowed his wayward emotions. "Say the word, and we're done. We can leave whenever you're ready."

The elevator dinged and the doors opened, revealing the lobby of the Freedom Ridge Lodge. Garland hung over every door, awning, and hearth, twinkling with white lights. An enormous tree stood imposingly by the huge staircase, and guests were scattered all over the large room. Tall windows framed the snowy scene outside.

He released her hand and gestured for her to lead the way. They were set to meet their instructor at the equipment rental shop in fifteen minutes. He had a quarter of an hour to get his head on straight.

A man wearing a blue outfit with the Freedom logo stood talking with another guy at their meeting point. When he spotted Beau and Anna walking his way, he lifted his chin and flashed a smile.

"Hey. Beau and Anna?"

"That's us," Anna said, extending a hand to the guy. "You must be Aiden."

"You bet. It's nice to meet you. Thanks for booking the private lesson."

"Well, I've never done this before, so I'm sure I'll need lots of help."

Aiden introduced himself to Beau, and they shook hands. "Is this your first time too?" Aiden asked.

"It's been a few years, but I've been snowboarding before."

"Sounds good. I can help both of you at different levels."

Beau raised his hand. "No need. Today is about her, so I'll stay at her pace." As fun as a free day on the slopes sounded, he couldn't miss the chance to watch Anna learn something new.

Aiden would probably understand if he was married or had a girlfriend. Beau had officially turned into one of those guys, and he and Anna weren't even together.

His chances of surviving this trip unscathed were looking grim.

Aiden nodded, grinning just a little bit. "Cool. That makes things easier."

Anna was smiling now, all traces of nervousness forgotten. Her smile lit something inside him he hadn't known existed. He quickly looked away, unwilling to be pulled into her siren trap.

Aiden walked them through basics, dos, and don'ts as they made their way to the lift. Anna started squirming again as they approached the line, and she didn't say much until it was their turn to get on.

As soon as they took their places in front of the next seat, Anna grabbed onto his arm with both hands.

Beau rested a hand over hers. "You okay?"

"Just a little scared of heights," she said, glancing back at the seat slowly approaching.

"Are you going to be okay? Now is the time to back out if we're not doing it."

She closed her eyes and shook her head. "No, I can do it."

When the seat reached them, she tightened her hold on him as the seat swung back and forth.

"Get comfortable before we're up in the air. Then you can close your eyes until we get to the top."

Anna shifted closer to him before improving her latch on his arm. "Just tell me when it's over."

"You don't like heights?"

"Sometimes I'm okay, and sometimes I'm not. I can be high up inside a building, and I'm okay until about the tenth floor. I don't do airplanes or high bridges, but if there's ground right below my feet, it's not so bad."

Beau reached the arm she held across her and grabbed onto the outside of her thigh. Maybe she'd feel better with a human seatbelt. "Just keep your eyes closed."

And she did. She didn't panic. She didn't complain. She just sat still with her eyes closed, holding onto him like he was the rope anchoring her to safety. Halfway up, she rested her head on his shoulder and relaxed.

Sitting this close to Anna should have felt weird, but it wasn't at all. It was exhilarating. He could jump from the lift right now, and he wouldn't get half the rush as he did with Anna snuggled up to his arm.

He was in trouble. So much trouble.

Once they were on the homestretch to the drop-off, he tapped her hand. "You can open your eyes now.

The air was thinner at twelve thousand feet, and his lungs were getting a workout. The freezing wind bit at any bit of exposed skin, and Anna remained quiet until it was their turn to exit.

Anna stumbled as soon as they stepped off the ski lift, and Beau grabbed for her arm.

"Whoa. You okay?"

Anna huffed as she stood, brushing the snow off her suit. "Sorry."

"It's okay. Get your balance."

She propped her hands on her hips and sucked in deep breaths. “I’m fine.”

She wasn’t fine, but Beau didn’t want to push her too much. She had to let him know if the altitude was getting to her.

They’d barely made it off the platform when her knees buckled. He grabbed onto her arm before she collapsed, but that was all he needed to make an executive decision.

Aiden jogged over and tucked his chin, studying her as Beau held her up. “Is it the altitude?”

“I’m not sure, but I think we need to skip the lesson. I need to get her back down the mountain.”

Aiden waved them over to the line to get back onto the lift. He spoke to another guy helping people on and off before gesturing for Beau and Anna to join him at the front of the line.

“When you get back to the lodge, ask for Joanna at the front desk. She’s my wife, and she’ll make sure you have everything you need.”

Beau offered Aiden a quick handshake before they hopped back on the lift. “I appreciate it.”

“Take care of her,” Aiden said as they rode away.

Wrapping an arm around her and pulling her close to his side, Beau whispered, “Just close your eyes.”

“I think I’m going to be sick.”

Great. They were hanging up in the air, and

there wasn't anything he could do to help her. Helplessness truly sucked.

Anna made it to the bottom of the slope without losing her breakfast, but she pointed toward the first sign for a restroom. "There."

Beau held onto her until they reached the door. "Hang on. I'll go get Joanna and she can help you."

"Nope. Can't wait." She leaned her shoulder against the door, using all of her strength to push it open.

There went the helplessness again. She could barely stand, but he wasn't welcome in the women's bathroom.

Beau paced outside the door, praying whatever was going on would ease now that they were back down the mountain. He pulled out his phone to call Travis when a loud thump came from inside the bathroom.

CHAPTER 17
ANNA

"Anna! Anna!"

Someone was calling, but she couldn't answer.

"Anna!"

Her upper body lifted, but her head was too heavy. Finally, her eyes opened, but she couldn't manage more than a few rapid blinks.

"Anna, talk to me."

It was Beau. The warmth of his chest settled into her as the fog lifted.

And everything hurt. A piercing in her head had her reaching for it, but she jerked as pain shot up her arm.

"Don't move. You hit your head."

That would explain the pounding. She tried again and failed to lift her arm without a shock of pain shooting up her arm. "My wrist."

"Looks like you landed on it." He shifted her in his arms. "I'm calling the front desk."

She rested in his arms as he made the call. The next second, the sound of multiple footsteps surrounded her.

"She hit her head?" a woman asked.

"Yeah. And she said her wrist hurts," Beau said.

A beautiful blonde woman appeared in Anna's line of sight. "I'm Joanna, Aiden's wife. He called and said you weren't feeling well. Our medical team is on the way."

Ugh. A dizzying sickness lingered, but it was nothing like it had been when she walked into the bathroom. She'd known what was happening seconds before she passed out, but there wasn't anything she could have done to stop it.

A few more people filed into the small bathroom. She hadn't even made it to the stalls, but thankfully, the nausea had eased.

"Miss Harris, do you remember what happened?" a man asked.

"I think it was the altitude. I was dizzy and nauseated." Her tongue was dry and too big for her mouth. "I came in here thinking I needed to vomit, but I passed out."

The man with dark hair and a red uniform crouched in front of her, studying her from all sides. "Is this where you hit your head?" he asked, pointing just above her right temple.

"Yes." Exhaustion spread over her like a weighted blanket. Could she just lie here until she felt better? Beau's arms tightened around her.

"You mentioned your wrist," the man said, gently examining it with small touches. "There's a little swelling, but I don't think it's broken. We'll need to get you in for x-rays to be sure." He pulled out a pen light and pointed it toward her. "Can you follow my light?"

She did as he asked, one thing after another, giving answers when prompted and resting during his exams.

Soon, she was being lifted and carried to a gurney with Beau at her side. He kept a hold on her as she slowly returned to her senses.

"I can walk. I think I'm fine now. I feel better," she said.

"Well, I'm not fine, so you're going to get checked out," Beau said with finality.

That made her chuckle, but the movement jostled her enough to aggravate the pain in her head.

He stayed quiet on the way to the hospital and while the paramedics transferred her to the emergency department. She didn't really feel like talking anyway. If only she could close her eyes and slip into a restful sleep for just a few minutes.

Once nurses started asking questions, Beau recounted most of the events when she got tired of talking. All she had to do was confirm what he said, and it was a great relief.

When they were left alone while they waited for her tests, she let her eyes close. Beau didn't so much as move in the chair beside her bed, but it was impossible to miss his presence. Knowing he was with her allowed her to rest.

Someone eventually returned to take her for x-rays and CT scans. After a long, boring wait, she was diagnosed with a sprained wrist and a mild concussion and released with a wrist brace and pain-relieving medication.

Beau sat quietly next to her in the back of the taxi as they made their way back to Freedom, but he glanced over at her every few minutes.

Her head still ached, but her pride took the biggest hit. Not only had she failed to snowboard, she'd skipped out before even trying. Then, she passed out. In the bathroom, no less. Poor Beau had to rescue her from the nasty floor.

Joanna met them at the entrance when they returned. "How are you feeling?"

The kind woman wearing a flowing lilac blouse and black pencil skirt gave a warm welcome as Anna stood from the back seat of the cab.

"Much better." Anna lifted her braced hand. "Sprained wrist and mild concussion."

Joanna clutched her hands to her chest. "I'm so glad you're feeling better." She handed Beau two cards. "This is my direct number. Call me if you need anything. Our employees are aware of what happened, and they'll do absolutely anything for you. No need to leave the room until you're ready."

"That's so kind," Anna said as she leaned onto Beau's sturdy side.

"The other number is for you to call whenever you're ready to eat. There's a menu for The Liberty Grill in your room, and you can order anything you want and as often as you want at no cost."

Anna brushed her hair behind her ear and winced. She'd forgotten all about the tender spot on her head. "You don't have to do all that. I promise I won't be filing a lawsuit. None of this was the fault of the resort. I just got a bad taste of altitude sickness."

"It's not about that. I'm sorry you had to spend part of your vacation with an injury. We want to make sure you're as comfortable as possible." Joanna reached out and grasped Anna's hand, and the warmth spoke of more than just protecting her job. "Aiden and I will be praying for you, but if you need anything else, don't hesitate to call me."

Okay, the emotional toil of the day must be getting to her because it took everything Anna had not to let the tears fall. "Thank you so much. That's really all I need."

Joanna smiled and turned to Beau. "They'll be waiting on your call at the Grill. I'm sure you two are hungry after the day you've had. If you want something warm and comforting, I recommend the potato soup."

Beau said his thanks to Joanna and wrapped his arm around Anna, tucking her close to his side. His strength was a huge help, and he guided her directly to the elevator where she leaned back against the wall. They'd been taking the stairs for the majority of their stay, but Anna happily accepted the ride after a day of fighting for balance.

When the elevator dinged and the doors opened, Beau reached for her, wrapping his arms behind her back and legs. Seconds later, her stomach dropped as he lifted her into his arms.

"What are you doing?"

He stepped out into the hallway and headed toward their room. "I'm not risking another fall."

Unable and unwilling to argue, Anna rested her head against his shoulder. "Thank you."

He stopped at the door and lowered her to her feet, continuing to hold her close as he pulled out his key card. Once the door was open, he picked her up again.

"This isn't necessary," Anna said.

"I don't care," was Beau's quick response.

He lowered her to the couch, and she missed the loss immediately. Everything inside her wanted to reach for him and never let go.

Beau turned around, grabbed a binder off the

table and handed it to her. "What do you want to eat?"

She took the binder and opened it to the menu for The Liberty Grill. If he wanted to revert back to his old stoic self, good for him. It would be easier to squash her feelings for him now before they got out of hand.

Who was she kidding? Things were already out of hand. Even when he sounded cold and uncaring, he was still carrying her and trying to feed her.

She rattled off her order and handed him the binder. While he called for room service, Anna checked her phone for the first time in hours.

Dozens of missed calls, texts, and emails waited. It was the same as every other day, except each one would deliver a tiny stab into her chest.

She'd gotten used to the encouraging messages from women who followed her fashion vlog and matter-of-fact emails from work. Now, she had to wade through speculation, assumptions, and opinions about her personal life.

She went for the texts from Olivia first.

Olivia: Are you okay? Beau texted and said you passed out. Call me!

Olivia: Beau said not to bother you, but I love you and I'm praying.

Olivia: Also, does Beau get brownie points for this?

The last message made her chuckle, but the others sucked all the fleeting joy away.

Anna: I'm fine. Beau has been taking good care of me. He gets all the brownie points.

Mom: I can't believe what you've done. Dean is trying to get in touch with you. If you had any sense, you'd beg his forgiveness.

So much for tiny stabs. Her mom always knew how to cut to the core.

Dean: Answer your phone. We have a lot to talk about.

No thanks. Could she skip to the part where Dean moved on and left her alone?

She clicked over to social media and skipped over any messages that looked even remotely aggressive, clicking on the one that promised some kindness.

Brittany: That's awful. Where are you now?

Anna rested her head back against the couch. Brittany was one of the kindest people Anna had met online. Brittany had been following the vlog since its early days, and she'd become a genuine friend.

After rehashing the story late last night, Anna had fallen asleep before reading Brittany's response.

Anna: I went on my honeymoon. I just needed some time away to wrap my head around things.

A response came immediately.

Brittany: What are you going to do with the dresses?

That was weird. Of course Anna had called each boutique and explained why she wouldn't be featuring the dresses they'd sent with the promise to return them in perfect condition. They hadn't been pleased, but she couldn't follow through with her end of the arrangement without a wedding.

Brittany knew a lot about how Anna handled her fashion vlog, but why would that be the one of the first things she asked?

Anna: I sent the dresses back to them and recommended a few other influencers who might be able to feature the pieces.

She tossed her phone onto the couch just as Beau ended the call.

"Food should be here in fifteen minutes."

Anna stood slowly, and Beau was at her side in an instant.

"What are you doing?"

"I need to get out of these layers." She reached her good hand up and touched her hair. "Gross. I just remembered I was laying on a public bathroom floor."

Beau reached for the zipper on her outer coat. "Let me help you out of these coats. You can take a shower while we wait for the food."

She winced quite a few times as Beau carefully removed layer after layer. The ones that went over her head were the worst, having to maneuver around her wrist and head.

When he'd helped her down to a tank top and thermal pants, she plopped onto the couch and stared at her useless hand. Showering was going to be a chore.

"I think I'll wait until after we eat to shower." Every last bit of her strength was zapped, and her stomach rumbled. It was well into the afternoon, and neither of them had eaten since their early breakfast.

Beau sat on the coffee table facing her, resting his elbows on his knees and pinning her with an intense stare. "Are you okay?"

She waved her good hand. "Of course. I'm fine now."

But his expression didn't change. His jaw was tight, and his gaze drifted slowly over her features.

"Are you okay?" she asked. He'd missed out on snowboarding—the only activity he'd been looking forward to on his trip—and instead, spent the entire day at the hospital with her. No doubt it was boring.

He looked down at his clasped hands and swallowed hard. "You scared me."

Anna sat forward and placed her good hand on top of his. "I'm sorry. I know you came on this trip because Olivia wanted you to protect me, but this wasn't something you could have prevented. It's not your fault. Plus, I'm fine now."

"You're not fine. You're hurt."

Then it hit her. His confession when they'd played twenty questions.

He was afraid of *her*. What did that mean?

Beau lifted his chin, and his gaze locked with hers. They were so close now—merely a breath apart.

Was he afraid because he cared? It was dangerous to hope, but it was impossible to ignore the way he'd tended to her. If love was something she could perceive and feel outside of her emotions, it was everything Beau had done for her since the moment he rescued her from a marriage that would have been a mistake.

His copper-brown eyes turned dark as his shoulders swelled with each breath. Lifting his hand, he brushed his fingertips over the bruise just above her temple.

All the air left the room. She couldn't breathe—couldn't think past the surge of hope hanging between them.

His fingers trailed into her hair as the pad of his thumb skimmed over the sensitive skin of her cheek. She leaned into his touch until he lifted his other hand, cradling her face and tilting her chin up to him.

At exactly the wrong moment, three knocks beat against the door.

But Beau didn't move. Neither did she. How could she pull away when everything inside her said this was right? The one thing she was dying to say was stuck in the back of her throat.

I'm afraid of you too.

The knocks came again followed by a deep male voice. "Room service."

Beau let out a huff and stood, letting his hands fall away as he moved to answer the door.

Beau, of all people. Why did Beau have to be the one to show her how broken all of her other relationships had been? It was obvious now. No other man had treated her the way Beau did. He encouraged her, answered her honestly, and shared parts of himself he didn't share with anyone else. He was right beside her when she needed help and was the first to tell her that she could do anything she wanted. He believed in her when no other man had.

He made her want to be stronger.

And she wanted to give all those things back to him. After seeing how hard he worked to build his business, treat people fairly, take care of his family, and study God's word, it was as plain as day.

She was falling for Beau Lawrence—not even a week after a breakup from her fiancé.

Everyone would say it was a rebound. Everyone would assume they'd been seeing each other behind Dean's back. Everyone would assume and assume and assume.

But she didn't care what everyone else would think. She cared about Beau, and the circumstances surrounding them didn't matter.

The question was, would all of those things matter to him?

CHAPTER 18
ANNA

"Absolutely not."

"Hear me out," Anna begged. Sheesh. He'd shut her down before hearing the whole request.

Beau crossed his arms over his chest. Was he flexing? "I'm not getting in the shower with you. Not happening."

"You make it sound bad, but we'll keep our clothes on." Anna lifted a clump of her hair. "I was laid out on the floor of a public bathroom, then I spent hours at the hospital. It's gross times two."

Beau leveled her with a tense stare. He really had the unwavering look down pat. "I am not getting in the shower with you. I can't."

"Clothes. On," Anna repeated. "I can wear this tank top and thermal pants, and you can put on your swimsuit. Just help me wash my hair, and I'll take care of the rest, but there's no way I can wash my hair with one hand."

Getting out of the wet clothes after her hair was washed would be a chore too, but asking Beau to help her undress was definitely crossing a line.

So was showering together, but it would be over in five minutes. They could handle it.

Well, *she* could handle it. Beau was still holding out.

He closed his eyes and pinched the bridge of his nose. "Anna, I'm trying here. Show me some mercy."

He was right. They'd been dancing around attraction and their new, unnamed feelings for days. Tempting him wasn't right.

"How about I wear a baggy, long sleeve shirt too?" she asked.

He lifted his head, giving her a look that said "Nice try."

"How are you going to get out of a wet, baggy sweater on your own when I'm finished washing your hair?"

Was it just her, or was he talking like he was going to do it?

He let out a deep, resigned sigh and headed for his suitcase. "Let's get this over with."

"Thank you. It'll be quick and painless," she promised. Darting into the bathroom to get the water warmed up, she vowed to do everything in her power to be grateful he was helping her while also making herself as unappealing as possible.

She was slipping off her socks when Beau knocked on the bathroom door.

"Come in."

Oh good. He'd already changed into his swimsuit, and he wore a white T-shirt to complete the very clothed, very modest look.

Then he reached behind his head and pulled the shirt off.

Why? Why, why, why?

She'd seen him without a shirt on when they got in the hot tub together, but it had been dark. So much for *him* being tempted. Beau needed to put his shirt back on, pronto.

Her attention caught on a long, slanting scar over his ribs. "Um, what's that?" she asked, pointing at the mark.

Beau glanced down before looking back up. "Crowbar."

Anna's eyes widened. "A crowbar? How?"

"I was pulling old boards up on a porch, and the crowbar slipped. Almost stabbed me in the heart."

Well, that was one way to distract her. There were other scars in lines, circles, and jagged splotches. "Good grief, where did you get all those?"

Beau shrugged. "I was reckless," he said, as if that explained a history of wounds.

"Why?"

"Why not? I thought I was invincible until I was about twenty-five."

Anna huffed out a sharp breath. It was the opposite of how she'd lived her life—careful and orderly.

"Do you have regrets?" The question was out before she thought about how he might feel about the scars that had obviously been painful in the moments.

His brow scrunched. "No."

Anna shook her head. "We are not the same."

"Wait." Beau held up a hand. "I do regret one." He turned to the side to show his bicep. A faint line ran horizontally across the muscle.

"I pushed Olivia off a tractor when I was about thirteen. She got up and grabbed the first thing she could get her hands on and threw it at me."

Anna leaned in to get a better look at the white mark. "What was it?"

"A saw blade. She threw it like a frisbee."

Anna gasped. "She did not."

"Oh, she did. She got in so much trouble. I did too, but at least I deserved it. She didn't speak to me for weeks. She also had to do my farm chores, and she hated it."

"But now she loves working on the farm. Her chickens are her life."

"She always liked the chickens. My chores included baling hay and milking the goats, and those were her least favorite."

Anna covered her mouth to hide her chuckle. Olivia still didn't like those things.

Beau reached into the shower and let the water run over his hand. "It's warm now."

"Wait, what's that?" Anna asked when she spotted the dark markings on the underside of his arm.

Beau lifted both arms, not only showing the tattoos but effectively flexing the muscles that needed no extra show. "Rock" was written on one arm, and "Solid" was written on the other.

"Rock solid?"

Beau jerked his head toward the shower. "Let's get this over with."

Anna stepped into the shower. "Fine, but I need you to tell me about that while we do this."

The warm water rushed over her, soaking her clothes, and she carefully held her braced hand out of the spray.

Beau stepped in behind her and engulfed any remaining room in the small shower. His large presence loomed over her, but instead of feeling trapped or suffocated, there was only peace.

She turned around to wet her hair, facing him in the small space.

He inhaled a deep breath before turning away from her. "Nope. Let me know when you're ready."

Her nerves kicked in, and every breath was thick and hot. Sure, she was fully clothed. Sure, they'd seen more of each other in the hot tub. But there was something inherently intimate about being in the shower together.

Anna quickly wet her hair, ignoring Beau's back muscles that were on full display for her. "Tell me about the tattoos?" she asked.

"It's not anything special. Everyone called me the Rock in high school. I was an offensive lineman when I played football, and no one could get past me."

"You protected the quarterback?"

"Basically."

With her hair drenched, she reached for the shampoo. "I'm ready."

When he turned around, she squirted the shampoo into his hand. He made a twirling motion, telling her to turn. She did as she was instructed just as he slapped the shampoo on top of her head and rubbed down both sides.

"What are you doing?" she asked through laughter and the spray of water around her.

"Washing your hair. This was your idea!"

"No, I mean why are you doing it like that?"

"If you want this done a specific way, you're going to have to walk me through it."

She used her good hand to show him the kneading motion on top of her head. "Like this. Or think about scratching a dog behind its ears."

"Okay. That I can do," Beau said as he adjusted his technique.

Her eyes closed involuntarily as she sank into the soothing feel of his fingers against her scalp. "You're good at this."

"No. I'm good at scratching dogs. I'm not taking appointments. This is a one and done deal."

A laugh bubbled out of her. "Got it."

After a few minutes, the lathered shampoo started running down her face. "Okay. I think that's good enough. Can you help me rinse it?"

Beau huffed, but he didn't say no. Anna turned to face him and tilted her head back into the spray of water. He lifted his hands and worked his fingers into her hair, massaging out the shampoo.

She needed to think about something other than Beau's hands on her, so she drifted back to their conversation. "I was a cheerleader for the varsity team when you were a senior."

Beau remained focused on rinsing her hair, not looking down at her. "I know."

"You were a sports legend in Blackwater."

Beau scoffed. "I was not. Also, who cares if you're the big fish in a small pond? I only had to be better than five other people to get noticed."

"You've never acted like you wanted to be noticed."

"I don't," he answered quickly.

"Why not?"

"Why would I?"

Beau was perfectly fine living his life on his own terms. No one told him where to go or how to act or when to speak. He was in charge of everything, and he did such a great job managing his business that no one ever saw him struggle.

Anna, on the other hand, never stepped out of bounds. Her life was dictated for her. Assistants scheduled her meetings. Her parents, and until recently, Dean, told her when to show up to charity events, networking parties, and social events.

The only thing she was in charge of was her fashion vlog, and she even had little say in that. Features usually had a schedule corresponding with the debut of a new line or trend.

"You okay?" Beau asked.

"Yeah. I think that's good. If you can brush this conditioner through the ends, I can rinse it myself." She grabbed the bottle and squeezed the conditioner into his hand.

When she turned around, Beau was careful not to pull too hard on any tangled pieces of hair. It probably took a lot of patience and restraint for him to be so gentle.

"I think that's it," he said, reaching his arms around her on both sides to rinse the conditioner off his hands.

"Thank you," she said softly. Appreciation

flooded her, mounting on the emotional toil she'd already been dealing with for hours.

His deep timbre was right beside her ear as he whispered, "You're welcome."

She couldn't turn around—couldn't face him. The tears would come, and he'd see them even through the running water.

And then he was gone, leaving her alone and overwhelmed.

CHAPTER 19
ANNA

Getting out of the wet clothes was more of a chore than she'd expected. By the time she was dry and dressed in warm pajamas, she could barely hold her eyes open. It would be great if her hair was dry before she laid down, but she wasn't about to ask Beau for another favor tonight.

Beau sat at the table, leaned over his open Bible with one hand wrapped around a steaming cup of coffee. When she made a noise while trying to get under the covers, Beau popped up.

"What's wrong?" he asked, suddenly at her side.

"Nothing. Just trying to get comfortable."

"Do you need the medicine?" He was already looking for the pill bottle.

"No, it's not that bad."

"Are you sure? What else do you need?"

She rested her head back against the pillow,

grateful to be clean and in the comfortable bed. "Nothing. You sound like a mother hen."

"Mother hens are vicious," Beau said, completely serious and not at all teasing.

"Well you're worrying too much. Go back to whatever you were doing."

"Are you ready to go to sleep? I'll turn the lights off."

Her phone rang across the room, and Beau went to get it. He handed it to her without looking at the screen.

"Dean. Again," she said with as much ire as she could muster.

"He's still calling?" Beau asked.

"I haven't answered yet." Just the thought of talking to him had her blood running cold. He probably had an excuse prepared to explain his affair. No doubt he thought it was justified somehow.

Beau held out his hand. "Allow me?"

Anna couldn't contain her smile. "That would be epic."

Beau's brow lifted. He was serious.

In a flash of boldness, Anna handed him the phone. He immediately answered and pressed it to his ear.

"Hello." He walked slowly around the foot of the bed and sat on the other side next to her.

"Beau."

Oh no. Dean was already shouting.

Beau looked over at Anna as he continued the conversation with Dean. “Anna can’t come to the phone now. She’s already in bed.”

Anna sat up quickly, completely forgetting the pain in her arm. She’d never gasped so loudly in her life.

Beau held the phone out to her. “Say hey, baby. It’s that loser from your wedding on the phone.”

The laugh bubbled out of her instantly. She slapped a hand over her mouth, but it was too late. Dean shouted a string of the worst curses she’d ever heard before hanging up.

Anna fought to catch her breath through laughter and terror. “I—I can’t believe you did that!”

Beau tossed the phone onto the covers. “I don’t know about you, but I feel better now.”

She gently rested her hand over the throbbing knot on the side of her head. “That was so much fun, but he’s definitely going to tell my parents.” All humor drained from her in an instant. “Oh no. He’s going to tell my parents!”

“And why is that a problem?” Beau asked.

Her heart rate jumped from jogging rate to running rate. “You don’t know my parents! They’re going to be so mad at me.”

“Anna, you’re almost thirty years old. You don’t have to report to your parents.”

“But—But I do. I live in their guest house. I work at their law firm.”

"I know you can afford your own place. Why are you still living at home?"

It was a good question, but she also had a good response. She still hadn't caught her breath from the phone call. "Because Mom is intense, to say the least. She lost her parents when she was young, and when she had my brother and me, she was always intensely protective."

"Controlling," Beau said. "The word is controlling."

He was right, and she had no rebuttal for that insight.

"She is. Mom and Dad always expected a lot from us. We were to always reflect well on them. Everything is about appearance."

Beau didn't comment. Instead, he leaned back against the headboard and listened.

"Drake left home as soon as he got the chance. Mom threw the biggest fit, but he didn't care. He was determined to get away, and I didn't blame him for that."

"But..." Beau added.

"But that meant they doubled down on me. Mom was absolutely not going to lose me too. I know how hard it was for her when her parents died, and I didn't want to put her through that again."

"That's not your fault, and there isn't a good

reason for her to use you like that. She held you back."

"I know," Anna whispered. "They didn't force me to become an attorney, but they definitely pushed for it. They wanted Drake to follow in their footsteps too, but he shut that idea down quickly."

"Where is he?" Beau asked.

"Moved to France. He's married with three kids."

Thinking about her brother was always tough. She loved Drake and missed him every day. He called often, but she'd never met her niece and nephews and probably never would unless she got over her fear of flying and hopped on a plane to the other side of the world.

"Is he happy?"

Anna nodded and settled back against the headboard beside Beau. "He is. He's very happy, and I'm glad. Mom and Dad disowned him, and he said he'd never come back."

Beau reached out and slid his hand into hers. "Not even for you?"

Anna threaded her fingers with his. It was difficult to focus on the conversation when Beau touched her. The anxiety that had gripped her since the phone call melted away, replaced by soaring hope. "That's okay. I know how hard it was for him before he left."

"Was it better for you when he was here?"

Beau released the grip on her hand, but he didn't

let go. His fingertips slowly brushed down her palm and back up her fingers.

"Yes and no. It was clear I was second best. Drake is incredibly intelligent and so likable. Everyone loved him."

"You're all those things too," Beau added quickly.

She rested her head on his shoulder. "You're so sweet to say that."

He reclaimed the grip on her hand again. "It's true," he whispered.

And that was the difference. She'd never lived up to her parents' expectations, but Beau had made her the light of his life for a few days, and it was glorious. For the first time, she was someone's number one.

"My parents aren't all bad. They provided for us, and we never wanted for anything. I don't take that lightly."

Beau loosened his hold again, tracing lines that were as light as air over every side of her fingers. Their hands slowly danced around each other, twisting and shaping together until they moved as one.

Beau pressed his bearded cheek to her damp hair. His voice was deep and soothing as he spoke. "I don't know them, but I don't think they respect you, and that's a shame because you're amazing."

And she was flying somewhere above cloud

nine, hanging on for dear life as her heart soared. Snuggling closer to him, she whispered, "You're pretty amazing too, but you do an awesome job of hiding it. It's like you don't want anyone to know."

He shook his head. "Nah. I just like to mind my own business."

"How do you do it? How do you not worry about what anyone else thinks?"

"I care about what people think to an extent. I want to be trustworthy. I don't want to treat anyone unfairly."

"I can see that. I just don't know how to do it the way you do."

"You want my opinion?" he asked.

"Yeah. I do," she whispered, hoping whatever he said didn't cut her to the core.

"You let go of yourself to be the person they want you to be. It's okay if they don't see you as perfect. God made you to be yourself for His glory. You're good at that, and that's all that matters."

She inhaled a deep breath as the sting of tears pricked in her nose and throat. "You're right. I've lost sight of that. Do you always read the Bible in the mornings?"

"I do. It helps me start my day with a reminder not to lose my cool when I have to deal with idiots at work."

She chuckled and twisted her fingers around his. "I think I should start my day that way too."

"Want to start tomorrow?" Beau asked.

"Yeah. Room service, coffee, and Jesus," she said as her eyes drifted closed.

"Sounds good to me."

"I'm tired," she whispered.

Beau pressed a kiss to the top of her head. "Good night. Wake me up if you need something in the night."

He stood and rounded to her side of the bed. After helping her ease down into the sheets, she grabbed his hand before he walked away.

"Thank you for everything," she said, grasping his hand with the force she wanted to convey.

He gave her hand a squeeze before releasing it. "Sweet dreams."

"Good night."

Despite the turmoil of the day, her mind and heart were more at ease than ever, and she pushed away any worries about tomorrow as she fell asleep.

CHAPTER 20
BEAU

Beau stood from a seat at the small hotel table and stretched his arms above his head. He'd been switching between reading the Bible and watching videos on his phone all morning, and the lack of movement brought on an ache in his back.

Anna sat on the bed, resting back against the headboard with her laptop open. She held her phone to her ear as she had most of the day. After deciding to stay in this morning, she'd thrown herself into work.

Well, aside from the hour-long nap she took after breakfast. The doctor at the hospital said she might feel tired.

Beau had not watched her the whole time while she slept. That would have been weird.

She let out a long sigh and reached up to touch the bruise on her head. She'd been twisting tighter and tighter with every phone call, and the happy woman he'd been spending his days with was almost completely gone.

Beau stepped to the bed and sat at the end. She glanced at him with that fake smile she'd promised not to use and held up a finger.

"Send me his number, and I'll take care of it. Thanks, Angie."

Anna ended the call and stretched her neck from side to side. "Sorry I've been on the phone a lot."

"Nothing to be sorry about. You want to get out of here for a little bit?"

She tossed her laptop onto the bed beside her. "Yes, I'm hungry."

"What if I took you into town? Did you see anything you wanted to try when we were at the tree lighting ceremony?"

And he was officially a puppy, following her around begging for her attention.

She bit at her bottom lip, making a show of thinking, and the expression wasn't doing anything for Beau's unhealthy attraction to her.

"I saw a sign outside a really cute house. I want to say it's called Evelyn's or something."

"You remember where it was?"

"Yeah. Just before we drove into town on the right."

Beau stood and offered her a hand. "I'll change, then you can have the bathroom."

She took his hand and stood, stepping close enough that the smell of her shampoo caught his attention. It was a scent that was embedded in his memory after showering together.

Nope. Don't think about the shower.

She squeezed his hand before letting it fall. "Any chance you could help me put my hair up in a ponytail?" Anna asked, holding up her injured hand.

"I have a better idea. Why don't we stop at the front desk and see if Joanna can help."

A smile bloomed over Anna's lips. "Perfect. Why didn't I think of that?"

Thirty minutes later, they were getting in the car and heading down the mountain. Fluffy snow covered the sides of the roads, and a white fog settled over the peaks. Anna sat forward in her seat taking photos after every switchback.

"There it is," she said, pointing to a two-story fancy house with a sign out front that promised delicious food with a view. Trees hid some of the dark-blue exterior with tall windows framed in bright white.

After parking along the sidewalk, Beau jogged around the car to help Anna. He rested a hand on her back as they walked up the steps to the entrance. "Any dizziness?"

She smiled at him then—the real one. "Nope. I feel good."

Food with a view was underhyped. They sat

at a small table for two in front of a big window showcasing the snowy mountains, and Anna absolutely glowed throughout the entire meal.

She talked too. A lot. He'd never been a fan of chitchat, but he'd do anything to keep her talking and smiling. He hung on every word she said like a total sap.

Shoot. This was bad. Awful. The worst. He was one hundred percent captivated by Anna, and he didn't have the willpower to pump the brakes.

Spending time with Anna was easy, and he wanted more.

After the meal, they headed back to the car.

"Where to now?" Beau asked.

"I'd like to go back to some of those cute shops we saw when we were here for the tree lighting. I think I could pick up some more Christmas presents."

"Okay." He reached for the passenger door, but she grabbed his hand.

Good grief. Why did he get a shock to his system every time she touched him?

"Could we walk? It's such a pretty day."

He released the door and returned to her side. She wrapped her arms around his, plastering herself to his side.

And he didn't hate it. Not one bit.

The first shop that Anna pulled him into was a

candle shop called Wick and Sarcasm. It was a whole store filled with shelves of candles.

A variety of scents hit him at the same time, but one overpowered all others—vanilla. It was as if Anna had just wrapped herself around him.

A short woman with sandy-blonde hair glanced at them over her shoulder as she placed candles onto a shelf from a rolling cart. "Hello! Welcome to Wick and Sarcasm. Our candle of the day is Stories and Scones named after the bakery here in town. It's a warm vanilla and pastry scent."

"It smells amazing. I definitely want one of those," Anna said.

The woman turned to face them, brushing off her apron. "We also make custom candles. You can pick your scent and give it a name. They're great for celebrating special occasions."

Oh, so they looked like a couple. Awesome. His journey into the Twilight Zone was complete.

"Can we do that?" Anna asked, looking up at him with wide eyes.

"If you want."

Anna squealed and followed the woman toward a room at the back. "Come on and we'll get started."

Beau tried and failed to hang out on the sidelines, but Anna asked his opinion about everything. If he was going to have a say in this special candle, he wanted it to smell just like Anna. Even without her standing right next to him, he'd memorized the scent that tangled around his thoughts day and night.

When they decided on a scent, the woman brought over a laptop where she pointed to a label template. "Now, what would you like to call your candle?"

"Candles have names?" Beau asked.

"Of course! And they're all unique and special," the woman said as if she were telling him something everyone else in the world already knew.

Anna looked up at him. "Can we call it Freedom?"

"Whatever you want." Whether she wanted to remember the place or her newfound freedom, the name was fitting.

"Perfect. I'll have this ready for you in about two hours. Let me get your information, and I'll call you when it's ready."

When they stepped out onto the sidewalk, Anna looked all around, completely thrilled by the decorations and flare of the Christmas town.

"Where to?" Beau asked.

"Can we go back to Stories and Scones? I could go for some more of those chocolate-covered strawberries."

"Anything you want," Beau said automatically.

Anna walked close to him, and he slipped his hand into hers, desperate to link himself to her in some small way.

She looked at him, radiating pure joy. "You should smile more. I like it."

If he'd been smiling before, it was gone now. He'd been *smiling*? He didn't smile. He wasn't a smiling kinda guy.

And she liked it when he smiled? What did it mean when his world flipped on his head whenever she gave him the tiniest grin?

It meant he was in trouble. Big trouble since they still had days left to spend together.

Beau opened the door to Stories and Scones, and Anna entered first. He heard the feminine greeting before he saw her.

"You're back!" Jan shouted, throwing her hands in the air. Her brow furrowed as she came to meet Anna. "And you're hurt."

Anna raised her braced wrist. "Just a sprain. I had a bout of altitude sickness the other day and passed out."

Jan wrapped Anna in a hug, careful not to jostle her wrist. "Wait a minute. Did you have a snow-boarding lesson with Aiden?"

Anna turned to look at Beau before giving her attention back to Jan. "How did you know?"

"Aiden is my son. He mentioned a young woman passed out yesterday, and he and Joanna were worried."

Anna pressed her good hand to her chest. "I love this small town. We saw Joanna this morning. She helped me put my hair up." Anna flicked her ponytail, emphasizing the subject.

Beau clenched his jaw. They needed to stop talking about Anna's hair because it only made him think about washing it for her last night.

"I'm so glad you're okay, and I'm happy to see you again," Jan said as she ushered Anna over to the pastry display case. "I have some samples of cranberry flapjack for you to try."

"I love cranberries!" Anna said excitedly.

"Anna."

Beau turned when someone called Anna's name. A young woman with brown hair and round glasses fidgeted with the strap of her purse. Could someone in Freedom, Colorado actually know Anna?

Anna's eyes widened, and her jaw opened for a few seconds before she spoke. "Brittany."

CHAPTER 21
ANNA

There she was. Brittany Diaz was here in Freedom.

After a second of shock, Anna recovered and hugged her friend. "It's so good to finally meet you in person. What are you doing here?"

Brittany hugged her back before pulling away and adjusting her glasses. "You sounded like you'd been having a tough time, so I thought I'd check on you."

Um, was that sweet or...something else? They'd known each other for years online, but even Freedom, Colorado was still a long way from Sacramento, California.

"That's so sweet of you." It was sweet—probably the biggest gesture anyone had ever done for her.

Brittany gently cradled Anna's braced hand in

hers. "Oh, you poor thing. How are you feeling today?"

"I'm much better. I had a bad experience with altitude sickness yesterday and passed out. It's just sprained." Remembering Beau, Anna turned and waved him over. "This is Beau Lawrence. He came with me on this trip because I didn't want to come alone."

Brittany looked him up and down, but her face didn't show much of a reaction. "I'm Brittany, Anna's friend."

Beau extended a hand to her. "It's nice to meet you."

"How do you two know each other?" Brittany asked, looking between them. "What does Dean think about the two of you traveling together?"

And there was the hit—the one Anna hadn't expected. Sure, Brittany was sweet, but she didn't always understand how her words could cut to the bone.

She wasn't intentionally insensitive, and this was only the first of what Anna had to look forward to when she returned to Blackwater and faced the mess she'd left behind.

"Um, well, Dean and I aren't together anymore. He cheated on me, remember?"

Anna had slowly told Brittany about the wedding over the last few days through messages. It had seemed like Brittany understood that Dean's infidelity wasn't something Anna was interested in working past. Maybe she hadn't been as clear as she'd thought.

"Oh, right." Brittany slapped her palm to her forehead. "Silly. I forgot. I guess I just got so used to you being with Dean that it hasn't sunk in yet."

"It's okay. And Beau is just a friend. We're not together." She turned to Beau for confirmation. "Right?"

"Right," Beau said with a single nod.

Though, Anna had found herself wishing more and more that they *were* together. She'd had the best time on this trip, and it was mostly because Beau had made it fun. She'd gotten a taste of pure happiness, and it seemed wrong to ignore it.

"Oh. Good to know," Brittany said, clutching the strap of her purse with white knuckles.

"How did you know I was here?" Anna asked. "I don't think we talked about Freedom."

Brittany tucked a strand of her hair behind her ear. "Oh, you mentioned this place, so I looked it up. This was the only Stories and Scones in Colorado."

The sweet scented air turned thin in the small bakery. "Oh."

Beau's hand rested on the small of her back. Had he picked up on her anxiety?

"After you said so many good things about it, I figured you'd come back here." Brittany opened her hands. "And here you are."

"Right. Um, are you staying in town?"

"Yeah, I got a room at a little apartment down the street. What are the two of you up to today?"

A flood of questions rushed through Anna's mind at once. How long was she staying? How long had she been waiting in this bakery? How had she gotten here from Sacramento?

"I—I think we're just doing some shopping around town." Anna paused to swallow past the dryness in her mouth. "Would you like to join us?"

"Sure!" Brittany said with wide eyes.

Okay, at least she'd have some time to talk to Brittany and get some answers. "Great. Do you want some coffee or a treat?" It was the least she could offer after Brittany came all this way.

Brittany stayed close to Anna all day as they wound in and out of shops on the main square in town. Aside from a few pointed looks at Beau, she didn't get a chance to ask him what he thought about the woman showing up out of nowhere and basically tracking her down.

No, she wouldn't be creeped out by that. No doubt Brittany saw it as kindness, not a breach of privacy.

They had a good time shopping for Christmas presents around town, and all of Anna's concern about Brittany vanished. She really had come just to check on her, and hanging out with a friend was just what Anna needed.

When Beau's arms were loaded with shopping bags, they started making their way back across town. The throbbing in Anna's head was back, and exhaustion was gaining on her like a cheetah chasing a gazelle. She pressed the heel of her hand against her temple.

"Are you okay?" Brittany asked.

"I'm getting tired. I think it's time to head back."

Brittany looked around the decorated town square. "Oh, okay. Where did you park?"

"Over by Evelyn's," Anna said, pointing in the direction of the restaurant.

"I'm parked this way." Brittany pointed over her shoulder in the other direction.

"Why don't you walk with us to our car, and I'll drive you over to yours? I don't like the idea of you walking alone," Beau said.

Brittany tilted her head as she looked at Beau. "Thank you. That's thoughtful of you."

That was Beau—thoughtful. He'd shown his true colors on this trip. Why hadn't Anna noticed it before now? He stayed close to Anna's side until they got to her car. He opened the doors for both her and Brittany before slipping into the driver's seat.

"Is this your car?" Brittany asked as she trailed her fingertips over the leather interior. "It's nice."

"Thanks." Anna hadn't gone for an over-the-top luxury vehicle, but it *was* nice. She'd chosen it because she could afford it, and paying for her own vehicle was something she was proud to claim.

"How do you afford it?" Brittany asked.

It wasn't the first intrusive question Brittany had asked, but the throbbing in Anna's head had her patience stretching thin. She rested her head back and took a deep breath before answering. "The fashion vlog is my job, but I'm also an attorney."

"Oh. I forgot about that," Brittany said, slapping her palm against her forehead again.

"I don't talk about it a lot on social media." It wasn't that she was intent on keeping her day job a secret. It just didn't come up in conversation about fashion often.

Brittany directed Beau to the lot where she'd parked, and they said quick goodbyes with promises to check in tomorrow. Beau and Anna waited until Brittany was safely in her car and had started the engine before pulling out into the snowy night.

Allowing her eyes to close, Anna whispered a soft, "Thank you."

"For what?" Beau asked.

"For shopping with me. For carrying the bags around all day. For being nice when Brittany showed up and plans changed."

"That's no big deal."

There was a beat of silence before Anna raised her head. "Is it weird that she found me here or that she came all the way from California just to see me?"

"I wasn't going to say anything, but it's kind of weird."

"But she's so nice," Anna added. "I hate to think bad of her when she was kind enough to check on me."

"If she's getting closer than you're comfortable with, just tell her."

Anna huffed. "It's not that simple."

"Yes, it is."

Okay, maybe in Beau's mind it was. He lived his life at face value, and it worked for him. If Anna told Brittany she was getting a little too close, she'd no doubt take offense. The last thing she wanted to do was hurt her friend's feelings.

Then again, if Olivia showed up in Freedom, Anna wouldn't question it. Maybe she'd been looking at her and Brittany's friendship differently because it had only existed online.

"I'm too tired to think about it today," Anna said.

Beau glanced over at her as he drove slowly up the mountain through gently falling snow. "Do you need a nap?"

"Yeah. I'll feel better after I rest a little."

CHAPTER 22

BEAU

Anna didn't stir for two hours, which gave him plenty of time to catch up with the guys at the garage and overthink every single thing Anna had said since the day he met her.

Things weren't going well. The tightness in his chest was worsening, and the impending separation coming for them after this trip ended hung over him like a rain cloud.

When Anna sat up in bed and stretched her arms above her head, Beau made every effort to ignore her.

"How long was I out?" she asked in that sleepy voice that zipped into his brain and paralyzed him.

"A few hours. Feeling better?"

"I am. Have you had dinner?"

Beau glanced at the clock on his phone. "Nope. You want me to go grab something for us?"

"Actually, I was thinking about a steak. I wonder if there's a wait at Liberty Grill."

"I'll call and find out."

Anna threw the blanket off her legs and slipped out of the bed. "I'll get ready."

Within minutes, they had a table waiting for them downstairs. They'd been together every moment for almost a week, and their time together was slipping away.

This was the last thing he could have seen coming. He'd gotten a peek at life with Anna, and now he wanted more.

Fifteen minutes later, Anna stepped out of the bathroom with wavy hair and wearing a shiny gold dress that should have been classified as a weapon.

He was staring—no, gawking—and he had zero motivation to stop as she casually slipped gold rings onto her fingers and hoop earrings into her ears.

Anna brushed her hands down the sides of her dress, looking down to inspect it before lifting her gaze to him. "What? Does it look okay?"

Beau looked away, scratching the back of his neck as he stood quickly from the couch. "Yeah. You look amazing. I should change."

Ducking into the bathroom, he had a couple of minutes to give himself a pep talk before facing Anna again. Never in his life had he been so flustered over a woman. Now, he was stuck in close proximity to the one who had gotten under his skin.

He could do this. He could have dinner with a beautiful woman and not lose himself.

What a joke. He was already gone. The damage was done, and he'd let it happen.

When they stepped into the empty elevator, Anna checked herself in the reflective walls, turning and swiping her hands over her curves.

Beau stuffed his hands into his pockets and stretched his neck from one side to the other. "Will you stop that? You look amazing."

Anna turned her bright eyes on him, and she might as well have pinned him to the wall. She reached up to adjust the collar of his shirt before sliding her hands down his chest.

Good grief, if she didn't stop touching him, his hands were going to come out of his pockets and do something they shouldn't.

"You look amazing too," she whispered.

Beau set his jaw. Why was the elevator moving at a snail's pace? He needed air and space between them.

Lots of space.

The torture chamber finally released them, and Anna slipped her arm around his as they made their way through the lobby to the Grill. The hostess quickly sat them at a small table for two next to the large windows overlooking the dark mountains.

They both skimmed the menu in silence. Beau

quickly decided on a pork chop, then made every effort not to stare at Anna.

How could he be expected not to look at her when she was two feet away? It was the equivalent of setting a hot steak in front of a starving man.

Anna finally laid her menu down and picked up her phone, immediately sighing at whatever waited on the screen.

"You can turn it off," Beau reminded her.

She scrolled through the notifications. "More calls from Mom, texts from Olivia, messages from Brittany. I should have invited her to dinner."

He'd keep his mouth shut on that point. Brittany did seem to like Anna, but she also overstepped her bounds a little too often for his taste.

"We don't have anything planned tomorrow except the church service in the morning. Should I ask her to have lunch with me?" Anna asked.

"If that's what you want. This is your trip, remember. You're in charge."

Anna's eyes widened. "Wow. Ten missed messages."

"From who?"

"Brittany."

Beau tapped his knuckles on the table. "I'm not trying to make decisions for you, but that's a lot. It might be a good idea to put some distance between you two."

Anna's shoulders rose and fell as she typed

quickly on the phone. "She sends so many messages. I can't keep up."

Reaching out, Beau rested a hand over Anna's braced wrist. "Stop. You don't have to reply to every message and email immediately. This is your time."

She looked up at him, and the crease between her brows disappeared. "You're right. I'll reply to the messages after dinner."

Great. Now that she wasn't on the verge of exploding, Beau released her hand. It wasn't a good idea to hang onto her longer than necessary.

She pulled her hands back and twirled the rings on her fingers. "This has been the best trip I've ever taken."

Beau sat back, crossing his arms over his chest. "I'm glad."

Their waiter appeared and took their orders before slipping away again.

Anna leaned forward, propping her arms on the table. "Where does this trip rank for you?"

"That's not really a fair question. I haven't been away from home many times."

"Still, would you rate this experience a five out of ten?"

Beau shook his head. This was a dangerous game. He didn't like lying, but telling her the truth was just asking for trouble.

"Higher or lower?" she asked, twirling her rings again.

"Higher."

"Seven?"

"Higher."

"Nine?" she asked, eyes wide and ridiculously beautiful.

Shoot. He might as well seal his fate. It was impossible to resist her when she asked for anything.

"Higher."

Anna's smile spread wide, and she clasped her hands in excitement.

Well, she clasped her right hand. The left one was still injured, and something shiny fell to the floor.

She gasped. "I dropped my ring."

"I'll get it." Beau slid out of his seat and knelt beside the table. The ring shone underneath the table. He picked it up and handed it to her.

A loud gasp from a woman behind him drew his attention. The woman was staring at him with a wide-open mouth.

"He's proposing!"

Good gravy, he was kneeling in front of Anna holding a ring between them.

When he turned back to Anna, her hand covered her mouth, trying to hide a mischievous smile.

Take the ring. Take the ring. Take the ring!

As soon as she removed her hand from her mouth, his stomach sank.

"Yes!"

Oh no. She was having the time of her life acting in front of a crowd, and he'd just gotten himself roped into it.

The entire restaurant erupted into cheers, and Anna sprang to her feet, practically jumping for joy.

Beau stood and pulled her close until they were nose to nose.

"What are you doing?" he whispered.

"Just having fun," she said, giggling through every word.

Beau shook his head, but she was actually cutting through his walls with her joy. "You're a menace."

Chants pulsed around them. "Kiss her! Kiss her! Kiss her!"

The warm vanilla of her hair drew him in as he leaned closer. "Sounds like they want a show," he said as the crowd chanted on.

Anna's smile faded as she glanced down at his lips before looking back up to pin him with her blue eyes. "What do you want?"

That was the moment that all restraint flew out the window. Without even stopping to think, he wrapped his arm around her waist and pressed his mouth to hers.

Her hand slid around his neck as she melted into his arms. The restaurant erupted into a wild roar, but he heard everything through a fog. Nothing existed except the woman in his arms. He kissed her madly, and she met each move match-for-match.

Someone behind him shouted, "Get a room!"

Remembering this was a family restaurant, he broke the kiss and blinked past the haze in his vision. Anna stared at him with a look that straddled the line between shock and terror.

Before he had a chance to freak out, she rose onto her toes and pressed a quick kiss to his lips.

Everyone was clapping and whistling, but Beau was paralyzed. Had he just kissed Anna for the first time in front of dozens of people?

Shoot, the fact that he was thinking about it as *the first time* wasn't good. He already wanted more.

Anna held out her hand, and Beau slipped the ring onto her finger. She held it above her head for everyone to see.

It was all for show. They'd just played a whole room full of people, and Beau's heart was about to tear out of his chest. He wasn't proposing marriage, but what would it be like if Anna Harris really said yes to him?

CHAPTER 23
ANNA

Beau reached for her hand as they walked out of the restaurant. A few of the other diners who'd witnessed the proposal clapped and whistled.

Anna snuggled to Beau's side with his fingers locked firmly between each of hers. Leaning closer, she whispered against his shoulder, "I can't believe we did that."

"You did that. You can't believe *you* did that," Beau corrected, but there was a hint of laughter in his voice—one she'd never heard before.

The lobby was bustling even at the late hour, and Christmas music was a low background to the festive room. Families gathered around the grouped seats, a line of customers led to Mountain Mugs Coffee counter, and groups congregated at the front desk.

It was a perfect night, and she was still riding

the thrill of Beau's fake proposal. Her heart raced like a herd of wild horses. It was all pretend, but her body hadn't gotten the message. She still hadn't caught her breath.

Dean had proposed at the local country club during a formal gala, and she'd been happy at the time—thrilled even—but tonight's proposal blew that one out of the water. No, it blew Dean's proposal out of the country.

Beau pressed the button for the elevator and tugged her arm until they were chest-to-chest. He wrapped his arms around her and leaned down to whisper, "Should I expect you pick out a house in the suburbs soon?"

Anna pressed her forehead to his chest. "Sorry."

"No, you're not. I have to keep my guard up whenever you're around. You're always getting us into trouble."

Us. She liked the sound of that way too much.

The elevator doors opened, and they stepped inside. A man and woman who looked to be in their late forties waved as they sprinted toward the elevator. "Hold it, please!"

Beau stuck an arm out until the couple made it to the elevator.

The man let out a deep breath. "Whew. I must be out of shape if I can't jog to catch the elevator."

The woman turned a sweet smile on Beau and Anna. "Thanks for holding it for us."

"You're welcome," Anna said.

The man pointed to Beau and Anna. "Wait, aren't you the two who just got engaged in the restaurant?"

Oh no. Faking it for a room full of strangers was one thing. Lying to someone's face was another.

Anna hunched her shoulders forward. "Actually, we're not engaged. I dropped my ring on the floor, and he just picked it up for me. Everyone thought he was proposing, so we played along."

The woman pressed a hand to her chest and let out a riotous laugh. "That's hilarious!"

"You two had us all fooled," the man said.

The woman chuckled. "That was some kiss. I'm sure the real thing is in your future."

Anna glanced up at Beau to find him staring at the floor. "We're not together. Just friends."

Why did it hurt to admit the truth? The lie sounded so much better.

The woman gasped. "You're joking. You two make such a great couple. And that kiss!"

The man shook his head and made a clicking noise behind his teeth. "I've got one piece of advice for you. Don't let a good one get away."

Beau pressed his lips into a thin line, biting off something on the tip of his tongue.

The elevator dinged, and the couple stepped out. "Have a nice evening," the woman said with a wave.

"Bye!" Anna shouted as the doors closed again. "They were nice."

Beau crossed his arms over his chest and glared down at her with a look that was probably meant to be intimidating. "You are trouble."

"I told the truth!" Anna argued.

"I can't trust you as far as I can throw you."

Anna propped her hands on her hips. "And how far is that?"

The elevator doors opened, and Beau's lips turned up into a playful grin. "I don't know. Let's find out."

One second she was an independent woman standing on her own two feet. The next, she was whisked into Beau's arms and carried out into the hallway.

"Beau!" Laughter spilled out of her as she clung to him. Nuzzling her face into the crook of his neck, the giggles died away, leaving a warmth that spread over her skin.

Lifting her head, she asked, "So, am I too heavy to throw?"

Beau huffed. "You weigh next to nothing. I could throw you ten yards."

She laughed again and tightened her hold around his shoulders.

"But I don't want to," he whispered softly as he continued carrying her toward their room.

When they reached the door, he rested her feet

on the floor. The excitement of dinner and the proposal had her mind zipping in a thousand different directions. Despite the late hour, she wasn't ready to settle down.

Beau walked straight to his bag and grabbed some clothes. "If you're all good here, I'm going to check out the gym."

"Go right ahead. I have plenty of work to catch up on."

He stopped just before the bathroom door. "Don't work too hard. You're still on vacation."

She couldn't resist the urge to roll her eyes. "Says the man who literally lives at work."

Beau shrugged. "Everyone needs time off."

He was right, but they'd both grown up hearing that hard work was the only way to keep your head above water. Beau and Olivia started farm chores when they were young, and Anna's parents had been training her at the law firm since she was old enough to read.

Anna grabbed her laptop and settled on the bed with her back propped against the headboard. She'd respond to emails until she got tired.

A minute later, Beau stepped out of the bathroom wearing a white T-shirt and black gym shorts. "I'll be back soon."

"Take your time. I'll be busy here for the next few hours."

Beau stopped in his tracks. "I'm serious. Don't overwork yourself."

The genuine care in his voice was more than she could comprehend at the moment. Her mouth went dry, and she cleared her throat. "I won't."

He gave her a small nod but didn't move to leave. "That was fun."

So he had enjoyed their little game of pretend. "Really? What part?"

His voice was deep and sure as he leveled her with his intense gaze. "Pretending you were mine."

CHAPTER 24
ANNA

The breath in Anna's lungs stilled as she watched Beau walk out the door. He had *fun* pretending they were together.

Alone in the room, the force of Beau's words struck her in the chest. It had been more than fun for her. She'd loved it—basked in his adoration and attention, took advantage of the opportunity to touch him, and finally said the things she'd been dying to say for days.

Her breaths came quicker as the realization took root. She was falling for Beau—fast.

She'd always been one to jump into love. It had always been easy to find the good parts of people and magnify them, but with Beau, everything was good. He put God first, he'd come on this trip with her, he'd taken care of her and protected her, he'd listened, he'd worked hard and helped others. What was not to love?

Anna grabbed her phone and called her lifeline —the one person who knew how to bring her back to earth when she got lost floating in the clouds.

"Hey!" A dog barked in the background as Olivia answered.

"I have a problem." Best to get right into it.

"What do you need? I'll be right there," Olivia said amidst rustling on her end of the call.

"No. Not that. I'm definitely falling for Beau. I mean, like *really* falling."

Olivia chuckled. "I thought you said you had a problem."

"This is a problem! I am head over heels!"

"Yeah, sounds terrible. Love is overrated," Olivia deadpanned.

"Why are you being sarcastic? I just got my heart stomped on. I don't know if Beau likes me back. What if people think I was cheating on Dean? It's too soon."

"First, who cares about what people think? If you two want to be together, don't let anyone tell you it's too soon after you broke it off with that loser. You deserve happiness, and you shouldn't have to sit on the sidelines for a socially acceptable amount of time."

Anna pinched the bridge of her nose. "But people will talk."

"Like I said, so what? Second, what makes you think Beau doesn't like you back?"

"Well, I actually think he might, but I am terrified of being wrong about this."

"Tell me about what's going on. What led to these feelings?"

Anna spent the next half hour telling Olivia about different things that happened over the last few days that showed Anna a different side of Beau. Reliving the moments only strengthened her feelings for him.

Finally, Olivia let out a long whistle. "Wow. Girl, I don't think you have anything to worry about. It sounds like he's in this too."

"You think?" She wanted to hope, but hope might only lead to more heartache.

"I do. I've never known Beau to act like that. This is different."

Anna huffed out a breath and relaxed against the headboard. "It's definitely different for me. I've forced more than my fair share of relationships, but being with Beau is as easy as breathing. I'm happy when I'm with him."

"Bingo! That's what I needed to hear. Just enjoy the rest of your trip and have a talk like responsible adults when you get back to the real world. If it's meant to be, it'll survive after the vacation is over."

The dog continued barking next to Olivia. "Hey,

let me call you back. Betsy needs to go out, and I have to suit up. It's snowing hard tonight."

"Go take care of your baby. We'll talk tomorrow. Love you."

"Love you too. Don't worry. It'll all be okay."

Anna dropped the phone onto the bed and allowed Olivia's encouragement to sink in. As expected, Liv had helped Anna breathe easily again. They knew each other so well, and they'd been friends since they were young. Even with the history, they still didn't shy away from telling each other the truth.

Her phone vibrated twice in a row, and she reached for it. There were multiple messages from Brittany.

Brittany: Who designed the beige trench coat you wore today?

Brittany: And were the boots Stella Artour? Have they been released yet? I can't find them.

At least Brittany had moved on from personal questions. Fashion was a safe subject.

Anna: The trench coat is Gretta Danse, and the boots are Stella Artour. Good eye! They're actually in next year's fall line.

Brittany would no doubt reply immediately, but Anna clicked over to check her emails. A message waited from TrueBlue, the exclusive boutique that designed and sent her custom wedding dress.

. . .

TrueBlue: Hi Anna.

We received the dress and wanted to confirm that it is still in good condition. It's unfortunate that you were unable to feature the dress since it was a custom creation. We also think it would be in poor taste to offer the dress to another bride in light of the negativity associated with your wedding.

Though we were grateful to have the opportunity to work with you, we have decided to terminate our business arrangement. The design and production of the dress was too much of a loss to overlook.

We wish you well.

Sincerely,

TrueBlue

Great. One of the biggest up-and-coming boutiques in America didn't want to work with her. Not only that, but they didn't care one bit that the day that was supposed to be the happiest of her life was a disaster.

It couldn't be helped. She couldn't feature the dress without a wedding, and she would not be getting married anytime soon.

Anna hung her head. She knew exactly the kind of bind she'd put these boutiques in, but she couldn't change it now. As much as she hated letting people down, this was a necessary step in regaining her independence.

More messages from Brittany came through, but Anna silenced the phone. Even fashion had a dark cloud hanging over it right now.

She got up, changed into comfortable pajamas, and washed her face. Exhaustion was catching up to her again despite the nap she'd taken earlier. When she slipped into the bed and wiggled into the warmth of the covers, her phone rang.

Her mom was calling...again. She hadn't answered a single one of her mom's calls since the wedding, and the longer she waited, the worse it would be when she finally confronted her mother.

When the call rolled to voicemail, Anna clicked to listen to the first message from her mother dated the same day as the wedding.

Her mother's irate voice greeted her, followed by strings of curses and threats. She'd seen her mother angry plenty of times, but this was worse than she'd ever heard. The names her mother called Anna made her want to sink into a deep sea to drown out the sound.

But she wrapped up in the covers and kept on listening—letting every word hit her like a bullet to the chest. The tears came quickly, sliding over her temples and soaking into her hair. She let the sobs have free rein. It was the perfect time to let it all out. No one was around to see her crumble.

There were so many messages. Some were long and hateful. Some were quick and sharp like a bee sting. Yet, Anna let them come. She let the blows hit their target and warp her into a bent and broken mess. Her mom didn't care that Anna had been betrayed. She didn't care that Anna was hurting or embarrassed. In Catherine Harris's eyes, Anna was the one to blame.

There were still more messages waiting, but Anna tossed the phone onto the bed and threw the covers back. She didn't have to listen to the messages. Her mother was supposed to love her and stand beside her, but Catherine had never been that way.

Anna stormed to the bathroom and wiped her face clean. So what if she didn't have a supportive mother? She had plenty to be thankful for, and she could still appreciate what her parents had done for her. She'd never wanted for anything, and she'd been allowed to pursue the best education. She had friends who would do anything for her. She had jobs she loved and a home in the best town in the world.

She stepped out of the bathroom with a clean, dry face and spotted Beau's Bible on the table. She hadn't even thought to bring hers on the trip, but Beau had brought his despite having only a few minutes to pack. Anna had been using the Bible app on her phone when they read together in the mornings over breakfast.

That was what she wanted. That was the happiness she should have been chasing all along. Love from an earthly man wasn't going to fill the hole in her heart. She needed Jesus. Only Jesus.

She sat at the table and brushed a hand over the worn cover. Beau's Bible wasn't pretty and pristine. The front cover had a slight hump in it, and some of the pages were bent.

Slowly, she opened it, only to find the spine separated from the pages. The title page was covered in scratchy writing. Verses, dates, and phrases covered the page. Things like "Shut up and listen" made her chuckle, while phrases like "Jesus wins" made her stop and stare in awe. Along the crease of the page was written, "Thank you for another day that I haven't earned and don't deserve."

As she scanned the page, one note stood out to her.

"Help. Psalm 34: 17-18"

Anna quickly flipped to the verses and read them aloud. "When the righteous cry for help, the Lord hears and delivers them out of their troubles. The Lord is close to the brokenhearted and saves the crushed in spirit."

That was her problem. She hadn't taken her anxiety to God. She hadn't asked Him to help her through it. She hadn't thanked Him for unanswered prayers. She'd been trying to do it all herself. No wonder she was lost. She'd turned her back on the One who promised to walk with her through everything.

Letting her chin fall to her chest, Anna closed her eyes and prayed aloud. "God, I'm sorry. I'm sorry I forgot about You. I'm sorry I haven't let go of my own selfish wants. I'm sorry I've been so caught up in being loved that I forgot I already am.

"Thank You for staying, even though I don't deserve Your love. Thank You for sending amazing friends.

"God, what I really need is You. I need to trust You, and I hope I can do that." She sniffed and wiped her cheek. "I don't want to live alone anymore, but I don't want to go against Your plan for me. Can You guide me? Show me when I'm on the wrong path, and encourage me when I'm heading in the right direction? I just want to do things right. For You.

"Yes, I want a man to love me, but only if it's the man that You know is right for me."

Images of Beau flashed in her mind. Sitting with her after she passed out and helping her after she injured her wrist. The way he listened when she spoke and encouraged her when she was afraid. Beau had been pointing her to God through all of this, and she'd been too self-absorbed to see it.

His name was on the tip of her tongue, but she couldn't force another decision when she was asking God to show her the way. She wanted Beau to be the man God had in mind for her, but His will was greater than her desires. Beau might be selfless and kind at every turn, but was he just the man God put in her path when she needed him most?

The proposal at dinner was fake, but she desperately wanted it to be real. If she was going to give it to God, she had to let go of all her own wants. If Beau was the man for her, God would show her.

Finally, the truth sank in. God had provided for her over and over again throughout her life, and He would continue to do it. Whatever He had in mind for her was better than her own desires.

They had a few more days left in Freedom, and Anna would make the most of them.

CHAPTER 25
BEAU

Freedom Bible Church wasn't very big, but the sanctuary held a bunch of people. They'd struggled to find seats even though they'd arrived early.

Locals came by to shake his and Anna's hands in a continuous line, and Anna had done a pretty good job of giving each of them her attention while still watching the door for Brittany to arrive.

Anna had been asleep when he got back from the gym, but she'd brought up Brittany during breakfast. After a little back and forth, Anna decided to invite her to join them for the morning service at the church Joanna at the hotel recommended.

For a brief second, no one was introducing themselves and welcoming them to the church, and Anna fidgeted like an energetic kid in her seat.

"You okay?" Beau asked.

"Just wondering whether she'll show up or not."

"She's not late. It was nice of you to invite her, but if she doesn't come, that's her choice."

Anna faced him, and the small crease in her brow disappeared. "You're right. It would just be great if she came."

Beau wrapped an arm around Anna's shoulders. "You're too good. You know that?"

Anna rolled her eyes. "Inviting someone to church is easy."

"No, it's not. I know as Christians we're supposed to go into the world making disciples of all nations, but it never dawns on me to invite someone to church."

"You barely speak unless you have something to say," Anna reminded him.

"Yeah, but that's not an excuse. That's something I *should* say, and I don't."

Anna could make a friend out of a stranger within five minutes, but Beau could count on one hand the number of new friends he'd made in the last ten years. Just because it came easy to Anna didn't mean it was an order from God that he was exempt from.

Anna smiled. "You're a good man. I wouldn't have thought to invite her if it wasn't for you."

"Me? I didn't do anything."

"You didn't do anything different. You woke up and read your Bible."

They'd been waking up around the same time to read together, and to be honest, it was Beau's favorite time of the day. Today, Anna said she wanted them to read the same passage. Beau had chosen the Beatitudes in Matthew.

"Do you remember what we read? Let your light shine before others, so that they may see your good works and give glory to your Father who is in heaven."

Just when he thought she couldn't get any better, she quoted Scripture and reminded him, again, of her pure heart.

Beau looked up just in time to see Brittany come to a stop at the end of the row. Slowly, he removed his arm from around Anna.

Brittany's expression was completely blank. Whether she meant to come off as unfeeling or not, he was having a tough time understanding her.

Anna stood with a smile. "Hey! I'm so glad you made it!"

Anna wrapped Brittany in a big hug, and Brittany returned the gesture with much less enthusiasm.

"Come sit with us," Anna said, dragging Brittany by the hand to their seats.

Seconds later, the worship leader began singing, signaling for everyone to settle down. He'd never paid much attention before, but Anna was a great singer.

Beau was *not* a singer. He mouthed the words. No more. But hearing Anna's voice lifted in praise was better than anything he could find on the radio.

Brittany sat quietly on the other side of Anna. It was impossible to figure out what she was thinking about the service, but maybe Anna had planted a little seed by inviting Brittany.

After the service, Brittany made a mad dash for the exit, and Anna quickly followed.

"Wait. I was hoping we could have dinner together," Anna said when they met up in the parking lot.

"Um. Sure." Brittany pushed her glasses up on her nose and kept a tight hold on the strap of her purse.

"Where do you want to go?" Anna asked. When Brittany didn't answer right away, Anna turned to Beau.

"I think I'll let you two go to dinner together. I have some Christmas shopping to do."

Anna's eyes widened. "Christmas shopping? We've already been shopping, and you didn't buy anything."

"We were shopping for you. I—I saw something I might get for Liv, and I can pick up your candle while I'm in the area."

Anna clasped her hands together as best she could with the brace on. "That's so sweet. Well, Brittany, how do you feel about Mexican food? I saw a place on the square called La Cresta that promised the best tacos in the Rockies."

Brittany shrugged. "That's fine."

The tightness in Beau's shoulders eased. He didn't like lying to Anna, but he couldn't exactly tell her he wanted to get a present for her, not Liv. He could always get something for his sister too. She'd like a book from that bakery that had the bookshelves in it.

The town square was packed with people and vehicles by the time they arrived, but they found a parking spot a few blocks away. Beau walked the women to the restaurant and headed for the store he'd spotted during the tree lighting ceremony.

Art and Soul Gallery was a small shop filled with paintings displayed against off-white walls and on stands dotted throughout the big room. A bell above the door jingled as he entered.

"Hey! Welcome to Art and Soul." A dark-haired woman wearing an apron covered in various colors of paint stepped out of a room in the back. "Can I help you find anything?"

"I'm looking for a painting for my...friend," Beau said.

The woman reached out her hand with a smile. "I'm Claire. Most of these are mine, but some of them are by students. All of the paintings in this room are local landscapes, and that room over there has a variety of paintings. Do you have an idea of what your friend might like?"

"You painted these?" Beau asked, kind of stunned at the perfection of each piece.

"I did," Claire said sheepishly.

Beau whistled low. "That's awesome. I can't even paint a wall."

Claire chuckled and propped her hands on her hips. "I've been painting for years."

Beau looked around. "I'm definitely interested in one of these," he said, pointing to the landscapes in the main room. "We rode snowmobiles over a ridge on our first day in town. Any chance you have something we might have seen there?"

Claire snapped her fingers. "I bet I do. Come here."

She led him toward a large painting covered mostly in white. Snow spread over the hill in the foreground, but a bright sun sat high in the sky, bathing the scene in an orange glow. The dark mountains in the distance looked just as awesome as they had on the day he'd seen them with Anna.

"That one. That's it."

Claire squinted at him. "Are you sure? You didn't look at the price tag."

Beau checked the label on the wall beside the painting. It was expensive but he'd already made up his mind. He wanted this painting for Anna. No matter how things went between them after they got back home, she'd like a memory of the trip.

"I'm sure. Can you ship it to my house? I'm with my friend now, and I don't want her to see it yet."

Fifteen minutes later, Claire had the painting packaged and labeled for shipping. Beau stepped out onto the sidewalk and came to a complete stop. He'd just bought a Christmas present for a woman he wasn't even in a relationship with.

It couldn't be helped. She had him wrapped so tightly around her finger that he could barely think of anything else.

But she was coming out of a long-term relationship—one that almost made it to the altar. A week ago, she'd intended to spend the rest of her life with Dean. There was no way she was ready for another relationship.

Here he was thinking about relationships. He wasn't a relationship kinda guy. He hadn't met a single woman he'd consider spending his life with.

Until Anna.

Beau's phone rang in his pocket, reminding him that he was standing on the sidewalk like a lost puppy.

"Hello."

"What are you doing?" Olivia said in greeting.

"Trying to decide how I got here." It was true. How in the world had he fallen for Anna in just a week's time?

"Dude, we have GPS now. There's no excuse for getting lost."

Beau pinched the bridge of his nose. "Never mind. I'm running some errands in Freedom while Anna has dinner with her friend Brittany."

"Oh, good. I'm glad she has a friend there with her. I was hoping I could come down sometime, but I had to work overtime. How is she doing?"

"She's fine. She actually seems happy."

Olivia hummed. "So I heard."

"What did you hear?"

"I might have heard she's having a good time with you."

"Explain. What did she say about me?"

Olivia laughed. Not just a tiny laugh. It was a long, drawn-out laugh that made him regret answering his sister's call.

"Stop laughing. What did she say about me?"

Liv's laughter turned to chuckles. "What do you think about her?"

He liked her. A lot. But he wasn't about to tell his sister about that before telling Anna.

"She isn't who I thought she was."

Olivia hummed. "Good or bad?"

"Good."

"Of course she's good. She's my best friend. There's a lot to love about her."

Yeah. He was figuring that out.

"Now, tell me what she said about me," Beau demanded.

"Oh, I can't. That would violate the girl code."

Beau gripped the phone and took an extra second to breathe. "You're kidding."

"No. I'm a good friend, and I keep secrets. Sorry."

"Olivia! Stop messing around."

"Okay. Okay. All I can tell you is that Anna needs a man. A good man. No, she deserves the *best* man. Do you think you can be that for her?"

Shoot. Liv was acting like this was the real deal, and it only solidified his feelings for Anna.

"I want to be," he said low.

"Then go for it. I think you could be good for Anna, but I also think she could be good for you."

"What do you mean?"

"I mean you seem happy too. I accept thank yous in the form of cash or gift certificates to Grady's Feed and Seed."

"I'm not thanking you yet. You could have just driven a wedge between your brother and your best friend. What if this is temporary and things are awkward between us from now on?"

"Not gonna happen. Best of luck to you. Don't screw it up."

"Olivia—"

"Gotta go, bro. Talk soon."

Olivia disconnected the call, and Beau was left

staring at his phone. Fear had a grip around his throat. He'd gotten a taste of life with Anna, and he had no idea how to talk to her about it.

CHAPTER 26
ANNA

Dinner with Brittany had been tense, to say the least. They'd talked a lot, but Brittany drove the conversation.

Her questions about fashion revolved around what Anna planned to do about the pieces she'd intended to feature during her wedding. An already sore subject needed to be picked apart and studied, laying Anna's biggest problems out on the table.

Still, she didn't have a good course of action. TrueBlue had already cut ties with her, and there was a good chance the other boutiques would as well.

One well-known boutique in particular had been extremely understanding. Not only had they asked Anna to keep the dress, but they'd sent a care package filled with beauty products that Olivia had intercepted from Anna's porch a few days ago.

Still, Brittany was only interested in knowing what Anna planned to do to make things right with the companies. Each working relationship was unique, and there wasn't a one-size-fits-all solution to the problems.

Brittany hadn't really made her mark in the fashion world yet, but it wasn't because Anna hadn't tried. Brittany had degrees in fashion and business, but her skill was in design. Anna had connected Brittany with a handful of boutiques, and despite her gorgeous designs, the jobs hadn't worked out.

Then, there were Brittany's questions about Beau. How could Anna really explain their relationship? A week ago, he would have been just her best friend's brother. This week, he was the person she'd leaned on the most and thought about more than anyone else. That was really saying something, considering her ex and her mom were both hounding her, making it impossible to forget about them.

Anna paid the bill for dinner and stood from the table. Hopefully, a change of atmosphere would bring on a change in subject.

"What are you doing later?" Brittany asked.

"I'm not sure. Beau has something planned for us, but he said it was a surprise."

"Oh. Well, I guess I'll talk to you later. I'm heading back home tomorrow morning."

"Thanks again for coming out here. It's been great to hang out with you in person."

Her earlier unease about Brittany was slowly fading. She just had an awkward way about her. It was their first time meeting in person. So what if it was a little different from an online friendship?

"Thanks for hanging out with me. Message me when you get back to the hotel and let me know you made it safely."

There. She was just being a thoughtful friend. How many people really cared if someone else had a safe trip home?

"You too. I'll be praying your trip home tomorrow is a smooth one too."

"Thanks. Bye."

Even the way Brittany said goodbye was stiff. Maybe she was still nervous about meeting in person.

Anna watched Brittany walk off toward her car and called Beau.

"Hello."

"Hey. We're finished with dinner. Did you eat anything?"

"Yeah. I had a sandwich at Stories and Scones. Jan can make more than cakes and cookies."

Anna chuckled, imagining Jan doting on Beau like a mother. "She's so sweet."

"Don't tell her, but I've missed Olivia this week. I

haven't had to think about what I would eat for lunch and dinner for years."

Even though Beau was the elder sibling, Olivia had taken it upon herself to care for him after their mom died. It was Liv's way of keeping her mother's memory alive. Beau occasionally complained about his sister taking care of him like a mom, so it was good to know Liv's efforts were appreciated.

"I won't tell a soul. Where are you?"

Before he could answer, her car pulled up to the sidewalk where she was walking away from the restaurant. Beau ended the call and reached over the console to open her door.

"Curbside service. I like it," Anna said as she slipped into the passenger seat.

Beau pinned her with a wicked grin. "Ready for some fun?"

Adrenaline tingled just beneath her skin. Beau's idea of fun was sometimes different from hers, but she was coming to trust him. "As ready as I'll ever be."

Fifteen minutes later, Beau parked in front of an old warehouse with a dilapidated sign on the front of the building. The place wasn't run down, and the wear on the sign was clearly intentional.

"Rage Room?" Anna asked.

Beau shifted into park and his smile grew. "Have you ever wanted to smash something before?"

"Um. No." It was the truth. Most of her emotions

weren't allowed to see the light of day. Anger was the number one no-no.

"You're telling me you didn't want to punch Dean in the face last week?"

Maybe she'd wished some kind of physical pain on him when Misty had gone on and on about their affair or when he'd gotten mad at Anna for leaving despite his infidelity.

"Okay. I'll admit it. I had some very unkind thoughts about him."

Beau jerked his head toward the building. "Let's go let it out."

Before she could really wrap her head around what Beau was suggesting, he was out of the car and opening her door. She followed Beau through the registration process, then an intimidating woman with an eyebrow piercing and arms covered in ink led them to a room filled with junk.

"You have thirty minutes," the woman said before closing the door on her way out.

"What do we do?" Anna asked. Vases, plates, old tires, and lamps were spread out around the room, while hammers, axes, and bats hung from the walls. A punching bag dangled from the ceiling, and a few logs were turned up on their ends.

Beau handed her a helmet, gloves, and goggles. "Whatever you want." He put on his equipment before picking up a wooden baseball bat and pointing it at an ugly, oversized table lamp. “This one is Dean’s head.”

Beau lifted the bat over his shoulder and swung, sending shards of the lamp flying toward the wall in a loud crash.

The sound alone stole Anna’s breath. He really smashed it. The lamp was reduced to dozens of jagged pieces.

Beau stretched his neck to one side, then the other. “That was fun.” He handed her the bat, and she took the heavy weapon in her gloved hands.

“I can’t just hit something like that,” she said, gesturing to the non-existent lamp.

“Why not?” Beau asked, crossing his arms over his chest.

“Because it feels wrong.”

“It’s wrong to trash our hotel room.” Beau held his arms out to his sides. “It’s perfectly okay to let it out here.”

She looked around at the mismatched, breakables scattered throughout the room. Was it really okay? She’d never broken anything on purpose.

Beau walked over to the wall and grabbed an ax. Lifting it above his head, he slammed it down on top of a thick stump where the blade jammed into the wood, splitting it in two.

The bat in her hands was heavy, and her palms itched. What would it feel like to break down the walls around her carefully guarded emotions?

Beau picked up a clear vase and rested it on top of a table in front of her before stepping back. She stared at the vase as she tried to talk her guarded mind into allowing her to break it. Why couldn't she just do it?

When she looked up, Beau was beside her. He reached for her hand, and she lowered the bat to her side.

Beau kept his gaze locked on hers as he said, "I know the difference in your smiles now. You've been pretending to be happy for a long time because you think it's expected, and I don't like it."

His light-brown eyes waited as she absorbed his words. She had been hiding behind a smile for as long as she could remember, but Beau was the one who noticed. He was the one who claimed to hate it as much as she did.

She allowed herself to think about the wedding—how Dean had betrayed her and embarrassed her, how he'd yelled at her and blamed her. She remembered his lies. He wasn't the Christian he claimed to be. At least he wasn't acting like it. He hadn't apologized or shown regret.

To top it off, he hadn't waited for her. She only wanted to share her body with her husband, but he'd given in to his physical desires with someone else.

Then her mom's angry words came to join the

party. Her mom had tried to convince Anna to do everything within her power to keep Dean happy.

There were years of pent-up anger and heartache locked behind a door with her mother's name on it. If she opened the door, could she ever stop the hurt inside from consuming her? Could she ever lock it safely behind that door again?

Probably not, but could she hang on the edge of this cliff her whole life? Would she ever be free if she didn't make the move in this moment when Beau was offering it to her?

Anna pulled her hand from Beau's and gripped the bottom of the bat with her uninjured hand. Pressure expanded and heated in her chest. Boiling with the lid on. Why didn't she have the luxury of feeling? She'd never been allowed to make a fuss over anything. She'd been pushed to the side and erased her entire life.

And for what? Love? If Dean and her parents didn't love her after she'd done all she could, maybe she was unloveable.

The vase sat temptingly on the table. When the pressure was too much, she raised the bat and swung, shattering it in one blow.

Her breaths came quick and hot. It wasn't enough. She'd only cracked the door open, and she wanted more.

Gripping the bat with white knuckles, she smashed one fragile item after another until she'd destroyed everything that could be broken in the room, including her heart.

Gasping for air, she dropped the bat and raised her hand to her throat. Hot tears slid down her cheeks as the sobs came, and her knees gave out.

Beau's arms wrapped around her before her knees hit the ground, but she pushed against him.

"No, let me go! I don't want to be babied!"

"I don't think of you like that. You're strong. You just—"

"Should just be perfect. I should be perfect!" she screamed.

"No, you're not perfect. No one is, but it's okay."

"I can't cause problems for anyone. I can't make mistakes. I can't inconvenience anyone!"

Beau swiped a hand over his face and propped his hands on his hips. "You're not a problem. You're not a mistake. You're not an inconvenience. You can cry and kick and scream, and I'll still think you're amazing. Anyone who doesn't isn't worth your time."

What was he even saying? Why was he here, begging her to be the person she'd tried so hard not to be?

Why did he make her want to be different? Why hadn't he seen the messed-up parts of her and run?

Anna swiped her hands over her cheeks, smearing mascara over her palm and wrist brace.

Beau stood right in front of her, witnessing her absolute meltdown.

He took a step toward her. Then another. His gaze remained locked on hers as he approached her the same way the Crocodile Hunter used to creep up on snakes.

When they were mere inches apart, he raised his hands and wiped her tears. His calloused hands were rough against her smooth skin, but she leaned into the touch. He wiped the tears on his jeans before running his fingers into her hair and cradling her at the base of her neck and jaw.

"You are amazing," Beau whispered. "Strong, smart, kind, beautiful."

Anna didn't care what else he had to say. She'd heard enough. Pressing up onto her toes, she met his lips with hers.

Beau caught her the moment she would have crumbled. His arms wrapped around her, holding her in the safety of his embrace as he moved against her.

And she took her first healing breath. This was what she'd been missing. This was real and unfiltered emotion.

To say it was the best kiss of her life was an understatement. She might have gotten the ball rolling, but Beau was in charge here. He took complete control, leading her out onto a raging sea.

Beau's movements slowed, and he tensed before ending the kiss. Her face heated as rejection burned hot inside of her.

"I'm...I'm sorry," she whispered as she took a step back.

Beau grabbed her hand, pulling her back to him. "No. It's not that. It's... You've been through a lot lately."

Anna shook her head. "No. This isn't a rebound or a trauma response. I...I like you. I've had the best time with you despite the mess waiting at home. You've been so good to me when you didn't have to be. You—"

Beau wrapped her up, crushing her to his chest. "Stop. I'm right here with you. I'm surprised, but I'm also one hundred percent sure this is real. At least it is for me."

Anna nodded against his chest. "It is for me too. I've never been so sure of anything. And the best part is, I'm not going to second guess the way I feel." She lifted her head to look up at Beau. "Thanks to you, I'm not afraid anymore."

Beau pressed another kiss to her lips that sent a shock racing down her spine. Being adored by Beau was both thrilling and calming at the same time.

He jerked his chin toward the shattered remains of the room. "Want to smash some more?"

Anna chuckled. The rage room was worth the

price he paid for half an hour. Beau knew exactly what she needed and made it happen.

"I don't need to hit anything else. Let's go have fun."

CHAPTER 27
BEAU

The rage room might have been a bad idea.

Anna definitely had no problems jumping right into something complicated with him while she had more complicated things going on at home, but Beau was still a little wary. Was he taking advantage of her? Was she looking for something to replace the hurtful things she'd gone through?

On the one hand, he wanted her to be bold enough to know what she wanted and ask for it. On the other hand, he wasn't the jump into things blindly kinda guy, and starting something with Anna could either be amazing or end in a cloud of smoke.

Either way, there were zero tears after that, so he was calling it a win. They'd sat side by side on the couch last night and watched a movie he couldn't remember a single thing about before they separated for bed. He should get an award for his self-control.

The next day, she told him she wanted to do something "fun," which gave him little to nothing to go on since they had very different ideas of fun.

In the end, they'd settled on a hike to Freedom Falls. The guy at the tourist stand in town said the views were not to be missed, and the trail was fine for beginners.

Anna skipped ahead as they entered the trailhead, looking back with a heart-stopping smile.

"Come on!" she said, bouncing over to his side to pull him along by the hand.

"What's the rush?"

She wrapped her arms around one of his and plastered herself to his side. Her happiness did weird things to his insides. "I want to see the waterfalls."

What was wrong with him? They were as close as possible, and he still wanted to be closer. They'd kissed only once—well, twice counting the restaurant—but now that he'd tasted her lips it was all he wanted.

He kept up with her brisk pace as they headed toward the falls. The trail was well-maintained, and they passed about a dozen people as they walked. Anna stayed close to him but pointed at anything remotely interesting with the same level of excitement as a kid exploring a new world.

Did he enjoy every minute of it? Absolutely.

When they reached the falls, Anna was giddy. She bounced up and down like he'd only seen Tigger do in *Winnie the Pooh* cartoons.

"Look how gorgeous! Can you believe this is just out here in the middle of the woods?"

Beau pressed his lips together as Anna went on and on about the waterfall.

"Don't you think it's great?" she asked.

"Oh yeah. It's nice," he offered. Reaching for her, he pulled her in and kissed her slowly, taking his time as she melted against him.

When he pulled away, she sighed. Even that tiny noise had every nerve ending in his body firing.

"I like seeing you happy. I would have hiked all this way just for that."

Anna's jaw dropped open. "Beau Lawrence, you are a secret romantic. I can't believe you've been hiding this from me!"

Had he ever smiled this much? He was living in an alternate reality where smiling was as natural as breathing and Anna was looking at him like she wanted him to kiss her again.

Anna's phone rang, and she pulled it out of her pocket. "It's Liv. I have to show her the falls."

Anna answered and switched to a video call. Holding up her phone, she flipped to the back camera on her phone. "Liv! Look at this place!"

"Oh wow. That's gorgeous! Where are you?"

"We hiked out to Freedom Falls. Totally worth the blisters I'm going to have later."

"You didn't say your feet were hurting," Beau said.

"Is that my brother? Is he being good?"

"He's being very good. He took me to a rage room last night, and I got to smash things! For fun!"

"Why didn't I think of that?" Liv asked.

Beau's phone rang, and he answered the call from Dawson.

"Hello."

"How's it going?" Dawson asked.

"Fine."

Dawson lowered his voice. "Give me the details. Olivia says you like Anna."

"I'm not talking about this."

"Oh, is it because she's right there? Blink once if you think she's the best thing since Dr Pepper."

"I don't even like Dr Pepper," Beau said.

"Pretend you're me for just a minute."

"I will never pretend I'm the guy married to my sister."

"Hmm. Good point. Just tell me if you like her."

"Why does it matter?"

Anna was holding up her phone, showing off the view. She was the best thing that had entered his life in a long time. Probably ever.

"Because Liv is ridiculously excited about this, and I'm kinda committed to her happiness."

Beau let out a deep exhale. “It’s like that over here too.”

“Woo-hoo!” Dawson shouted.

“But don’t print it in the newspaper. This is really new, and given the state of things when we left Blackwater, I don’t think this new development is going to be easy for her.”

“Got it. Cross my heart and hope to fly.”

Being friends with Dawson was exhausting.

“Oop. Gotta go. Liv is off the phone, and she wants to talk about you and Anna. Have fun, and make good choices.”

Beau hung up the phone just as Anna was walking back toward him. She held up her phone between them.

“Any chance I can convince you to take a selfie with me by the falls?”

Beau raised a brow. “A selfie?”

“Please,” she begged.

Good grief. Why was it impossible to say no to her? “Fine, but this doesn’t get posted anywhere on the internet.”

Anna bounced on her toes. “Promise.”

Beau took the phone from her just as she pressed her body against his side. With one arm around her and one holding out the phone, he took the first selfie of his life.

Dinner at the Liberty Grille was out, considering they didn't want to be recognized after the fake proposal. They ran into Joanna in the lodge after their hike, and she suggested the restaurant on a nearby mountain.

Anna radiated joy the entire time. Her smile never fell, and she even silenced her phone a few times without wavering.

When Anna asked about his biggest fear on the elevator ride up to their room, even he was laughing.

"Just tell me. I promise to keep your secret," she begged with her arms wrapped snugly around his right one.

"I can't. You'll laugh at me."

"I'm already laughing!" she pointed out.

"Nope."

"Please." The single word was drawn out and sultry.

Oh no. She couldn't be this close and using that voice on him right before they locked themselves in a room alone for the next twelve hours.

Yeah, he had to do something. Sharing a room with a friend was different from sharing a room with a woman he was not only attracted to but also falling for.

The elevator dinged, and the doors opened.

"Come on. I promise I won't tell."

Maybe his irrational fear would come in handy.

She'd be completely unattracted to him after finding out.

"It's pigs."

"What?"

"Pigs. I hate pigs."

Anna stopped and stared at him. "Pigs?"

"Yep. Pigs."

She covered her mouth a second before the laughter burst from her. She doubled over, cackling like a hyena.

"I told you it was embarrassing," Beau said as he turned and headed for the room.

"No. It's okay. It's okay. I'm sorry I laughed."

She was running after him now. Still laughing.

As soon as he reached the room, she wedged herself between his chest and the door.

"I'm sorry. I think it's cute."

"Cute," Beau huffed, grabbing the key card from his pocket.

"I mean, you're not cute. You're handsome. And sweet." She slid her hands up his chest. "And manly. Not cute."

Beau lowered his chin, brushing the side of his nose against hers. "You're cute." he pressed a quick kiss to her lips. "And smart." Another kiss. "And strong."

Anna wrapped her hands around the back of his neck and pulled him down until his lips crashed against hers. Pinning her against the door, he forced the kiss to a slower tempo while Anna tried her very best to stoke the flames.

She needed to know he was interested, but she would also need to understand why he had to leave.

At the brink of his control, he broke the kiss and opened the door. “I’ll be back in a little bit.”

Her brows pinched together, creating a tiny crease. “Where are you going?”

“I need to get my own room. I can’t stay here with you.”

Anna’s eyes widened, and she wrapped her arms around herself. “Oh. Yeah. That makes sense.”

He lifted her chin with a finger until she was looking up at him again. “It’s not because I don’t like you. It’s because I do. Too much. And while you can rest assured I would never take advantage of you, I don’t want there to be any doubts.”

“Right. I mean...” She let out a short, nervous chuckle. “I guess it’s kind of out in the open that that’s one reason why Dean cheated. Because I wouldn’t have sex before we were married.”

Beau pressed his eyes closed. “Dean is stupid. Trust me, you and I are on the same page. You won’t ever have to worry about that with me. Okay?”

Anna nodded. “Okay.”

“I just think a little space would be good for us tonight.” He pressed a kiss to her forehead. “Does that sound good to you?”

"Actually, it's probably the best thing you could have said."

Too bad the woman working at the front desk didn't think it was so great. He'd tried his best to negotiate himself into a new room for twenty minutes, but she must have been serious when she claimed they didn't have any rooms available. She'd gotten a little snappy with him toward the end of the conversation.

Returning to the room he shared with Anna defeated and tired, he knocked on the door.

A few seconds later, Anna appeared wearing the new pajamas she'd bought at the lodge gift shop. They were blue and white with the words "I'd rather be in Freedom" across the front of the shirt.

"Why are you knocking? You have a key."

"Unfortunately, it's the only key I have. There aren't any rooms available."

Anna opened the door and waved him in. "Come on. We can handle this."

"I think we need to make a rule," Beau said as he toed off his shoes.

"No kissing in the room?" Anna asked.

"That's the one. Glad we're on the same page."

Anna clasped her hands behind her back and grinned up at him. "Is it bad that I want to kiss you right now because that was so sweet and thoughtful of you?"

Beau plugged his ears with his fingers. "Stop. No talking about kissing."

Anna laughed before heading to the bed and slipping beneath the covers. "I'm going to bed so I won't bother you anymore."

"What time do you want to head out in the morning?" Beau asked as he grabbed a T-shirt and sweats to change into.

Anna sighed. "I'm not in a rush to get back home, if that's what you're asking."

"You're not going home alone, Anna. Between me, Olivia, Lyric, Hadley, and Bella, you have an army to protect you. I dare anyone to say a cross word to you."

"I appreciate that, but even my friends have their own problems. It's not right for me to ask them to fight my battles too," she whispered.

"You're not a problem. They're your friends, and that means they care about you."

"I know they do. I'm sure I'm just being dramatic about going home." Anna flipped onto her side and bundled the blankets around her shoulders. "Do you want to leave at seven?"

She'd just changed the subject, but should they really drag out a conversation made up of what-ifs?

"Seven is fine."

"Good night, Beau. Thank you for coming on this trip with me. I've had the best time."

Beau thought back over the last week. He'd be

lying if he claimed it was anything less than the best week of his life. They'd carved out a tiny slice of life together and found something good in the middle of a storm.

"Me too. Good night."

He could handle Dean, but her ex wasn't the only one Anna was afraid to face. If things between them were going to last more than a week, they'd have to face her mother.

CHAPTER 28
ANNA

Anna was going to miss the coffee from Mountain Mugs. The cafe conveniently located in Freedom Ridge Lodge was some of the best she'd ever had. If only the line were longer, she could drag out the leaving.

They'd slept late, then taken advantage of the hot breakfast at Liberty Grille. That was another thing she wanted to take home to Blackwater—the food.

Beau joined her as she stared at the menu written on a chalkboard high on the wall. He wrapped his arm around her as if it were the most natural thing in the world. "What are you getting?"

"I think I want to try the peppermint mocha. You?"

"You get three guesses, and the first two don't count."

"Black coffee," she said, rolling her eyes at the simplicity of his order. "Don't you want to try something new?"

"No. I know I like black coffee."

Anna leaned her head on his shoulder. "That's one of the many things I love about you. You know what you want."

He pressed a kiss to her hair. "I think you know what you want too. You're just afraid to speak up and go after it."

She angled her head toward his face. "You're right, but there's this great guy who is teaching me how to do that."

Beau squeezed her tighter. "It's all you. Reminding you that you're awesome makes me a cheerleader, not the one who gets the credit."

She thought about what Beau said as they got their coffee and stepped out into the cold December morning. Snow covered every surface for as far as she could see. It settled on rooftops, roads, and mountains for miles. She was used to snow, but this level of coverage was reserved for the high elevations of the Rocky peaks.

Soon, they were venturing north, and a nagging sat low in her gut along with the coffee. What was she going to do when they got back to Blackwater? What did she *want* to do?

It was both freeing and terrifying knowing she

wasn't beholden to anyone anymore. She could make her own decisions—something she hadn't been able to do since she started dating Dean. Actually, her parents had been pressuring her into making decisions her entire life.

Whatever was building between her and Beau was a completely different animal. Sure, she still wanted to be one part of a whole, but Beau made it easy. It was as if they fit together like two pieces of a puzzle. Making decisions was simple because they understood each other and actually communicated.

Dean hadn't liked talking. He made decisions for himself and did what he wanted without considering her. He'd also shamed her whenever she brought up something she wanted to do, or flat-out refused to do things with her if it wasn't something he was interested in too.

What a contrast to the entire week she'd spent with Beau.

She glanced over at him as he drove. Would he eventually get tired of being around her too? Would he ignore her calls and claim she was too needy the way Dean had?

They were chasing sunsets with the darkness at their backs, ready to claim them. Was the trip meant to be a fleeting moment of happiness and then just a memory?

"What's going on in that head of yours?" he

asked, giving her a quick glance before turning back to the road.

"Just wondering about...life. My future. Our future."

"Well, that's a lot. Care to share with the class?"

Anna rested her head against the seat. "Will you forget about me?"

Beau swallowed before answering. "I could never forget about you."

"I couldn't forget about you either. I don't want to go back to the way things were before. I want to be able to talk to you and be happy with you. My old blissfully ignorant life has disappeared, and I can't get it back. I don't want to."

Beau reached for her hand. "It'll be tough. You might lose everything, and I can't live with that."

"I won't lose everything if I have you and my friends. I'll be happy. That's all I want."

Beau let out a deep sigh but kept his attention on the road.

"Can't we just stay? I bet Jan would give me a job at Stories and Scones, and you could lead snowmobile tours over the mountains."

Beau glanced at her again. "That's tempting, but I think Olivia would show up at the door to yell at us."

Anna sank into the seat. "I love Blackwater. It's my home, but it's more than that. I really have the best friends."

Dean had put a strain on all of her friendships. Actually, she'd let him, all in the name of love. How could they forgive her for taking his side all this time? Her friends had only been looking out for her. They were the ones who'd begged her to stand up for herself, but she hadn't listened until Misty metaphorically slapped her in the face.

Not having Dean in her life was one problem solved, but no matter how supportive her friends were, they couldn't protect her from her mother's sharp tongue.

After a few minutes of silence, Anna whispered, "I want to go home, but I want to run away too."

Beau adjusted his hand and threaded his fingers into the spaces between hers, careful not to move her wrist too much now that she wasn't wearing the brace. "If you're running away from your problems, I'm glad you ran away with me."

"Me too." Her voice broke on the two simple words. He'd given her a safe place to heal and get her feet back under her, and words couldn't express what that meant to her.

"I have a theory, if you're interested in hearing it," Beau said.

"By all means, please share."

"The happiness of this week wasn't because of where we were or how far away your problems are. You were happy because you were just being you. No fake smiles, no putting on a show, no bowing to someone else's orders. I know it won't seem as easy as it was in Freedom, but you can still do that at home."

Anna lifted his hand and turned it over until his palm was exposed. She focused on the lines, calluses, and curves as she explored the man who continued to surprise her. "I need to be a better me."

"That doesn't mean you have to do everything alone," Beau reminded her.

Anna swallowed hard, dreading the conversation they needed to have before they crossed the town line back into Blackwater. "Where do we go from here?" she asked.

"What do you mean?"

She brushed her fingertips over the lines on his palm before trailing up each finger. With a deep inhale, she asked, "What are we? Do we have a label? What do you want?"

Beau lifted her hand in his and kissed her knuckles. "I want you to be happy. As much as I really, really want to jump into things with you, I think you need time to find out how strong you can be."

Anna's chest tightened. It sounded a lot like he was letting her down slowly. "What are you saying?"

"I'm saying I want to make sure this is what you want. You have a million things to take care of when we get back, and I don't want to get in the way of that."

"You're not in the way," she quickly added.

"Listen, nothing that I'm saying is bad. I'm not going anywhere. I'll be here. Just don't stress too much about us when you have other things going on. I'm not going to be upset if you don't call, because I know you're busy. I'll be happy to hear from you when you do have time for me."

"That's...good, I guess."

When she stopped exploring his hand, he began to lazily explore hers where it lay on the console between them. "I'm trying to say I'll give you time to realize that you can do things on your own without questioning every move you make. You don't have to worry about what I think because I'm on your side. Always."

Beau was giving her a gift, and it was the best thing anyone had ever done for her. It only made her want him more.

"Is that what you want?" she asked.

"What do you mean? This isn't about me."

Anna leaned closer to him, propping on the console between them to whisper, "Ask me what I want."

He gave her a playful smirk before facing the road ahead. "Okay. What do you want?"

"I want you. I also realize that you're right. I trust you, and I'm not afraid. I've never had this before—a relationship that was stronger than the storms life throws at us."

"See? You can do this." He blew out a quick breath. "I can't believe I'm saying this, but *we* can do this."

Anna chuckled. "Yeah, it sounds strange to me too. I don't think anyone could have seen this coming. Me and you!"

Beau narrowed his eyes. "I'm starting to think Olivia pushed me to go with you because she knew."

She hadn't thought about it before, but she certainly was now. Had she missed Liv subtly prodding them toward each other? "You think? She's never said anything to me about the two of us."

"I wouldn't put it past her. She's sneaky like that."

A carefree laugh burst from Anna's chest. "Do you think she saw an opportunity and ran with it?"

"You're laughing, but I think I'm right."

"I think you are too. I don't know whether to kick her behind or send her a thank you card."

Beau was quiet for a few moments, but he held onto her hand with an unwavering grip. "I think we should wait to tell people."

Anna could easily spiral into doubt, but none of that feeling made an appearance. Beau wasn't ashamed of her, he was protecting what they were building. "I agree. It would take a lot of the pressure off, at least in the beginning. Liv and Dawson know."

"We could ask them not to tell," Beau said.

Anna nodded, then squeezed his hand in a show of solidarity. "I like that idea."

Their week in Freedom was only the beginning. The new relationship they were bringing home was worth protecting at all costs.

CHAPTER 29
BEAU

Days without Anna were incredibly boring.

The guys had kept the shop running smoothly while Beau was away. No one had called him with business-breaking news, and the first thing he thought of in the morning was Anna.

He'd worked all morning doing the same things he'd done every other day of his adult life, but everything was lackluster. He measured every minute against the ones she'd claimed. Was he even living if she wasn't there—reminding him to find the color in a world of gray?

He'd gotten up, read his Bible alone, and forgotten to eat breakfast, all after a night of tossing and turning. He couldn't get Anna out of his head.

Then, Gage had asked about the trip, and Beau had never been so tempted to spill his guts. Luckily, Beau maintained a shred of self-control because he would have to hand over his man card if he ever engaged in girl talk with any of the guys.

Olivia walked in carrying a greasy brown bag with a burger logo on the front. "Lunch is here!"

Beau checked his watch. How was it lunchtime already? He'd barely accomplished anything.

The guys disappeared from the garage following the smell of the warm burgers, and Beau kept working on the Ford F-150. For some reason, the silent garage didn't help his focus.

A few minutes later, Olivia showed up beside him, propping her elbow on the truck. "How's it going?"

"Fine."

"What are you doing?"

Beau shot a warning glare at his sister. "Working. Can I help you?"

"No. Last I checked, our relationship is kinda one-sided on the help front. I'm always helping you, but the brother benefits are seriously lacking."

"You never tell me you need help. How am I supposed to know if you don't say something?"

"Relax, Rocky. I don't need help."

"Liv, I'm really busy. Get to the point."

"I'm just waiting around for appreciation. I accept thanks in the form of cash or chicks, remember?"

Beau braced his hands on the frame of the truck. "So you did set us up."

Liv shrugged. "It wasn't my direct intention, but I did think the two of you could be good for each other."

"Don't meddle in my life."

"I'm not meddling. You two started things up on your own."

Beau pulled the rag from his back pocket and wiped his hands. "I'm not thanking you yet. I don't even know if this is going to work out."

"Oh, it will."

"I appreciate your eternal optimism, but I don't need your false hope."

Olivia leaned closer to him with a stone stare that would have impressed him if he didn't know she used the same stare on her chickens when they pestered the goats. "I know it'll work out because I can tell you want it to. Ask me about the only other time I've seen you this determined."

"How do you know how determined I am?"

"It was when you were starting the business. Dad wanted you to stay and work the farm, but you had your heart set on owning your own business doing what you love."

Beau rubbed his grease-stained hand down his face. "You make it sound as tough as climbing Mount Everest."

"But I'm seeing a change in you, and I like it. Now, tell me how you feel about her. I want details."

Beau shook his head and turned back to the truck. "I'm not talking about Anna with you."

Olivia chuckled. "You are so adorable."

Good grief. The sides of his neck were itching. His blood pressure was probably through the roof. "I'm not adorable. I'm big and ugly and gross. Tell your friends."

"You're in love, and it's so sweet!" Olivia said, high-pitched and giddy.

"I don't feel sweet. I feel like I'm going to puke."

She squealed again, clapping her hands.

Beau turned to her, making eye contact as he whispered, "Will you keep your voice down. Someone might hear you."

"Oh, they'll all know soon."

"Liv! You told Anna you wouldn't tell anyone."

She held her hands up in the air. "And I won't, but I have a feeling the two of you aren't going to be able to resist telling the world."

"I'm not telling the world about my relationships. Do you know me at all?"

"Everyone hates Dean, but everyone wants Anna to be happy. We all swallowed our tongues for months because we wanted to believe she really was as happy as she claimed. But I know my best friend," Olivia said, pointing at her chest.

"And I think you know me too. I don't want to talk about it. I don't talk about my feelings."

Olivia pointed a finger at him. "I knew it! You do have feelings!"

"Please shut up. I'm begging you."

Her arms wrapped around him, squeezing him as hard as she could. "I'm just so happy."

"Don't be happy. Just tell your little brain not to care."

"Sorry, but you're not raining on my parade today." She released him and brushed a hand over her scrubs. "Actually, I'm hoping you'll give her the courage to stand up to her mother." Olivia shivered and grimaced.

"Okay, what's up with her mom? I've heard some horror stories." Anna's reaction to her mother's phone calls on the trip was all he needed to see.

"She's awful," Olivia whispered.

"Now you decide to lower your voice. I need more details."

"This isn't girl talk?" Olivia asked. "It won't hurt your devil-may-care reputation if someone sees us being very secretive after you just took a week off work to run away into the Rocky Mountains with a beautiful woman?"

"Liv, focus. Mom details." Good grief, his sister could narrate her trip to the grocery store and make it into a soap opera screenplay.

"Be very careful. She's super strict, and she's mean to Anna. She's controlling and unreasonable."

"And you're not exaggerating?" Beau asked.

Olivia crossed her arms over her chest and straightened her posture. "Rude."

"As if it wasn't a valid question."

"Fine. No, I'm not exaggerating. She doesn't like that Anna is a Christian, and she's very vocal about it. I'd call it blasphemous."

"How does Anna take that?" Beau asked.

"It's the one thing Anna will stand up about. She lets her mom walk all over her in every other part of her life except that one."

Hmm. Until now, Beau would have bet he couldn't be any prouder of Anna. Knowing she wouldn't bow to anyone when it came to worshiping the one true God had heat rising in his chest.

Oh no. It was heartwarming. Anna had softened his rough edges in a mere week. At this rate, he'd be watching those made-for-TV Christmas movies before the end of the month.

Beau rubbed the back of his neck. Dean was out of the picture, but her mom was still a threat to Anna's happiness. He'd never had an enemy before, but anyone who bothered Anna was going to get bothered by him.

"Tell me everything you know about Catherine Harris."

CHAPTER 30
ANNA

Walking into Harris and Associates after the week spent with Beau was like stepping into a time machine. She'd worked at the family firm since she was old enough to file and water plants, but nothing about the place welcomed her back to the real world.

The receptionist, Katie, raised her head as soon as Anna stepped through the door. The young girl's eyes widened, and she straightened her back.

"Hi. How was your...trip?" Katie asked, stammering over half the words.

"It was great. How have you been?"

Katie had been with the firm since early October, and she probably deserved some kind of award. Anna's parents did a fantastic job of running off employees who were too sweet.

"I'm fine. It's just..." Katie glanced at the

doorway leading to the attorney offices. "Things have been tense."

That wasn't news. Her parents and the other attorneys were always upset about something or fuming whenever the smallest things went wrong. It was a pretty toxic work environment.

"Oh? What's happening?"

Katie glanced one way, then the other before leaning in to whisper, "They're not happy about the wedding." Katie's nose scrunched. "Sorry about that, by the way. You deserve better."

Right on cue, Anna's stomach clenched. Of course her parents were making the employees miserable because they were mad at her. Heat crept up her chest and neck, tightening her throat until her words were hoarse. "I'm really sorry you're having to deal with that because of me."

"Oh no. I just wanted to give you a heads-up. I don't know if you've talked to them since you got back, but maybe tread lightly."

Katie was a gift from the Lord and way more mature than most eighteen-year-olds.

"I haven't talked to them yet, but hopefully it won't be a big deal." Who was she kidding? Her parents were going to lay into her as soon as they found out she was here.

Katie lifted her hand in a small wave. "I hope you're right. I'm glad you're back."

Anna flashed a sweet smile. She wasn't so glad

to be back, but there hadn't been any catastrophic damage since her return.

Yet.

"Thanks. I'll see you at lunch," Anna said as she headed for her office.

The whole place was eerily quiet. When she peeked into a few offices to say her hellos, the conversations were short and stilted. She'd been lulled into a false sense of security while she was on the trip. Freedom was just far enough that she could avoid her parents and ex, but now she was home, and the air was charged like the calm before the storm.

She slipped her purse into the bottom drawer of her desk and pulled her laptop out of its case. At least there wouldn't be a ton of work waiting for her. She'd taken care of most things for the firm on the drive home yesterday, and she'd stayed home this morning to process all the mail she'd received while on the trip. She must have had fifty packages from boutiques waiting for her.

The quick, heavy beat of her mother's footsteps echoed down the hall, and it took everything Anna had to keep her shoulders pulled back. Beau had taught her well, but he wasn't here. Her instinct was to cower and please.

Not this time. She wouldn't let her mother make her feel like an abused animal.

Catherine Harris dressed the part perfectly. Her

hair was slicked back into a tight bun, her navy blazer matched her pencil skirt, and her scowl could terrify a grown man. Somehow, Anna lifted her chin in the face of the tongue-lashing to come. She thought of Beau and the way he built her up, and her insecurities faded from a burning wound to a dull ache.

Catherine didn't give Anna a chance to greet her before she let the daggers fly. "How dare you."

"Mom, please. We don't have to fight like this."

"Oh, really? You think you can walk out of a wedding, disappear for a week, and have no consequences?"

The burning in Anna's core stoked to a raging flame. "I didn't do anything wrong." She pointed to her chest. "He cheated, and I cleaned up the mess."

Her mom laughed, and the sound sent a chill down Anna's back. "You didn't clean up any mess. You're an embarrassment. You made us a laughing stock. You ruined everything!"

"Please keep your voice down. People can hear you," Anna pleaded.

Her mom pointed a thin, manicured finger at her. "Don't you dare tell me what to do. This is what *you* are going to do. You're going to really fix this mess. Dean is expecting your call, and I've smoothed things over with the vendors. They're willing to work with us again, but we have to make quick decisions to get on their schedules again."

"Do you hear yourself? I'm not going back to Dean. He cheated on me. The woman he was seeing showed up at my wedding! It's not happening."

There. She'd said it, and it felt good to let the truth out. Not only had she healed from the betrayal, but she was happy about the outcome. If Misty hadn't shown up when she did, Anna would have tied herself to a man who wouldn't be faithful to her.

Catherine took two steps closer until they were mere inches apart. Glaring down, she set her jaw and pointed a steady finger at Anna. "You are going to make things right. You have one week to come to your senses and make all of your apologies. I suggest you get started immediately."

With that final order, Catherine walked out of Anna's office, slamming the door behind her on the way out.

Anna's knees weakened, and she lowered herself to the office chair. She'd held firm against her mother, but had it actually worked? She wasn't any better off than before. Nothing had been resolved.

She grabbed her laptop, ready to shove it back into her bag and head home, when an invisible force stopped her. She paused, frozen in place with a white-knuckle grip on the computer.

You can do this.

Could she do this? Could she stand up for

herself? Could she be firm when the one person who terrified her demanded obedience?

Yes. Anna didn't serve her mother. She served the Lord, and there was a newfound determination to remain bold on this front.

Slowly, she released the laptop and sat back in her chair. The tension from her encounter with her mom eased as she closed her eyes and prayed.

Father, help me remain strong. I can't do it on my own. I need help.

She sat there until her breaths came easily, then she straightened her spine and got to work.

CHAPTER 31
ANNA

Anna stepped into her cottage and leaned back against the door. The silence was both welcome and unnerving. She wanted to hide away from the world, but the thought of being alone kindled a familiar fear.

Closing her eyes, she prayed for the tenth time today. It was the only thing that had given her the strength to stay at the office when she really wanted to run home and hide.

Her mom hadn't returned to her office, but their next meeting lurked somewhere in the near future. Catherine wasn't one to give up without a huge fight.

The sounds of an approaching vehicle turned Anna's attention to the window by the door. Olivia stepped out of her car and bounded up the porch steps.

Flinging open the door, Anna wrapped her arms around her friend.

"I'm so glad you're back," Olivia whispered against Anna's hair.

"I'm so glad you came." She needed a hug in the worst way.

Olivia pulled back to get a good look at Anna's face. "What's wrong?"

Anna didn't try to stop the instinctual eye roll. "Mom."

Liv huffed. "I knew it. She won't let you have a minute of peace."

"The good news is that I stayed at work all day after she brought out her sword the minute I got to the office."

Liv resumed their hug. "That's my girl! I'm so proud of you."

It wasn't much to some people, but Anna's first instinct was to either run from conflict or cower and submit. Standing up for herself was going to take practice.

Anna pulled Liv toward the door. "Come in. I'll make us some baked chicken while we talk."

"I can never turn down your food. Other than your unwelcome visitor, how was work?"

"Pretty good actually. I tried to focus on the things I needed to get done instead of the awful conversation with Mom."

Olivia stopped and propped a hand on her hip.

"Was it really a conversation, or did she yell at you and storm out?"

Anna gathered the ingredients she'd need while Olivia searched for a pen and paper. She always wrote down the recipe whenever Anna cooked dinner for them. "You're right. Not much of a conversation if she didn't hear or care about anything I said."

Liv sat at the table and clicked her pen open. "Enough about her. Tell me about the trip."

Reliving the trip only reinforced Anna's feelings for Beau. He'd put himself and his wants aside for her multiple times, and the longing in her heart grew deeper.

Anna checked the potatoes in the oven and tossed the potholder aside. "Would you mind if I invited him to have dinner with us?"

Olivia smiled and propped her chin on her hand. "Not at all. Do I need to make myself scarce?"

"No way. Beau isn't like Dean, and to be honest, I'm not the same as I was when I was with him." Anna wrung her hands. "I'm sorry I wasn't the best friend to you. I shouldn't have let him come between us."

Olivia stood and wrapped her arms around Anna. Hugs so good for aching hearts.

"I forgive you, and I'll always be here," Olivia whispered.

Anna tightened her embrace. "I'm so glad you're my friend."

"Always and forever," Liv confirmed. "Now, call Beau, and tell him to hurry because I'm starving."

Anna didn't have to be told twice. Beau had sent her a good morning text, but they hadn't talked since. When the call rang the third time, she was sure he wouldn't answer.

"Hello."

"Hey!" Okay, maybe that was a little too peppy. Everything with Beau was new, and the last thing she wanted to do was scare him off by being too excited. At least, Dean had always been annoyed by her happiness. She'd been told to "chill out" more times than she wanted to admit.

"How was your day?" Beau asked.

"It was fine." There. She hadn't made a big deal over the encounter with her mom, but she also wasn't giggling with excitement, though that was exactly what she wanted to do now that she was talking to Beau.

"That's it? You don't want to tell me about it?"

Anna glanced at Olivia, not sure how to answer Beau's follow-up question.

"I doubt you want to hear about it."

"Of course I do."

There were plenty of noises in the background. It was almost seven thirty, but he was still in the garage and giving her his full attention.

"Oh, well would you like to come over for dinner? Liv is here too, and I'm making baked chicken."

"I need to shower, and I'll be on my way. Give me twenty minutes."

"You don't have to rush."

"Anna, I'm on my way. I'll see you soon."

"Okay." He didn't sound put out or irritated that she'd clearly pulled him away from work. "See you soon."

Anna ended the call, and Olivia was standing right beside her with a smile that could rival the Cheshire cat's grin.

"He really likes you. Did you know he works until about nine every night?"

Anna looked at her phone. What had she done? He said they needed time to get things in order after being gone for a week, and here she was already asking for his time. "I shouldn't have called him."

"You most certainly should have. He needs a life outside of the garage. There just hasn't been anything else he cared about until now."

Oh no. Anna's defenses were crumbling. There was a tingling in her nose and a lump in her throat that refused to be ignored.

"I...I just..."

Olivia opened her arms and patted her shoulder a mere second before Anna's tears made their abrupt appearance. The sobs wracked her frame as Olivia brushed a hand over Anna's hair.

"That's it. You haven't done enough crying since that bad man hurt you. Let it out so you can move on."

"I'm not crying over him! I don't even care anymore."

"I know exactly what you mean. Even if you're happier without him, you were still betrayed, and it's okay to be hurt by that. I think anyone would be."

That was it. The betrayal hurt, not the loss of Dean in her life. Actually, not a single one of her tears was for him. It was the look in her mom's eyes that upset her the most.

"And I'm so proud of you," Olivia continued. "You've handled it all really well, and I'm excited about all the happiness you have ahead of you."

"What about my mom? She's not going to be happy."

Olivia chuckled. "We don't care if she's happy. She could stomp on you all day and still look like she ate a handful of sour grapes. Don't let her hurt you."

Liv was right. Catherine would never be happy, and there wasn't anything Anna could do to change that. Trying would only make both of them miserable.

Anna lifted her head and wiped at her tear-stained cheeks. "You're right. I don't think there's anything I can do that would make her happy besides go back to Dean."

Olivia's nose scrunched. "Ew. That's the worst thing you could do."

"I know, but Mom thinks I should just act like it never happened. I can't be in a relationship like that. I won't. If that's how Dad has treated her, then I feel really bad for her."

Olivia reached for Anna's hand and squeezed. "My mom was the happiest woman on Earth, and there were two reasons for that. She put God first, and she had a good man standing beside her who reminded her to keep doing just that."

"Yeah. My parents despise anything to do with God. It makes me physically ill when I think about how closed off they are to any talk about God."

"That's because you care about them despite the way they treat you," Olivia said. "And we should all feel that way. We're not called to only share the gospel with the people we like. We're told to go into the world teaching all nations about Christ."

"I just wish it didn't hurt so much."

Anna was used to her parents' dismissal, but most times, she couldn't discern whether they were rejecting God or her.

Olivia squeezed Anna's hand, reminding her of the ever-present and unwavering friendship that was always a phone call away.

"Your parents are human and fallible. Your heavenly Father is not, and His love is unconditional. You're doing great."

Olivia was right. Anna had too many blessings to sit around letting the bad control her life.

The oven timer beeped, and the women separated. Anna grabbed two oven mitts and reached for the hot casserole dish. "You always know just what to say. Do you get that from Beau or does he get that from you?"

Olivia blinked a few times before stammering, "Um, I'm not sure I was aware that Beau was capable of saying the right thing at the right time."

Anna set the baked chicken dish on the counter and covered her mouth with the back of her mit to hide the chuckle.

"What are you laughing about?" Olivia asked, clearly outraged.

"It's just that Beau isn't who I thought he was at all. I feel so stupid. Why did it take me this long to see him?"

Olivia shrugged and pulled a fork out of the silverware drawer. "There's a time for every purpose under heaven I guess."

Anna swatted Olivia's hand as she reached the fork toward the chicken. "We're not eating until Beau gets here."

"Are you kidding me? I'm starving, and the food is right there!"

Grabbing Olivia's hand, Anna pulled her friend toward the hallway. "Come on. You can help me organize the clothes that came in while I was out of town."

Olivia threw her head back and groaned. "I just need food."

There was a knock on the door, and Olivia quickly shouted, "Come in!"

Anna glared at her friend. "So much for stranger danger."

"It has to be someone with the gate code. I texted it to Beau."

When Beau walked in, the whole world stood still. He wore a plain blue T-shirt and faded jeans, and he was completely and perfectly himself and nothing else.

His gaze lifted straight to her, and the grin that still felt like a secret between them spread over his lips.

Letting go of Olivia's hand, Anna closed the distance between her and Beau. As soon as his strong arms were around her, peace settled over her tired bones.

This was it. This was everything she'd been missing. Beau wasn't her crutch, he was her motivation when times got tough. He was peace and hope and safety all at once.

His breath was warm as he whispered against her ear, "I missed you."

Beau was patching up her heart with pieces of his and wrapping himself around her, protecting her from anything that could ever hurt her again.

CHAPTER 32
BEAU

The minute Olivia finished eating, she picked up her plate and headed for the sink. "Gotta run. The chicks wait for no one."

"Thanks for coming. I missed you," Anna said.

Olivia turned and flashed her friendliest smile. "You're never allowed to leave me again."

The same possessiveness reared up inside Beau. Now that he'd spent a week with Anna, the thought of being separated made his stomach roll.

Good grief. He was in trouble.

As soon as Olivia left, a thick silence settled in the room. Beau hadn't ever been inside Anna's house, but it suited her. Even the dark night couldn't mute the whites and light colors. Her home was as bright as her personality.

Anna grabbed both of their empty plates and

took them to the sink. Still turned away from him, she wiped at her face with the dish towel.

Beau stood, pulled by an invisible force to her side. The makeup around her eyes was smudged, and he brushed his thumb over the soft skin of her cheek. "Have you been crying?"

"It was a moment of weakness. I probably look like a mess."

Beau's chest swelled. A twinge shot through him every time she talked about herself as anything less than perfect. "You're so beautiful, you make the stars jealous."

Anna covered her mouth, but a laugh escaped. "That's very sweet but so untrue."

Reaching for her, he pulled her to his chest where she belonged. "I don't tell lies, Anna. I don't like knowing you've been crying, and I don't think you could ever look bad."

She nuzzled closer to him. "I can't believe you said that. No one would believe me if I told them you were a secret romantic."

"If you tell, I'll plead the fifth."

She looked up at him with the most gorgeous eyes he'd ever seen. She was so beautiful it hurt. "I would never tell. And thank you for coming."

"All you have to do is call," he reminded her. It was true. He had five vehicles waiting at the garage, but nothing could have stopped him from seeing her tonight.

Her eyes glistened, and she blinked rapidly before whispering, "Thank you."

"I didn't do anything."

His hand rose on its own and brushed over her cheek. He was still living in some dream where he got to touch her now. A humming vibration shot through his arm from the fingertips that trailed over her skin. She leaned into his touch, and the tingling only grew stronger.

But the tightness in her jaw and brow said something wasn't right, and he couldn't shake the unease. "What's got you upset?"

Anna sighed and took a step back, running her hands through her long blonde hair. "Mom. It's no surprise that she's still angry about the wedding." Throwing her hands out to her sides, Anna huffed. "She wants me to go back to Dean!"

The blow hit Beau in the chest. He had no illusions that Dean was anything but an idiot, but what if Anna listened to her mom? What if she took the easy way out and went back to her ex because it was a sure thing?

Anna had always been looking for something, and she'd sacrificed a lot to make squares fit into circles when it came to Dean. Was that still what she wanted?

"I mean, she thought we would just set another date and make it happen. I don't get it," Anna said as she marched toward the living room.

Beau swallowed, trying and failing to be patient long enough for Anna to explain. “And what do you want?”

She stopped her pacing in front of the couch, and her shoulders sank. “I’m finished with Dean. Misty can have him for all I care. I’m never going back to him.”

Oh good. Beau’s lungs still worked. Their paralysis for the last fifteen seconds must have been a glitch. “What did you tell your mom?”

“What I just told you. It’s not happening. Then she gave me one week to patch things up with Dean and reschedule the wedding.”

“Or what?” Beau’s eyes widened. “That’s ridiculous.”

“Tell me about it.” Anna fell onto the couch, her perfectly styled hair billowed out around her. “She didn’t hear a word I said.”

Beau took the seat beside her, trying his best not to scare her off. “What can I do to help?”

Anna turned to him with a tired smile before letting her eyes drift closed. “Nothing. This is all I need.” She reached for his hand and squeezed it.

“Anna,” he whispered.

When she opened her eyes, the tension was nearly gone.

The heavy footfalls on the porch came a mere second before the front door opened, and Catherine Harris barged in.

Beau sat up quickly. He'd been so focused on Anna that he hadn't heard her mother coming.

He'd seen Catherine Harris before, but they'd never been officially introduced. Actually, she'd given him plenty of glares over the years.

She could throw dirty looks all day long. Nothing was going to make him cower to this woman.

"Mom." Anna jumped to her feet. "What are you doing here?"

Catherine let out a maniacal laugh. "Are you kidding me? I own this place," she seethed, pressing a manicured fingernail to her chest. "The question is, what is he doing here?" She turned her finger to Beau.

"This is Beau Lawrence," Anna said, moving to his side. "I invited him over for dinner." Her chin was held high, and her voice didn't shake.

"Do you think I'm an idiot?" Catherine asked, glaring at Anna. "I know you were with him last week. I know he went on what should have been your honeymoon."

Uh-oh. Surely, that wasn't something Anna wanted her mother to find out about. How had word gotten out?

Catherine chuckled, but the sound held no humor. "Do you seriously have the nerve to pretend like this is perfectly normal? How long have you been sneaking around with him?"

"I have not been sneaking around with anyone. I was faithful to Dean. He was the one who cheated."

"And so what? That's what men do!"

Beau squared his shoulders, ready to set things straight. "No, that's not what men do. Good men are faithful and—"

"Who said you could speak? I'm talking to my daughter," Catherine spat.

Beau allowed himself half a second to rein in his irritation at the interruption. "You're not talking to her like she's your daughter. You're treating her like a criminal, and I don't like it."

Catherine huffed a small, humorless chuckle. "This conversation is private, and you're not allowed on my property. Leave now, or I'll call the police."

"Mother! Stop talking to him like that!"

Catherine shot a glare Anna's way. "You shut up and listen. This is my estate, and he is never allowed here again. Is that understood?"

Anna's jaw dropped open, and she stammered, "What?"

The look on Anna's face said it all. She'd been given an ultimatum—her family and her home or him. She'd lost everything last week, but apparently she had more things she cared about to be stolen.

Anna reached for Beau's hand and squeezed tight. Keeping her gaze firmly locked with her mother's, she begged, "Don't do this. Let's talk about it."

"There's nothing else to talk about. I won't watch you throw your life away."

"I'm twenty-eight. I stayed here because you wanted me to. I've been obedient to you my whole life, but this has to stop."

Beau's jaw tightened. Anna was finally speaking for herself, but what would she lose because of it?

Was she standing up for herself, or was she standing up for him?

Catherine took one more step toward Anna, keeping her icy glare on her daughter. "You stayed because you have no business running your own life. You can't do anything without me."

"What makes you think that?" Anna asked with shoulders pulled back. "I graduated from law school. I'm a successful attorney and a business owner. I manage my life just fine."

"You can't even associate yourself with decent company!" Catherine spat. "Olivia is a chicken farmer, and her brother is no better," she said, pointing at Beau.

He'd been called a lot of things in his lifetime, but to be compared to his sister wasn't a bad thing. Olivia was one of the best people he knew, and Anna was better off with a friend like Liv.

Beau loosened his hold on Anna's hand. If he stuck around much longer, he'd tell her mom exactly what he thought.

"If he goes, I go too," Anna said.

Beau's heart sank. Anna's entire life was burning, and she'd be the one left in the ash when all was said and done.

Catherine's nostrils flared, and her lips pressed tight together for a mere second before she stepped to the side. "You can go with him. Find somewhere else to live."

There it was—the blow he'd been dreading. Catherine hadn't listened to a word Anna said, and she never would. Anna had a million problems sitting on her shoulders, and he'd just become another.

Pulling his hand, Anna marched for the door. "I'll be back to get my things later."

"Don't you dare walk away from me!" Catherine shouted.

Anna's hand shook in Beau's as she grabbed her purse from a hook by the door with the other. "I'm not going back to Dean, and you're not listening to me."

Beau grabbed the knob and shut the door behind him as they walked away from her family and her home without looking back.

CHAPTER 33
ANNA

Flurries of soft snow rushed over Anna's windshield in the dark night as she followed the taillights of Beau's truck. The hands that gripped the steering wheel ached, and her wrist throbbed. Her entire body shook as she gasped for air.

I left. I just...walked out.

The adrenaline pumping through her veins was either excitement or fear, but none of it mattered. She needed to use the energy to figure out what to do next.

"Father, I need some help. What am I doing? I want to honor my parents, but at what cost?"

Her parents didn't love God. Did they even love her? She'd blindly trusted that they'd had her best interest at heart her whole life, but did they? It certainly didn't feel like it at the moment. Was blind obedience at twenty-eight the only way to honor?

She'd left her mom—the one thing she'd always said she wouldn't do. Her mom's parents had been taken from her, but this was different. Anna had left on her own.

But it was time. She knew it. She wasn't ready, but for some things, she might never feel ready.

"God, help me. I—I don't know what I'm doing. I don't want to hurt her, but I don't like it when she hurts me either." Her breaths were ragged as her tight muscles racked her whole body. "Help me, please!"

Then the tears came again, blurring what little she could see of the road in front of her. Beau's taillights were the only thing guiding her now.

"Am I supposed to follow him? Where is he even going?" Anna asked as tears rolled down her face, chasing each other before falling onto her lap.

The rest of her prayers were more of the same. What else could she do but beg for help? She was as lost as the hundreds of snowflakes that peppered her windshield.

Beau parked behind Blackwater Automotive, and she followed. She spent a lot of time hanging out with Olivia and their friends at Beau's place, and while she knew he lived in the back, she'd never had a reason to explore that area..

He met her at her car as she stepped out. Snow crunched under his boots as he wrapped her in his arms and settled his stance around her.

Beau huffed a warm breath against her hair. "I'm sorry. I didn't know what to do or say. I wanted to fight her for you."

"You were great." She was still shaking, but hopefully he wouldn't notice. "I don't think I could have done that if you hadn't been there."

"You might not have had the same conversation if I hadn't been there."

Anna was already shaking her head. "No. It's not your fault. She'd already made up her mind before she showed up. I could tell. She was going to push me to the limit."

Beau pressed a kiss to her head and took her hand in his. "Let's go inside. You're freezing."

She wasn't shaking because of the cold, but she didn't correct him as they entered the back of his building. He took her straight to the kitchen that served as the break room and pulled out a chair at the table for her.

He opened a cabinet and grabbed two mugs. "You want coffee? I think Olivia keeps hot chocolate here somewhere."

"Coffee sounds good." She brushed her hands into her hair, trying and failing to shake off the exhaustion of the day.

While the coffee brewed, Beau pulled a chair away from the table and rested it in front of her before sitting down. He cradled her hand in both of his and propped his elbows on his knees. "What can I do?"

"I don't know." Her mind was still inconveniently void. "I have no idea what to do."

"Do you want me to schedule a moving company to come? Dawson, Asa, Travis, and Gage would all help you move since your mom has evicted me from the property. I'm sure Olivia is on her way here right now."

Anna hadn't made a single phone call on the drive to Beau's. While she'd been praying, Beau had been making a plan for her.

"Thank you. Yes, I do need a moving company and plenty of friends. I'm still in shock."

Beau straightened his shoulders and gently tugged her hand. She moved from the chair to sit on his lap where he wrapped his strong arms around her, forming a fortress around her that shut the rest of the world out.

"You're not alone. You have plenty of friends, which means you have options on where to stay until you can find a new place. That is...if you want to."

"What do you mean?" Anna asked.

"I feel like this is my fault. If I hadn't been there, she wouldn't have told you to leave. I don't want to cause any more problems between you and your family."

Anna raised her head and cradled his face in her

hands. Beau might have a masculine look about him, but there was a vulnerability in his words she'd never heard before.

"Newsflash, Mom and I had problems before you came along. Beau, this is not your fault. Well, actually, it is. You're the one who believed in me and made me believe I could do it."

His arms tightened around her. "I'm really proud of you. I just hope you did it for you and not me."

Her heart still pounded hard and fast, but the fear had disappeared. There was a peace about what happened with her mother, and she had to believe that was a sign.

Anna slowly dragged her fingernails through his short beard, and he closed his eyes at her touch. He was so calm and steady—he was the rock they'd always said he was.

"I did it for both of us. Do you have any idea what you did to me on that trip?" she asked.

Beau slowly shook his head, never breaking eye contact with her.

"I was a mess after the wedding, but I didn't stay that way. I was looking for myself, and I found you."

"I don't want—"

Anna pressed her lips to his in a quick kiss. "I'm not finished. What I mean is, you showed me how to be myself. You gave me hope and courage. You can't possibly know what that means to me."

Beau nuzzled his head into the crook of her neck,

and she held him close. Last week, he was an acquaintance—her best friend's brother. This week, he was her confidant and teammate.

"What do you want me to do? How can I help?" he asked.

"You've already done it. You stood beside me."

He raised his head and set his jaw. She was used to his stern demeanor, but this wasn't the grumpy attitude so many of their friends teased him about. This was bold determination, and it was all in defense of her.

He brushed a hand over her cheek and into her hair. "I told you I'd always be here for you, and part of standing beside you means guarding your heart when someone tries to hurt you. So when you need me to, I'll stand in front of you and take the hits if it means you get to be safe and happy."

A lump sat heavy in Anna's throat, and she tried and failed to swallow it. "Thank you," she whispered.

He pulled her head toward him until her forehead touched his. As her eyes closed, she took her first healing breath.

Beau's hand fisted in the hair at the nap of her neck. "I don't want to cause you any more problems, but I will fight for you. All you have to do is ask."

CHAPTER 34

ANNA

Anna pulled a blush sweater dress from the pile on the bed and hung it in the closet of Dawson and Olivia's guest room. The clothes were the only things left to put away after two days of moving everything Anna owned from her parents' guest house.

It hadn't even been her home in name, but all the work she'd put into making the small cottage into the place she loved was a wash now. She'd stayed close to her parents at their request, but looking back, they'd actually ordered her to stay. She'd just agreed without protest.

How different would her life be now if she'd moved away when she wanted to the way her brother Drake had? She'd tried to please them, and she'd ended up failing anyway. She'd stuck around so they could push her away when she refused to bend to their will.

Olivia shuffled into the room carrying a mound of Anna's clothes draped over her arms. "Good grief. Are you sure these had to come?"

Anna rushed to take them from her friend. "Sorry. They just arrived, and I have to take photos before I can donate them."

Olivia propped her hands on her hips and huffed out a breath. "Have I told you lately that you have a strange job?"

"Which one? Both are a little weird."

"The one where businesses send you free clothes and you take photos of yourself wearing them, post them on the internet, and get paid to do it."

"Oh, I thought you were talking about the one where I argue with adults and try to convince strangers to pay my clients money."

"That is weird too. Although I am super proud of you for being brave enough to stand up to strangers, even if it took you long enough to stand up to your mother."

Anna sighed. "It's easy to be confident when I have evidence to back me up. I don't have any of that when Mom comes at me in a rage."

Olivia slid her arm around Anna and squeezed. "You do now. From what I heard, you put your foot down. I just wish I'd been there to see it."

"Thanks for letting me stay here. I promise I'll be out of your hair as soon as I find a new place."

Liv plopped on the bed beside the piles of clothes. "Take your time. I have no complaints about having my bestie stay with me all the time."

"Yeah, but you and Dawson just got married. You need space and privacy."

Dawson and Olivia decided to tie the knot in a private ceremony and have a reception party in the spring before Wolf Creek Ranch opened for the season. With Olivia's possible infertility, they didn't want to wait to try for a family.

"It's not like our rooms share a wall. We're on the other side of the house, and I don't expect you to show up at my bedroom asking for a glass of water."

Anna chuckled. "You're right. I'll stay on my side."

Olivia grabbed the next few pieces of clothing and handed them to Anna. "You know, Beau is welcome here too."

Beau. She barely went ten seconds without thinking about him. The way he supported her. The way he'd assured her he would be by her side. The way he'd worked hard to help her get moved into Olivia's place on short notice. He was a man of few words, but actions told her more about him than anything he could say.

"Thanks for that. I hate that I've already taken

up so much of his time since we got back. I didn't expect to have to move on such short notice."

"Can I tell you something?" Olivia asked.

"The fact that you're asking is a little scary. Since when do you think before you speak?"

Liv rolled her eyes and handed over another dress. "Ha-ha. You're so funny. In that case, I'll just say it. I think you and Beau have something really special."

Anna's heart rate picked up speed as if she were running a marathon instead of hanging up clothes. She smiled, then quickly squashed it. "I think so too, but I'm terrified."

"Why?"

"Because I always think with my heart and don't always use my head. What if I'm so excited that I mess it up again?"

Olivia held up a finger. "Hold up. The fiasco with he-who-shall-not-be-named was not your fault. I'll agree that you were a little stubborn and had some pretty strong blinders on, but I admire your strength in the aftermath. You did the right thing walking away from him and standing up to your mom."

"I'm glad I did it too, but it's hard to know which way is up when my world is turning upside down. It all happened so quickly."

Olivia reached for Anna's hand. "But I'm right here, and I'll keep you on the right path. I love you, girl, and I know you're going to be better off after the dust settles. I just want you to know that Beau is going to stand by you too. He's good for you, and you're good for him."

Anna let out a sarcastic chuckle. "Beau doesn't need me. He's got it all figured out."

"He needs you, *and* he wants you. You're going to be so good for him."

"I'm glad you think that. Sometimes I feel like this whole thing is one-sided."

Olivia's mouth turned up in a mischievous grin as she pulled her phone from her pocket. "Look at this."

She turned her phone around to show Anna the screen. It was a photo of her friends as they unpacked yesterday. The bedroom was filled with boxes. Bella sat on the bed handing books to Anna from an open box. Dawson and Beau stood in the corner of the room next to the dresser.

"Why are you showing me this?" Anna asked.

"Look at Beau."

Beau's arms were crossed over his chest, and Dawson was clearly talking to him. "Yeah."

"He's staring at you like you're the only woman in the world."

Anna took a better look at the photo. He was looking at her, and his features were softer than usual. His brows weren't pinched together. He wasn't frowning at whatever silly joke Dawson was probably making. He wasn't even listening to whatever his friend was telling him.

Liv was right. Many men had looked at Anna before, but the looks were usually followed by a cat call or a creepy wink.

As far as she knew, no one had ever looked at her the way Beau did. Sure, the photo captured a small moment in time, but was it wrong to hope Olivia was right?

Anna handed the phone back to Olivia. "Please don't get my hopes up."

"I'm doing no such thing. I'm telling you it's okay to be scared, but don't let the fear keep you from seeing the one thing you've always wanted."

Anna pinched her lips between her teeth and nodded. She'd always trusted Olivia but never more than now.

Grabbing her phone back, Olivia glanced at the screen. "Let's get these put up. I don't want to be late for the Christmas party."

Christmas party? Shoot. Anna had forgotten all about the casual Christmas party at Travis and Bella's house. "Let's just hang these up, and I'll sort through them later. I need a shower. What am I going to wear?"

Olivia's eyes widened as she glanced at the full closet and the piles of clothes on the bed. "You're kidding, right? That was a joke."

Anna squinted. “Not really. I want to wear something Beau would like.”

Olivia patted Anna on the shoulder and walked toward the door. “Wear something warm and comfortable. I heard there will be a bonfire. Whatever you decide to wear, I guarantee Beau will like it.”

It took more time than expected to get ready. She’d misplaced her favorite curling wand, and the shoes that matched her green sweater dress were nowhere to be found.

Oddly enough, getting ready at Olivia’s house wasn’t so bad. There were plenty of cabinets and drawers in the bathroom, and the shower had the perfect water pressure. She would miss the towel warmer and built-in heater at her old place, but those were luxuries she could live without.

A text from Beau came in just as Anna slipped into the passenger seat of Olivia’s car.

Beau: Are you on your way?

Anna: Leaving now.

The short text from him awakened a bubbling joy in her chest. Beau had never been much of a talker, but he didn’t skimp on the check-ins when they were apart.

Olivia let out a long, dramatic sigh. “Is that Beau? I’m not going to lie. I’m jealous.”

“Of what?” Anna asked. “Dawson is practically attached to your hip.”

"But he's working tonight."

"Sorry, but I've been the third wheel for too long. It's my turn to get the guy."

Olivia shoved Anna's shoulder and squealed. "Do you hear yourself? It's your turn! I'm so excited for you!"

Okay, so she was excited for herself too. After the roller coaster of the last two weeks, it was starting to sink in that the changes might have all been for the good. If God was working in her life, she'd trust His plan.

The moon was barely a sliver in the dark sky when they pulled into Silver Falls Ranch. Travis and Bella's cabin was small, but they were excited to host their friends for a casual Christmas get-together.

This was Bella's moment, not Anna's. After all her friend had gone through since her accident and the awful run-in with her ex, they really should be throwing a huge party to celebrate.

Travis had been just what Bella needed after her accident, and Anna had been the first one to remind her friend that men like Travis were few and far between.

Anna had been struggling with her own relationship at the time, and seeing Travis's kindness to Bella should have been Anna's wake-up call. She and Dean had done nothing but fight for months.

Oh, but she could see it all clearly now. Beau was

everything that Dean wasn't. Beau treated her like a woman, not a toy.

"Are you sure we didn't need to bring anything?" Anna asked.

"Positive. No presents, and the guys are taking care of dinner."

Firelight led the way through the trees to Travis and Bella's cabin. Trees sheltered the clearing as Olivia's lights shone on the cars and trucks parked on the sides of the path.

Anna spotted Beau instantly. He stood with Gage in front of a grill just past the fire pit. By the time Olivia pulled into a parking spot, Beau was already making his way toward them.

Anna stepped out of the car and pulled her jacket tighter around her. The snow had melted to almost nothing in the open areas, but a few mounds of dirty white lingered beneath the dense trees.

Beau was only a few feet away, but she didn't wait for him to reach her. Breaking into a sprint, she rushed into his arms, burying her face in the collar of his coat.

She could barely breathe, but everything was perfect. The lingering worry that whatever they'd started in Freedom would fade when they returned to Blackwater melted away. Beau was the same no matter where they were. He was beside her. His strong arms wrapped around her, protecting her when she didn't feel strong enough to protect herself.

She was falling again—falling for Beau Lawrence—and, once again, he was there to catch her.

CHAPTER 35
BEAU

Drops of water dripped from Beau's hair onto his face as he brushed his teeth. Was he going to regret leaving Tim in charge for a few hours on a Saturday? Probably. Could he skip Jacob's birthday party? Not without getting an earful from Olivia.

Jacob was young, but the kid practically worked at the garage. Maybe in a few years Beau could add him to the payroll. Jacob knew more about cars than Tim.

"Beau! We need to leave. Chop, chop!" Olivia shouted.

Spitting his toothpaste into the sink, Beau grabbed a towel and rubbed it over his dripping hair. "Get out of my room!"

"You two sound like siblings," Dawson said.

Dawson and Olivia stood in the bathroom

doorway looking way too excited to be going to a pre-teen birthday party.

"Ever heard of boundaries? Personal space?" Beau asked.

"What's that?" Olivia asked, scrunching her nose the way she used to do whenever she caught their parents kissing when she was a kid.

Beau ran a brush through his hair and reached for the shirt draped over the towel bar. "I said I'll be there. You don't have to watch me until I walk out the door."

Olivia crossed her arms and leaned against the doorframe. "I just wanted to tell you that Anna is waiting on you. She's in the kitchen."

"Lead with that next time," Beau said as he pushed past Dawson and Olivia.

"Do you two want to ride with us?" Dawson asked.

Beau slid the shirt over his head and grabbed his wallet and keys from the dresser. "Nope. I need a getaway vehicle."

"Don't you dare have fun!" Olivia shouted behind him.

"I did that once. It was awful," Beau said as he headed toward the kitchen.

Anna stood at the sink washing dishes. The sleeves of her white sweater were pushed up past her elbows, and her blonde hair was pulled back in a high ponytail with stray pieces framing her face.

"What are you doing?" Beau asked as he stepped up behind her. His arms wrapped around her waist, and he breathed in her warm vanilla scent.

"Washing dishes. I thought I'd make myself useful while I waited."

"That is one hundred percent Tim's job today." Beau pressed a kiss to Anna's temple at her hair line. "You never have to lift a finger when you're here."

"That's sweet, but I would feel horribly useless if I didn't." She turned to look over her shoulder at him and pressed her lips to his cheek.

The woman was intoxicating. Every nerve ending in his body roared to life like a diesel engine whenever she was around.

Beau handed her a dish towel. "Are you ready to go?"

She dried her hands and hung the towel carefully on a hook by the sink. "Yep. I can't believe Jacob is growing up so fast. I feel like he was a kid just yesterday."

Beau reached for Anna's hand as they made their way to his truck. "He's still a kid. He's just smarter and way more mature than your average pre-teen."

"What did you get him?"

"Custom floor mats for his Porsche," Beau said as he opened the passenger door for her.

"He's going to love that! I got him a new bat he's been wanting."

Beau slid into the driver's seat and headed for

the main road. He was getting used to having Anna beside him in his truck, and reaching for her hand was becoming his new favorite thing to do while driving.

He was still getting used to this alternate reality where Anna wanted to kiss him—where he could touch her and hold her. Every step of their new relationship had come and gone in the blink of an eye. His entire focus had changed in a few weeks' time, but not one part of him wanted to pump the brakes.

Still, there was the annoying reminder that everyone in town had shown up to Anna's wedding. Actually caring about what people thought was new to him, but every time he thought about someone judging Anna, a low roar crawled up his chest.

"So, what are we telling people today?" Beau asked.

"You mean when people see us looking cozy?"

He glanced over at her and was greeted with her playful smirk. At least she didn't seem worried about it. "Yeah. That."

She rested an assuring hand on his arm. "It might be a good idea to lay low for a little bit. I mean, people are going to talk no matter what, but I'd like a chance to breathe before the rumor mill comes knocking."

"It's not like I'm big on kissing in public anyway. We can just play it cool, and maybe no one will notice."

Anna leaned toward him, and it took every bit of his self-control to focus on driving. "You mean you don't want to kiss me in front of a bunch of preteens and their parents? I'm crushed."

Beau glanced at her. She was close enough he could lean over a few inches and press his lips to hers, but a new and urgent instinct demanded he drive safely when she was in his truck. "I always want to kiss you. Make no mistake, that's at the top of my list every day."

Anna leaned closer until her warm breath brushed against his ear. "Can we do a little bit of that before we join the party?"

The air in the cab of the truck grew thick and hot as his entire body heated. He swallowed hard and tightened his jaw before his body allowed him to respond. "Anything you want."

Anna bounced in her seat and pressed her lips to his cheek. "You're fun, you know that?"

Beau huffed. "You are the first person to ever say that to me."

He parked as far away from the house as possible and shut off the truck. He didn't waste any time pulling Anna in for a deep kiss. Her soft lips molded to his, sending sparks down his spine.

He broke the kiss long enough to say, "Let's just skip the party."

Her forehead rested on his shoulder as she laughed. The joyful sound vibrated into his skin and found a direct path to his heart. "We have to at least make an appearance."

"Ten minutes? No one will miss us."

"Olivia would send out a search party. She'd recruit all of the kids to find us."

"Not if she valued her life," Beau added.

"Actually, she might let us run off together. She's definitely cheering us on."

"For once, I can't hate her for getting in my business."

Anna pressed her lips to his one more time before reaching for the door handle. "Let's go. Everyone is going to wonder why we're parked but haven't gone inside yet."

"I don't care what they think," he reminded her, and tugged her back into his arms to nuzzle the back of her neck.

"I know you don't, but I do. Hop to it, Mr. Lawrence."

The party was a circus of kids running around screaming. Did they have to shout all the time? The boys had a paintball war in the backyard while the girls stood off to the side with their heads together whispering to each other. Every once in a while, they'd point and giggle at the boys.

"Aren't they cute?" Lyric asked as she glanced out the window into the backyard.

Asa watched the kids with his arms crossed over his chest. "Jacob is going to be one solid bruise tomorrow. He can't stop looking at the girls long enough to keep from getting shot by the paintballs."

"I think the girls can't stop looking at him either," Anna said, pointing to a girl who tossed her hair whenever Jacob looked her way.

Olivia joined the viewing party and rubbed her hands together like an evil mastermind. "Looks like the guys are out of ammo. Time to stir the waters."

"Hide-and-seek!" Dawson shouted as he burst into the backyard.

Olivia grabbed Beau and Anna's hands and pulled them toward the door. "Let's get in on the action."

"No thanks. I'm just here to eat cake," Beau said, pulling back on his sister's hold.

Olivia tightened her hold on his hand. "Shut up and quit being a buzzkill."

Anna leaned over and whispered, "She won't let you out of it. Ask me how I know."

Outside, Dawson and Olivia gathered the kids and explained the rules of hide-and-seek as if it were an Olympic sport while Beau formed a game plan.

When the kids scattered, Beau took Anna's hand in his before she had a chance to run off after them.

He jerked his head in the opposite direction. "This way."

He kept a tight hold on her as they approached an old shed close to the tree line. Olivia had deemed this section out of bounds, which meant it was the perfect place to "hide" with Anna.

"Ten seconds in, and you're already breaking the rules," Anna said.

"I don't care about Olivia's rules." He reached behind a bush near the door and fumbled around until he found what he was looking for. A black box with a key inside.

"Is Asa going to be mad at us for breaking and entering?" Anna asked, glancing back over her shoulder as if the officer himself would appear with handcuffs.

"I'm not breaking anything. I'm using the door." Stepping to the side, he let Anna enter first.

Faint light drifted through the dirt-caked windows, and dust floated in the cold air, mixing with the cloud of Anna's warm breath.

"No one will find us here."

He didn't have to see Anna's face to know she was smiling. She radiated happiness over small things all the time, and he could tell when she was smiling even on phone calls now.

Beau reached through the dim light until he found her hand. Pulling her to him, he skimmed the tip of his nose over her jaw and up to her ear to whisper, "Found you."

Her hands slid up his chest and around his neck to pull him down to her. Their mouths crashed together in a rush, leaving a roaring in his ears that drowned out everything except the feel of Anna in his arms. The world could crumble around them, and he wouldn't notice. Anna was his new center of gravity, and he was more than happy to be locked in her orbit.

Was this it? Had God jerked Beau out of his content life to place him beside Anna? It was improbable. Impossible. Yet, his world had shifted, and he didn't want to set things back in order.

When she broke the kiss, Beau rested his forehead against Anna's. There was a hungry lion in his soul that settled whenever he could hear the steady rhythm of her breaths.

"I have a surprise for you," she whispered into the darkness.

"What is it?"

She quietly laughed. "If I told you, it wouldn't be a surprise."

"Why did you tell me about it then? That's just mean."

She traced her fingernails over the back of his neck, playing in the short hairs at the nape as if it didn't light a fire that raced down his spine. "I'm a little nervous, but I think you'll like it. Well, you may be proud of me, but I'm not really sure if it's going to be a good thing or a really tough thing."

Nothing about her vague explanation gave him the slightest hint at what she meant, but one thing stood out that he couldn't ignore.

She took a deep breath and tucked her chin to her chest. The shadows fell on her face in all the wrong places, so he lifted her chin with a finger.

"I'm always proud of you." He didn't whisper this time, and he wouldn't leave room for misunderstanding.

Her smile was back, and he kissed her slowly, careful to let her know with each movement exactly how much he adored her.

The shed door burst open, letting in a flood of light. Anna broke the kiss and took a step back as Jacob peeked his head through the doorway.

"Um, Mom said to let you know that we're going to cut the cake and sing happy birthday now so Aunt Olivia can leave for work."

"We'll be right there," Anna said, not moving to follow Jacob as he closed the door.

When they were alone again, Anna patted Beau's chest. "I need to go anyway. I don't have long to make my move."

Beau grabbed her hand in a show of solidarity. "Do you need me to do anything?"

"Not this time. It's something I have to do on my own."

Man, it was good to see her taking control of her own life. She'd come so far in such a short time. "You're amazing. You know that?"

She pressed a soft fingertip to his lips. "I don't

know how this is going to go yet. Save your excitement for later."

Sliding his hand around her wrist, he removed her finger from his lips, then pressed the palm of her hand against his chest. "When can I know about the surprise?"

"Hopefully, we can talk about it later tonight."

Beau jerked his head toward the door. "Then let's go."

Anna lifted onto her toes to press a quick kiss to his neck just above his pounding pulse before darting out of the shed.

What was happening to him? He wasn't a stranger to taking risks, but Anna was the most dangerous thing he'd ever loved. Cars could break him, speed could kill him, but Anna would consume him.

CHAPTER 36
ANNA

The emails were relentless. Anna dealt with dozens of messages on a daily basis, but this onslaught would be a part of her life for a while. You don't shake things up without having backlash to deal with.

Christmas tended to be a slow time at the firm. Many attorneys and judges took weeks off in December only to pick back up with a renewed force after the new year.

Her parents had never fit that mold. Every Christmas growing up had been a rat race at the office, and Anna couldn't remember a year when her parents hadn't brought her with them to the office after opening presents on Christmas morning.

A ding alerted her to a message on a different app, and she flipped over to read it. The emails weren't going away, and they'd be waiting for her tomorrow and the next day too.

Brittany: What did Cynthia DeSilvio send you?

Anna glanced at the clock. Five minutes until her meeting. She had some time to decompress.

Things with Brittany had been easy and comfortable since the trip, and Anna's previous unease about her friend had almost vanished. She could chalk up the awkwardness of their meeting to nerves.

Anna: It's gorgeous. A periwinkle skirt with cerulean ribbon detail. It's light and flowy, and will be a hit this summer.

Brittany: I have to see it. Video chat tonight?

Anna: I can't tonight. I'm shaking up my life today, so I'll be busy.

A quiet vibration tingled beneath Anna's skin. Between Beau, Olivia, and Bella, she'd heard plenty of pep talks this week. Why was her stomach still flipping like a gymnast?

Brittany: What do you mean? What's going on?

Anna's five minutes were almost up. There wasn't enough time to get into the story now.

Anna: I'll tell you on our video chat tomorrow. I want to see your face.

Brittany's response was immediate.

Brittany: Are you sure we can't just talk tonight?

Anna: Positive. See you soon.

Anna closed her laptop and stood, pushing out a

deep breath through rounded lips and brushing her hands over her charcoal-gray slacks. She made it all the way to her office door before she stopped with her hand on the knob.

"God, I need Your help this morning. I need Your strength and comfort. I can't do this on my own, but You've asked me to trust You, and I'm doing all I can to follow You. Please give me boldness."

Anna tightened her hands into fists before flexing them as she walked down the hallway. Her attention remained focused on the door at the end.

It'll be over in just a few minutes.

They won't hurt you.

It's only words.

You are loved.

The words she'd repeated all morning were true, but the mind was its own entity. Why did it take so much to convince herself that there wasn't a hungry bear waiting in her dad's office?

Her mother's loud voice drifted down the hallway to meet her before she stepped into the room and closed the door. Her mom stood by Anna's dad's desk with her arms crossed over her chest. The conversation died as her mother faced her.

Her dad checked the time on his monitor. "You have four minutes. I have a call at 10:15.

Anna clasped her hands, determined to stop the shaking. "I'm leaving the firm."

Her mother didn't miss a beat. "You're what?"

"Leaving." It was a miracle she'd gotten the words out without stuttering. "I'll send you an email confirming my two-week notice, effective immediately."

Catherine's arms dropped to her sides, but her hands were clenched into tight fists. "You're going to allow that piece of trash to disrupt our business. You're more stupid than I thought."

They're words. Just words. Beau was so much more than a piece of trash, and Anna was not stupid. In fact, she was coming to believe she was making more intelligent decisions every day.

"If I'm being honest, I don't like the work environment, and the firm's goals do not align with my own."

"No one asked for your thoughts!" Catherine shouted. "We have deadlines, hearings, and trials scheduled, and you think you can just leave because you're running around with a filthy man who works on cars?"

Anna took a deep breath, refusing to react to the hateful words. "You don't love me," she whispered.

"What?" Catherine wasn't quiet. The rage in her tone carried through the room. At this rate, everyone in the office was going to hear the news before the meeting was even over.

"You don't love me," Anna repeated slowly, clearer this time.

They were just words, but these did hurt. They ripped open her soul, leaving her empty and cold.

Her mom scoffed. "You've been making decisions that we don't agree with. You're not thinking clearly. You're not being responsible or mature—"

"I'm not doing everything you tell me to do. There's a difference. I can make decisions for myself without your consent. I'm not a child, and you don't own me. You kicked me out, then—"

"You left!" Catherine exclaimed, pointing a stiff finger at Anna. "You left. We did not kick you out. You made a poor decision."

"I made a decision for me. There's a difference."

Catherine scoffed. "It was a ridiculous decision!"

"I understand that you believe that, and I can't change your mind. Still, I didn't make a ridiculous decision. I made a choice for myself, and I don't regret moving out."

The last word cracked. Could she get another adrenaline boost to finish this conversation without breaking? She wanted her family—craved them—but nothing she did would truly make them happy. Even when she'd been meek and compliant, they weren't satisfied.

The frowning lines on her mother's face smoothed. Catherine stood tall, glaring at Anna. "You can't make it on your own. You can't make it without *me*."

The old fear rose up inside her, hot and firm as it tightened in her throat. "I don't want to do this." Great. Her voice was shaking now. She wasn't bold enough to break all ties with her parents without shedding tears.

"Then don't. Get rid of that creep and right the wrongs you've made recently. You've been throwing your life away ever since the wedding."

"I don't believe that," Anna said quickly. "I've never been happier."

"That's a lie," her mother spat. "That stupid boy is feeding you lies. Life without structure and success is lazy and useless. He can't give you the life we have. You'll be knocked up, broke, abused, and homeless before you know what hit you."

Anna jerked back. None of those things would come from a life with Beau. He'd done nothing but nurture and support her—things her parents had done only with money and social standing.

"I'm sorry." Anna sniffed and wiped the moisture from her eye. "Your love costs more than I can afford. I'm my own person, and I need to live my own life."

Her mother's hand slapped onto her father's sleek, mahogany desk with a bang that reverberated through the room. "How can you say that? We've given you everything!"

Despite her initial bravery, Anna's shoulders shook as she gasped for breath. "Except the ability to choose. I've chosen my faith, where I'll live, and now, I'm choosing my job. I love it here, but I want to do things my way. I'm choosing God and myself."

Catherine lifted her chin, looking Anna up and down the way someone would assess a threat before battle. "What are you going to do?"

Anna shook her head. "I'm not ready to tell you that yet. I might never be, and I'd like to settle into my new job without complications."

"You won't be getting a letter of recommendation from me," her father said.

Any hope she'd held onto that her dad might support her vaporized like steam above boiling water. The rolling in her empty stomach begged her to double over. Did it have to be this way?

Yes. She'd tried to comply. She'd bent over backward to please them, but even her best efforts hadn't done any good.

They didn't love her. They controlled her. All the years of showing only her best and smiling through the hurt were for nothing.

Maybe one day she could have a relationship with her parents, but it wasn't today. If they wouldn't listen, she couldn't change their minds.

Her mother crossed her arms over her chest, bunching her pristine blouse. "And don't bother showing up for the next two weeks. You'll need to file a notice of withdrawal in every lawsuit you're associated with and turn in your keys by the end of the day."

The tears did come, but they were mercifully silent. After years of loving her job, she was leaving everything behind with one decision.

Was she being selfish by leaving the clients she'd promised to represent? Of course. Was she willing to continue being her mother's punching bag? Not at all.

She turned to leave, desperate to escape before her parents saw the weakness streaming down her face, but her mother's sharp voice called her back.

"Oh, and Anna."

Turning, Anna let the woman who'd raised her see the hurt in her eyes. Would she even care?

"That man is not allowed here. Understood?"

"Yes." It was all she could muster before the floodgates opened. She rushed down the hall, clamping her hand over her mouth to muffle the sobs that ripped from her chest. Tears rolled over her fingers until she slid into her office and closed the door.

It wasn't even her office anymore. She wouldn't come here anymore. It would become a strange place to her soon. Would she even miss it?

Pressing her back against the door, she let the tears fall. Gasping for air, she choked on the sobs. The tears fell until her shoulders sagged with the weight of her sadness.

She didn't want to keep her job. She wanted her parents to care about her the way she cared about them, but that prayer wasn't meant to be answered today.

Her phone on the desk dinged, and she swiped at the tears on her face as she pushed away from the door that held her upright. A text from Beau lit up the screen.

Beau: Meet me outside.

She grabbed a tissue from the box on her desk and dried her face. Beau knew about the meeting with her parents, but it was the middle of a workday, and he should be at the garage.

Her breaths evened as she neared the lobby, and she stormed straight through the exit without saying a word to anyone.

Beau leaned against the front of his truck in the parking lot. His head lifted as she burst through the door, showing off his gentle smile.

Who cared if she was wearing heels? Anna tore across the lot toward Beau, but he met her halfway. The truth clicked into place the moment she crashed into him. She loved Beau Lawrence with all her heart.

His arm held tight around her back, and his hand cradled her head. "I'm here. It's okay."

The tears started anew, but her heart was at war with itself. Beau's love healed the fresh wounds her parents had created. "I don't know what I'm supposed to do now. I don't know where I belong," she said, wiping her tears on his shirt.

"You belong with me," Beau said, deep and sure as his hold tightened around her. "And you've already done everything you need to do. You start working at Camille's office in two weeks."

He was right. She had a new job—a better job—waiting for her.

"Anna."

She wiped at her face. She probably looked horrible with a red nose and makeup smeared around her eyes. "Yes."

Beau brushed his hand over her wet cheek and waited patiently until she looked up at him. Instead of a look of horror, Beau's light-brown eyes peered straight into her soul.

"I love you, Anna."

She sucked in a quick breath. "What did you say?"

"I love you. I know it hasn't been long, and I know you're going through a lot right now." He cradled her face in both of his strong hands. "I have no right to love you, but I do anyway. You're the most amazing woman in the world. They may have hurt you today, but you will always be loved. You're strong, funny, smart, beautiful, and the kindest—"

"I love you too. I love you so much."

Her arms tangled around his neck the moment their lips touched. Beau met her kiss with an intensity that brought her back to life. His kiss was hard and forceful but slow and sure. There wasn't an ounce of hesitation as he showed her the depth of his love.

She broke the kiss to breathe but didn't move out of his embrace. Cradled against him, she could believe that everything would be okay.

"I don't know what I would do without you," she whispered.

"You could have done all of this on your own. You're stronger than you realize." He pulled back just enough to wipe the tears from her cheeks. "I know you'll miss them, but you never needed them to be complete. You just needed someone to tell you that you already are."

She sniffed and wiped her nose. "Do you mean that?"

"Of course I do. You're a rockstar, Anna." He jerked his chin toward the door of the building. "Do you need help moving things out?"

"Actually, you're banned from the building."

"Well, I think that means we should go get lunch and come back with some friends who aren't banned."

Anna chuckled and blinked away the last of the moisture in her eyes. "Let me get my purse."

Beau tugged on her hand. "You don't need it. Let's get out of here."

How could she refuse that offer? She let him

walk her to the passenger side of his truck and open the door for her. When she was settled inside, he leaned in to press a quick kiss to her lips.

"I love you."

Would she ever get tired of hearing those words? "I love you too."

CHAPTER 37
ANNA

Bright lights shone through the windows of Barn Sour as Beau parked in the gravel lot in front of the restaurant. The orange glow faded into the dark night before reaching them, and flurries of snow drifted gently toward the white ground.

"Asher and Hunter know how to draw a crowd," Beau said as he turned off the engine.

Anna unbuckled and reached for the door. "It's always a good show. I'm glad Donna lets them play so often, even if most of the people they bring in don't buy drinks."

Beau rested a hand on her arm. "Don't move." He hopped out and rounded the truck to open the door for her.

Anna took his offered hand and stepped out of the truck. "You're such a gentleman. Are you going to dance with me tonight?"

Beau chuckled under his breath. "Like we did in Freedom? No way."

The intimate dance class they'd taken in Freedom felt like a lifetime ago, but she couldn't forget the way he held her or the way he'd whispered silly things in her ear. "We'd have every jaw in Blackwater dropping if we showed them what we know."

Beau pressed a kiss to her temple. "I think that kind of dance should be our little secret. Maybe we can practice again sometime."

A full-on belly laugh gripped her as Beau opened the door and raised voices rushed at them. It was just past seven, and the bar was already packed. Friends crowded in groups around tables laughing, while Asher and Hunter Harding set up their equipment beside the stage. The platform was only a couple of feet high, but it was enough to give the whole room a good view of the musicians.

Anna leaned in close to be heard above the noise as they weaved their way through the crowded room. "I haven't heard the Hardings play in a while."

"Me neither." Beau leaned from one side to the other, scanning the room. "You see Travis? He's supposed to have a table for us."

Anna spotted Lauren across the room, waving. The two usually helped out with children's activities at church together, but with the move and changing jobs, Anna hadn't spent a lot of time hanging out with friends.

"Hey, girl! I've missed you!" Anna wrapped Lauren in a hug. "How are you?"

"Great. I just graduated with my master's in psychology. I'm a licensed counselor now!"

"Congratulations! How many degrees is that now?"

Lauren rolled her eyes, but the smile on her face said it all. "Three, but who's counting?"

"I'm counting. Tonight, we celebrate! A round of water and totchos for the whole place!" Anna shouted.

Lauren covered her mouth as she bent over in laughter, and the light in her eyes reflected pure joy. She'd overcome so much in her life, and she'd never once let the darkness win.

Lauren had lost family and friends. She'd been used for selfish gain by the people she loved most and had almost lost her life. Yet, she never let her chin fall.

Could Anna be like that? Could she be strong when she was losing the only life she'd ever known?

Anna wrapped her friend in a hug and held on. Lauren was living proof that anyone could be strong in the face of struggles.

"You're amazing, and you're going to change lives as a counselor," Anna whispered against Lauren's hair.

"Are you saying I haven't been changing lives as a librarian all these years?" Lauren joked.

"You most certainly have, and you're the best Sunday School teacher ever. I'm just happy you're going after your dreams."

Lauren stepped out of the hug with a huge smile on her face. "Thanks, girl." She pointed behind Anna and gasped. "Look who's here!"

Camille stepped through the crowd with her husband, Noah, and their little boys, Evan and Taylor.

Evan ran straight up to Anna and Lauren and wrapped both of them in a hug around their legs. "I didn't know you'd be here!" the six-year-old boy shouted.

Lauren ruffled his hair. "I just saw you Sunday morning. That was only two sleeps ago."

"I know, but I missed you." Evan released them and looked around. "Where is the food?"

"You just ate!" Camille said, leading Taylor by the hand toward the nearest table. "I swear he's a bottomless pit."

"Wait until they're both teenagers," Anna said.

Camille bit her lips between her teeth and leaned closer to Anna and Lauren. "There might be three teenage boys running around the house one day."

Anna gasped. "Are you serious?"

Lauren grabbed Camille's shoulder. "You're joking!"

Camille shrugged, but a playful smile lingered on her lips. "Well, there might be two boys and a girl. We're not sure yet."

"Congratulations!" Anna and Lauren shouted in unison.

"We have so much to celebrate tonight," Lauren said. "Anna's new job, Camille's growing family, and my expensive diploma."

Bella stepped up beside the women and elbowed her way into the huddle. "Did someone say celebration? If nothing else, we should celebrate Anna's new freedom."

Bella had lived with Anna for a little while over the summer, and their friendship had only grown since then. Bella had needed a place to stay and friends in a strange new place, but Anna had gained a friend during the rockiest time in her relationship with Dean and her mom. How would she have handled those tough times if God hadn't given her a roommate to lean on?

Now, Anna knew freedom in more ways than one. She'd found hope and healing in the town of Freedom, and she'd brought home a new boldness that was changing her life for the better every day.

Lauren held up a plastic cup filled with water. "Amen!"

Beau's warm hand rested on the small of Anna's

back, and she leaned into him as he appeared at her side. "Can we join you ladies?"

Travis nudged his way into the group with a playful smile. "Yeah. Beau is the object of someone's affections."

Beau huffed and rolled his eyes. "You don't have to make it into a big deal."

"It's just funny." Travis jerked his head toward the bar. "That waitress over there can't leave Beau alone. She just asked him if he'd meet her after they closed tonight. Or should I say in the morning?"

Heat crept up Anna's neck. Dean had never seen the harm in flirting with other women and even made sure Anna knew women wanted him, but Beau had made every effort to assure her that she was the only woman he was interested in. Still, her body's instinctual reaction was unavoidable.

Beau leaned in to whisper in Anna's ear. "I let her know I am happily taken."

Anna lifted her chin and gave him a tense grin. She really believed him, but her immediate reaction wasn't fading quickly.

Beau brushed the side of his nose against hers and pulled her closer, pressing her whole body against his as he whispered, "I love you."

Well, that was one way to make her body forget to be jealous. The tension from mere seconds ago melted away as he pressed his lips to hers.

The relief swept over her like a tidal wave. Beau

was fixing parts of her he didn't even break. Between his love, God's guiding hand, and her friends' encouragement, Anna could make it through any storms life could throw at her.

The short kiss was all she needed to reset her fluctuating emotions. A peace settled over her as she blinked in the bright lights. "Thanks for that."

"The pleasure is all mine," Beau said before flashing her a wink.

Anna's stomach was still doing somersaults when she caught sight of movement behind Beau. Her grip tightened on his arm as Brittany Diaz stepped into view.

CHAPTER 38
BEAU

Every alarm in Beau's head went off in unison when he saw Brittany. He'd been on high alert for weeks, but Anna had gone to great lengths to assure him Brittany was a friend.

Friends were supportive. Friends were there when you needed them. Friends did not travel across the country *twice* and show up unannounced.

Anna kept a firm grip on Beau's arm as she greeted Brittany. "Hey. I didn't expect to see you here."

That was one way to put it. Anna had a lot more tact than Beau.

Brittany kept her gaze locked on Anna as she pushed the bridge of her glasses up her slender nose. "You haven't answered my messages."

Her monotone words were so matter-of-fact, but her reason for traveling so far to find Anna didn't add up. If she was outraged enough by Anna's lack of replies to travel this far, where was her emotion? There wasn't a frown line or wrinkle on her face.

Anna rested a hand on her chest and gave Brittany her full attention. "I'm sorry. I've been really busy the last few days."

Brittany only stared. "Okay."

That was it? *Okay?*

Nope. Not gonna work for Beau.

He reached for Anna's hand just as she gestured for a table their friends had claimed.

"Do you want to sit and talk?"

Brittany gave a single nod, and Anna moved toward the booth. Beau's hand kept a firm grip on Anna's while he watched Brittany.

She was the last person anyone would expect to be a threat with her thin build and big-framed glasses, but Beau wouldn't underestimate her or anyone else when Anna's safety was at stake.

A hand rested on Beau's shoulder, and Lauren appeared at his side.

"Let me," Lauren whispered.

Beau glanced at Anna and Brittany before turning back to Lauren. She could take his place at the table, but he wasn't leaving Anna's side.

Lauren jerked her head toward the nearby bar where a few of their friends watched intently.

He had zero problems leaving Anna to girl-talk

with her friends. Leaving her with someone he didn't trust was a whole different story.

"Trust me," Lauren said before sliding into the chair across the table from Brittany. A friendly smile lit up her features, and Anna made introductions.

His chest rose and fell in deep waves. He could stand five feet away. He could give Anna space and trust that she and Lauren knew what they were doing.

What kind of help could he provide anyway? None when the game was being played with words instead of fists.

Dawson welcomed Beau to a different table where the Harding family waited to hear Asher and Hunter play. "Hey, man. Who's that?"

Beau leaned over the table without sitting and rested his palms flat on the wooden surface. "Her name is Brittany. Anna knows her from her online stuff, but she lives somewhere in California."

"That's cool. I didn't know Anna was expecting someone. Is she planning to stay at our place? We don't have any more beds, but there's a couch available."

Beau glanced at the table where the women talked. "Anna didn't know she was coming."

Camille leaned in, jumping into the conversation. "Is that the girl who showed up in Freedom when you were there?"

Dawson's head jerked from Camille, to Beau,

and back to Camille. “Time out. She showed up in Colorado too? Unexpected?”

“Yep. It’s as weird as it sounds,” Beau said.

The women at the table seemed calm enough. Anna smiled and leaned one elbow on the table. If her alarm bells were going off right now, she was hiding it well. His feet wanted to do the walking for him and march right over to Brittany and lay down some boundaries.

But Anna was thriving in her new independence. How much would it set her back if he barged in and took charge?

Camille watched as Anna and Lauren talked with Brittany. “I’m going to trust that Lauren is using everything she learned in those psychology classes right now.”

Just as quickly as she’d come, Brittany stood and walked out without looking back. She didn’t storm out angry. She just...left.

Beau met Anna and Lauren halfway between the two tables. “What did she say?”

Anna reached for his hand immediately, and he welcomed the connection. Hopefully, he was just overreacting about a long-distance friend.

“The last time I talked to her, I told her I quit my job at Mom and Dad’s law firm, but I haven’t replied to her messages since.”

“You’ve been busy. Changing jobs is a lot of work,” Camille said.

"Who is she? Tell me everything," Lauren demanded.

Anna looked at Beau, and all of her casual calm from a moment ago was gone. "I met her online through the fashion vlog, and we've been friends for a few years. She lives in California, and since I'm afraid to get on an airplane, I figured we wouldn't ever meet in person. Then she showed up in Freedom when Beau and I were there."

"Out of the blue?" Lauren asked.

"Right. She was waiting at a bakery just assuming I would stop by because I had told her about how much I liked it when Beau and I went earlier in the week."

Lauren's eyes widened. "And she showed up in Blackwater unannounced too?"

Anna nodded. "She seems awkward in person, but she's very relaxed when we talk online, even in video chats."

Yeah, hearing about the ways Brittany had crossed lines only confirmed his reasons for sitting on high alert. "Where did she go?"

"I invited her to stay and hang out with us, but she said she was tired from traveling. She's staying at the Kellerman Hotel in town."

Camille shook her head. "Sounds like she's obsessed with you. Has she ever asked you for anything? Money? Products?"

"No. Actually, I've helped her make connections

in the industry because she's an aspiring designer." Anna glanced toward the crowd where Brittany had disappeared. "I can't figure it out. She's usually so casual, but tonight she seemed guarded."

"What is she looking for?" Lauren asked. "She came all the way here, but she didn't hug you, and she only talked for about three minutes before she left."

Beau listened while the women worked through the conversation with Brittany. Was he missing something?

Camille rested a hand on Anna's shoulder. "I know she's your friend, but I would feel a lot better if we looked into her. It seems very sweet and thoughtful that she came all this way to check on you, but something is off."

Anna's chin fell with a sigh. "I know. It's just... she's never done anything like this. She has always been so kind and friendly. These few meetings don't show who she truly is."

Camille's hand rested on Anna's shoulder. "I believe you, but I think we'd all feel better with just a little more information on our side."

Olivia bounced up between Anna and Lauren, draping her arms around both women. "Sup, ladies?"

Beau pointed a finger at his chest. "Not a lady."

Olivia shrugged. "You're over here girl-talking like one. What's with all the whispering?"

Asher stepped to the microphone and strummed his guitar. The crowd went wild with hoots and cheers. “Anybody ready to get the party started?”

Dawson grabbed Olivia’s hand from Anna’s shoulder and pulled her toward the dance floor. “Dance now. Talk later.”

Lauren turned as Asher started singing and couples made their way to the open area. “He’s right. Let’s worry about Brittany later. Go dance with your man.”

Anna turned a wide smile toward Beau. Shoot. He should have known he couldn’t come here with Anna without being pressured to dance.

After making a show of a huge sigh, Beau slid a hand around Anna’s waist, pulling her in until her chin rested on his chest as she looked up at him.

“Just once?” she pleaded.

A deep hum rumbled up his chest at her sweet request. “You think I could ever say no to you?”

Anna hightailed it to the dance floor without missing a beat, dragging Beau behind her through the horde of people. When she’d settled on a spot, she turned toward him, fanning her blonde hair out around her.

Remembering the intimate dance instructor’s directions to explore his partner’s body, Beau slowly ran his hands from Anna’s waist up her back. Her warm vanilla scent had his mouth watering.

"Easy, tiger. There are small children here," she whispered in glee.

"They have to leave at nine," he reminded her. "They might serve food, but this is a bar."

She slid her hands up his chest and around his neck, sending a shiver down his spine. "Do you remember the last time we danced?" she asked.

His lips brushed against the shell of her ear as he whispered, "Lucky charms."

The laugh was expected, but the sound was more than he could handle. He finally understood what the Grinch felt when his heart grew two sizes.

He loved Anna Harris, but it was never enough. Every time he saw her—spoke to her—he fell harder. It was as if love were a free fall from an airplane, but the ground was nowhere in sight.

When her giggles faded, he whispered, "I love you."

She leaned in closer. "That's the sweetest thing you've ever said to me."

The song ended, and Lauren released the cowboy she'd been dancing with to lean close to Anna. "Hey, I forgot to ask how the house hunt is going. Find anything yet?"

"Not yet. In the chaos of changing jobs, I kind of put my search on hold. Though, I'm sure Dawson and Liv are ready to kick me to the curb."

"Not true!" Olivia shouted from where she

remained snugly in Dawson's arms, ready for the next dance.

"Want me to call a real estate agent and get you set up for a meeting?" Beau asked. "I have a whole lot more time than you right now."

"Says the guy running a business," Anna countered.

Beau pressed a kiss to her jaw. "Let me help you. Please."

Anna hummed. "That would actually be very helpful. I love how you always look out for me."

"Can't think about much else," Beau admitted.

"I have one tiny favor to ask," she said, pinching her finger and thumb together.

"Anything," Beau drawled. If she asked him to jump off a cliff at this point, he'd probably do it.

"Will you go with me?" she softly asked.

Beau rested his forehead against hers. With his eyes closed, he could imagine they were the only people in the world. "I'll be with you every step of the way."

CHAPTER 39

ANNA

Anna hummed the chorus of "Amazing Grace" as she waited by the door. Well, it was Dawson and Olivia's door, not hers. That was a line that was blurring the longer she stayed with them.

In the chaos of changing jobs, she hadn't found the time to really focus on finding a new place to live. What kind of place did she even want? With so many uncertainties in her life, she felt a lot like a lost ball in knee-high weeds.

"Will you stop fidgeting? You're making Betsy nervous," Olivia crooned against the tiny dog's cheek.

"Sorry. He said he would be here at five-thirty." She fought the urge to check her watch for the tenth time.

"He's one minute late. Quit worrying." Olivia

gave Anna a once-over. "You look amazing, by the way. Green is a good color on you."

Anna brushed her hands over the shimmery dress. It was a perfect shade of green for the Heart Springs Pregnancy Resource Center's Christmas gala. "Thank you."

"Beau is going to lose his mind," Liv sang, loud and high-pitched.

Betsy, who was used to Olivia's dramatics, didn't flinch. She was literally the perfect dog for Dawson and Olivia, especially since she was the only dog who'd never bitten Dawson.

Headlights shone through the window, and Anna glanced out into the dark night to see Beau's truck coming to a stop in front of the house.

"See! Told you he'd be here soon," Liv said.

Anna reached for the door, but Olivia's hand rested on her arm. "Let him come get you."

"I don't want to be late to the gala."

A second later, Beau knocked.

"Showtime," Olivia said as she flung the door open.

Anna's breath hitched in her throat. Beau wore a black suit with a green tie that matched her dress perfectly. She had Olivia to thank for that. No doubt there had been photos and information exchanged between the siblings in the weeks leading up to the gala.

Oh, and he held a bouquet of red roses—at least two dozen.

Olivia waved her arm in front of Anna. "Look at your gorgeous date!"

Beau's jaw tensed, and he nodded. "Gorgeous is an understatement." He reached for Anna's hand, pulling her in to press a kiss to her forehead. "You're dangerously beautiful," he whispered against her hair.

Anna cleared her throat. "You look great too."

He lifted the bouquet. "These are for you."

She accepted the roses and hugged them to her chest. Dean had gotten her flowers once, but they'd been delivered to her office after an extremely nasty argument. They were meant for show—meant to butter her up and buy his way back into her good favor.

Beau bought her roses because he wanted to. There weren't any strings attached. The simple gesture made an emotional pressure swell in her chest.

"These are beautiful. Let me put them in some water."

"I'll take those." Olivia grabbed for the bouquet. "Go have fun, have her home at a decent hour, and don't do anything I wouldn't do."

"Let's go," Beau said, tugging her by the hand toward the truck.

The ride into Cody was quick and easy. Anna did

most of the talking, but Beau was definitely listening. He asked questions and added his thoughts regularly.

After they handed over the keys to the valet, Beau reached for her hand.

She laced her fingers with his and stared up at the stately marble building. Beau had to be out of his element at a place like this, and she'd spent way too much time leading the conversation instead of asking about him. "I'm sorry I talked so much."

He squeezed her hand. "You don't have to apologize for talking. I like it."

"But you never talk to people. In fact, you spend a lot of time telling people you don't care to hear what they have to say."

Beau glanced at her with narrowed eyes. "That's true, but I do care about what you have to say. I just don't like petty gabbing or gossip."

An older man in a suit opened the door at the top of the stairs and bowed his head to them. "Welcome. May I take your coats?"

Beau grabbed the collar of Anna's coat as it slid off her arms. A waiter met them a few feet into the cavernous foyer, holding a tray of champagne flutes filled with bubbling liquid. They both declined the drinks, and Anna took hold of Beau's arm as they entered the main room.

The Florentine Mansion was well known for its grandeur and elegance. It had been owned by the same family for over a hundred years and was a popular venue for weddings and events. Even growing up in a wealthy family, Anna had rarely seen anything as opulent as the Florentine.

A crystal chandelier hung in the center of the ballroom where men in suits and women in elegant gowns mingled around high tables.

The Christmas gala was Heart Springs Pregnancy Resource Center's biggest charity event of the year, bringing in hundreds of thousands of dollars from wealthy donors from all throughout the state.

Anna had been attending since her teen years and always made a sizable donation to the non-profit that provided prenatal care to women, as well as help and supplies for struggling families with young children.

Anna's phone vibrated in her clutch, and she pulled it out to read the message.

Brittany: Hey. What are you doing?

Anna released Beau's arm to type out a quick reply. Things had returned to normal after Brittany left Blackwater, but Anna stayed on high-alert. The last thing she wanted to do was cause Brittany to worry enough to show up for another visit.

Anna: Hey. I'm at a charity event right now.

She slid the phone back into her clutch and looked up at Beau. He was already watching her with a silent question in his eyes.

"Brittany," Anna explained.

Beau's jaw tensed. Camille and Anna had delved into a search on Brittany, but their resources hadn't produced anything alarming. Still, Beau openly didn't trust Brittany, and Anna kept him in the loop about everything that went on.

There was another message from Brittany a few seconds later.

Brittany: What kind of charity event? Where is it?

Anna turned the phone to show Beau.

She'd been walking a thin line in their conversations lately. If she didn't respond, Brittany might do something drastic. If Anna did keep up the conversation, she'd spend the evening on her phone instead of enjoying the event.

There was also a warning that stayed front and center in her mind. Every bit of information she gave Brittany felt like an invasion of privacy after the way she'd showed up at random places where Anna just happened to be.

Beau shook his head. "Maybe ask if you can call her when we leave so you can tell her all about it."

"Good idea." Anna typed out the message and got a quick response from Brittany.

Brittany: Sounds good.

Okay, that went well. Now she could enjoy the evening with Beau.

But as soon as she pushed the phone back into her clutch, Beau's hand rested lightly on hers. "Heads-up. Your parents are here."

Every bit of joy she'd brought with her died. She wanted to see her parents more than anything, but would they want to see her?

She turned slowly, scanning the suits and ball gowns. The sight of her mother in a shimmering gold dress stopped Anna cold.

"Do you want to talk to them?" Beau asked.

Anna ducked her chin before looking up at him. "I'm not sure."

CHAPTER 40

BEAU

The vulnerable look in Anna's eyes gutted him. How could her parents live with themselves after the way they'd hurt her? It made Beau physically sick to see her like this.

He rubbed his hands up and down her arms. "I'll be right beside you, no matter what you decide."

Her shoulders lifted and relaxed as a smile lit her features. "I know. I can't thank you enough for that."

Oh no. She had that glassy look in her eyes. He leaned in and pressed a kiss to her forehead. "You okay? What can I do?"

She shook her head. "You've done everything. You always know how to cheer me on, and I love that you're always on my side. I love *you*."

Good. At least they were on the same page, because he loved her more than life itself. "I love you too. Now, do you want to go check out the silent auction?"

Anna carefully wiped at the edges of her eyes. "Yes. That's my favorite part of this gala."

"I'm not going to pretend like I know what it is. I've never done this before."

Anna's earlier tears were forgotten as she dove headfirst into the silent auction. They slowly made their way through the room bidding on the items and talking with people Anna knew. Fortunately, no one gave him a second look. They were mostly interested in catching up with Anna.

When they moved out of the auction room, her parents were nowhere in sight. Anna was in a brighter mood, and Beau didn't bring up the elephant in the room. If she got a chance to talk to her parents tonight, maybe it would be in God's perfect timing.

The dinner was a plated, five-course meal, and Beau held up the set menu between them, whispering behind the thick paper. "Is this a different language? What is camembert? Why is the turkey stuffed with prune and juniper?"

Anna giggled, and the sound was a jolt straight to his heart. He'd do anything to keep her happy like this.

Beau glanced up as a couple walked by their table. Anna's parents passed so close to them that her father's coat brushed Beau's arm.

In a desperate attempt to distract Anna from her parents' dismissal, Beau asked, "Do you think they'd let me substitute the pavlova for Froot Loops?"

Anna's smile faded. Shoot. She'd noticed.

Beau reached for her hand beneath the table. "Don't worry about talking to them right now. We can't exactly switch tables during dinner, so this is your time to relax."

A bright-eyed woman in her early fifties let out a controlled gasp when she spotted Anna. "Anna Harris, it is so good to see you!"

Beau relaxed as soon as Anna stood to greet the woman. "Sharon! It's so good to see you too."

The woman embraced Anna, then stepped back to give her a once-over. "You look amazing. You are practically glowing."

Anna reached for the woman's hand. "Thank you, but I was going to say the same about you."

Sharon pointed at a man a few feet away. "Mark retired, and it has been the best thing for us."

"That's amazing. Congratulations to both of you."

Sharon leaned around Anna to lock her attention on Beau. "And who is this?"

Beau stood and offered his hand, but Anna beat him to the introduction.

"This is my boyfriend, Beau Lawrence. Beau, this is Sharon Black. She and her husband own hotels in and around Jackson Hole."

Wow. They owned multiple hotels in one of the country's top vacation destinations? Even knowing Sharon and her husband were probably loaded, the woman was friendly and down-to-earth. "It's a pleasure to meet you," Beau said.

Sharon's brows rose as she took his hand with a playful smile. "The pleasure is all mine. I hope you're treating Anna well. She's the sweetest woman I've ever met."

Yep. Beau and Sharon were going to be good friends. "My mission is to make her happy for as long as she'll let me."

Sharon pinched her lips together, trying and failing to hide a grin. "Well, that's good." She leaned closer to Anna and held up a hand in a show of sharing a secret. "He's a hundred times better than that sour-faced man I saw you with last year."

Anna chuckled. "You have no idea."

"And what line of work are you in, Mr. Lawrence?" Sharon asked.

Oh, great. The question he'd been waiting to rear its ugly head. "I'm a small business owner."

Sharon made a rumbling sound in her throat. "Really. That's impressive. I admire anyone who has the guts to step out and take a risk these days. I've never understood the appeal in working for anyone but yourself."

Beau raised his glass of water. "I agree."

Sharon reached for Anna's hand and whispered, "I like this one."

And with that, the nervous energy Beau had been carrying around all night slipped away. Sharon had a gift for making people relax in the most uncomfortable situations.

Beau pulled Sharon's chair out for her to sit next to Anna. Once the two women settled into a conversation, Beau leaned over to whisper to Anna.

"I'll be right back." He gestured toward the alcove where the men's room was discreetly labeled.

Anna nodded, clearly happy to have a friend next to her.

Beau was washing his hands when Anna's dad walked in. He'd met her father before, and the encounters had always been polite but petty.

Donald Harris lifted his chin as he stopped next to Beau. There wasn't an ounce of emotion in his voice as he said, "This could all be over if you would leave her alone."

Oh, good. A solution.

Too bad it wasn't a solution. Not one that Anna would like. It was just another way her parents could dictate her life.

"Polite decline. I think Anna is tired of someone else calling the shots in her life, but you're welcome to take that proposition to her yourself. You'll be digging your own grave, but that's your call."

Donald's eyes narrowed. "Is that a threat?"

"It's a figure of speech. Anna wants you in her life, but she doesn't need someone making decisions for her anymore."

With a huff, Donald lifted his chin again. "Catherine has big plans for Anna without you. Bow out now and save yourself the embarrassment."

Beau dried his hands and shoved them into his pockets. "Why do you care? You don't care about Anna, so what's your endgame?"

Donald made a tsk sound behind his teeth. "You don't understand. We have a reputation to uphold, and we didn't raise Anna to throw it all away on trash who will find some other tramp within the week."

Beau took a deep breath. "I hope you're not implying Anna is a tramp because that won't end well for you."

"The point of this conversation is to convince you that leaving Anna now is what's best for her."

Well, Beau's patience was officially at its end, and a few more words with this guy might earn him a trip to jail before the end of the night.

"She's twenty-eight years old. Twenty-eight. You have to trust her to make her own decisions now. She's not a pawn in your networking game. She isn't your employee anymore, and calling her your daughter is kind of a stretch when you've turned your back on her. So, I think it's weird that you assume she'll come running back, asking for you to manage her life again."

"Obviously, she can't make decent decisions on her own. You're living proof of that."

Beau stepped closer to the man he wanted to throat punch. "Here's a decision Anna and I made together. We're committed to each other through the good and the bad. I'll love her without strings attached. I'm not asking for your blessing. I just wanted you to know that I'll be taking care of your daughter from now on. She'll have everything she needs and wants, and I'll do whatever it takes to make her happy."

If Donald was bothered by Beau's admission, it didn't show. Instead, the man continued to stare Beau down as if he could set him on fire with a look. "Success isn't about happiness. It's about determination."

The skin on Beau's arms prickled, and he forced out another deep breath that was anything but relaxing. Still, falling into Donald's trap wasn't on Beau's list of things to do today. "I can see this conversation is getting us nowhere, but I have one thing to ask of you."

Donald huffed a single laugh. "That's incredibly bold of you."

"Hear me out. Anna still cares about you and her mom, despite the way you've shut her out. I know she would like to at least hear from her parents on Christmas."

"That's—"

"Just think about it," Beau said before stepping around Donald and out the door.

CHAPTER 41
ANNA

On Christmas morning, the warm scent of coffee woke Anna from a restful sleep seconds before her phone dinged with a text. Blinking through the soft light of the morning, she stretched her arms above her head and reached for her phone.

Beau: Good morning beautiful. Breakfast is here.

She tossed the blanket off and grabbed her robe from the hook on the back of the bedroom door. Sneaking into the bathroom, she brushed her teeth and hair in a rush. Beau wouldn't mind seeing her in her pajamas, but he might be put off by morning breath and bedhead.

How far had she come from when she would've never let a man see her without makeup and hair styled? She would have panicked if Dean showed up at the door and she didn't have breakfast made for him.

Her idea of a healthy relationship had changed drastically in the weeks since the wedding that never happened. She never worried what Beau would think of her without makeup or how he would react if she had an opinion.

And her feelings for Beau? The way she loved him paled in comparison to anything she imagined love could be.

When she stepped into the kitchen, Beau handed her a mug of steaming coffee. He wore a gray thermal shirt and jeans, and his hair was tousled from sleep.

Anna took the mug and rested it on the counter before reaching for him. "Good morning, handsome."

Beau slid his arms around her waist and pulled her to his chest. "Merry Christmas."

"Merry Christmas indeed." She glanced at the table where plates were rounded with food. "Did you do all of this?"

"I can't take credit for cooking it, but I picked it up from Mrs. Scott on the way over. She said Asa, Lyric, and Jacob are having breakfast at home before they stop by to hang out here for a little while."

"That's so sweet of her. And you."

How many times would Beau do more than

repeat his love for her in words? He went above and beyond on a daily basis, and she never took him for granted.

Beau rested his forehead against hers and closed his eyes. "I haven't really enjoyed Christmas since Mom died."

Oh no. The loss of Beau's mom had hit everyone in Blackwater. Mary Lawrence was a pillar in the community, and everyone loved her.

Anna had been there for Olivia during that time, but what had Beau gone through?

Her hand slid over his short beard and into his hair. "I'm sorry."

Beau grasped her hand and lowered it, cradling it in his. "Don't be. For the first time in years, I'm looking forward to it."

Olivia bounced into the kitchen. Her dark hair was piled into a messy bun, and she had way too much pep for the early hour. "Good morning!" she sang.

"Merry Christmas, Liv." Anna turned and gestured to the coffeemaker. "Grab a cup while we wait on Dawson."

"Ha! As if I would be late when food is involved," Dawson said as he reached for a slice of bacon.

Olivia slapped his hand, sending the bacon flying across the kitchen. "We haven't blessed that food yet!"

Dawson gawked at Olivia. "Look what you did to that poor bacon."

Beau reached into the cabinet to grab plates for everyone. "Well, you tried to eat unblessed food."

"Shame on you," Anna said, frowning at Dawson who crossed his arms and pouted at being called out.

"Beau, bless this food before my husband gets himself in trouble again," Liv demanded.

Anna bowed her head and closed her eyes. Whether they'd blessed the food or not, there was no doubt that the Lord had blessed these relationships and friendships. She'd been homeless and jobless just a few weeks ago, but here she was, celebrating Jesus's birth with everything she needed and more.

After breakfast, everyone moved to the living room and settled around the fire. Beau found a seat on the couch, and Anna scooted in next to him with her feet tucked beside her and a blanket over both of them.

They took turns reading different accounts of Jesus's birth in the gospels while they waited for Travis and Bella to arrive. Anna rested her head on Beau's shoulder and silently prayed, thanking God for these moments of peace. They'd all signed up to hand out toys to kids at church later, but they had a few hours to enjoy the quiet, still morning and remember why they celebrated.

When Travis and Bella arrived, everyone moved closer to the Christmas tree, sitting on the floor and on ottomans to gather together. Anna sat on the floor in front of where Beau stayed on the couch. His knees bracketed her on either side.

Dawson clapped his hands to rally everyone's attention. "Listen up. We're gonna pray, then we can rip into the presents."

Their friends bowed their heads as Dawson prayed, "Almighty Lord, we come to You with grateful hearts. Thank You for sending Jesus to die for our sins. Thank You for loving us and forgiving us when we make mistakes. Thank You for the gift of salvation. We are nothing without You, and we humbly bow ourselves before Your mighty name. In the name of Jesus Christ I pray. Amen."

Olivia clapped her hands and squealed. "I'll hand out the presents!"

Dawson held out an arm, blocking her from the tree. "No way. This is every man for himself. It's a grab-fest."

Olivia rolled her eyes and bent to pick up a present with her name on it. "Whatever. We're not kids."

Bella pushed past the bickering couple. "Got mine!"

Anna made her way over to the tree and found hers and Beau's. Both were in the same cube shape big enough to grip with one hand.

She handed Beau's to him with a smile before sitting down at his feet. "It's not much, but I thought of you when I saw it."

Beau leaned down and kissed her forehead. "Yours isn't much either."

Anna's Christmas mornings as a child had looked different from Beau and Olivia's. Anna woke up to dozens of expensive gifts she wasn't allowed to play with, while Beau and Olivia received a few small things they'd really wanted. After talking about past Christmases and the true meaning of the holiday, they'd decided on simple gifts with no expectations or pressure.

Anna held up her gift. "Open them together?"

Beau aligned his fingertips on the edge of the paper. "Ready, set, go."

She tore through the wrapping and opened the box, lifting out a white mug with blush-colored letters on it. Laughing, she read the words. "Practically perfect in every way."

Beau held up his mug with a smile. "Rock solid."

Bella crooned, "Aww. That's the cutest. You got mugs for each other."

Beau shrugged. "I figured one day we might get back to reading the Bible together in the mornings."

"With coffee," Anna whispered. The memory of the peace of those mornings on the trip to Freedom squeezed her throat.

She'd always been the one looking to the future.

She was the romantic one who dreamed of a perfect family full of love and happiness.

But Beau could see that future too, and he imagined it with her. His gift wasn't small at all. It was all she'd ever wanted.

"You actually have another one," Beau said.

Anna frowned. "What? I only got you one. That's not fair."

Beau stepped behind the tree and pulled out a flat, rectangular present. "I bought this one a while ago."

"How?" She took the gift from him and slowly peeled back the paper.

It was a painting—one she thought she'd seen before. It was so familiar. A white landscape with snow-capped mountains and a bright sun shining over them.

"Where did you get this? It's beautiful."

"I bought it in Freedom. The artist is local," Beau explained.

The familiarity hit her. "It's the view from where we rode on the snowmobiles! I love it!"

Beau grinned. "I thought you'd like it."

Anna stared at the painting that transported her back to that day when she'd wrapped herself around Beau and trusted him to take her on an adventure she'd never dreamed of before.

"This is so thoughtful." Her heart radiated inside

her chest as she reached for him. "I love it. I love you."

"I love you too. I think I knew then."

Anna's smile bloomed. "I think I knew I loved you too. It's been a whirlwind."

"But I wouldn't change it for anything."

After everyone had opened their gifts and started chatting, Anna rested her hand on Beau's arm. "I'm going to try to call Brittany."

Beau nodded. He'd been supportive as they tried to piece together Brittany's actions. Still, they were missing something, and Anna couldn't give up until she knew the truth.

Slipping into the kitchen, she dialed Brittany's number but didn't get an answer. Maybe she'd return the call later.

Anna cradled the phone in her hands. There was one more call she needed to make. Could she work up the courage to press the button?

Beau walked in with his hands in the pockets of his jeans. "What did she say?"

"Nothing. She didn't answer."

He slid his hand behind Anna's neck, threading his fingers in her hair. "Did she sound okay last time the two of you talked?"

"She did, but I don't know anything about her family. She doesn't talk about them. What if she's alone on Christmas?"

He pressed a kiss to Anna's forehead. "You've done all you can do for now."

Letting her chin dip to her chest, the words sank in. "I know. I just wish I could help."

"You're a good friend—better than any I've ever seen," Beau said.

She didn't feel like a good friend while she worried over Brittany. "Thanks. I have one more call to make."

"You want me to stay?" he asked.

"Would you?" She could do the hard part on her own, but knowing Beau would stand beside her through anything was a reminder she needed.

She dialed the number and pressed the phone to her ear. Listening to the ringing, Anna reminded herself that words could hurt, but there wasn't an actual threat waiting on the other side of the call.

"Hello," her father answered, clipped and short despite knowing exactly who was calling.

"Hey, Dad. Merry Christmas."

There was only a small pause before he cleared his throat. "Merry Christmas to you."

Anna's pulse pounded in her ears. "Is Mom around?"

"Just a moment."

Anna glanced up at Beau and stretched a smile as her dad's "moment" stretched over fifteen seconds.

Beau shook his head and brushed the pad of his

thumb over her bottom lip. "No fake smiles," he whispered.

Right. She'd promised him honesty in all forms, and it felt good to be vulnerable when she knew he wouldn't leave.

"Hello."

"Hey, Mom. I just wanted to call and wish you and Dad a merry Christmas."

"Well, Merry Christmas to you too. I hope you're happy."

The words may have kind meanings, but Catherine's snide tone said anything but.

"I am. How have you been?"

"Just fine. Thanks for calling."

The conversation was over before it began, and Anna lowered the phone. "I guess that went as well as could be expected."

Beau wrapped her in his arms, and she melted against his warm chest. "I love you so much," he whispered against her hair.

"I love you too. I'm not going to let it ruin the day." It was a promise she made to both of them. She wouldn't keep waiting for people to love her when she had plenty of love already.

A commotion came from the living room, and she released her hold on him. "Sounds like more people are here."

Jacob burst into the kitchen with snow-dusted hair. "Come on, we have news!"

Anna grabbed Beau's arm as they followed the excited teenager into the living room. "You think—"

"Yep." He rested a hand on top of hers. "Pretend to be surprised."

"Trust me, there won't be any fake smiles when Asa and Lyric tell us they're expecting a baby."

CHAPTER 42

BEAU

Anna practically glowed in the orange sunset filtering through the French doors on the back side of the house. She'd taken her time, strolling through each home as if she were getting to know the very framework. Judging by her wide-eyed expressions and soft smiles, Beau had no clue which one she liked best.

"This place is gorgeous," she said as she made her way back to his side, holding onto his hand with both of hers.

"It is. I take it you like this one?"

She nodded and rested her cheek against his shoulder as they made their way back to the front door where the realtor waited, holding a tablet in one hand.

"Did you find what you were looking for today?" Jenny asked.

Anna chuckled. "I guess so. I love them all!"

Jenny opened the front door and moved to the side. "That's great. Do you want to see anything else here?"

"I think we saw everything," Anna said. "You've been amazing. Thank you for showing us around. I'll be in touch later this week."

Jenny exited behind them and locked the door. "It's my pleasure."

Anna released a long sigh as she settled into the passenger seat of his truck.

It had been a long day of exploring house after house, but she'd seemed happy. Still, the stress of choosing a house to buy was probably getting to her. "Everything okay?"

"Everything is great. This is just such a big deal. I don't want to buy a house and decide I hate it after six months."

"I highly doubt you'd hate any of those houses," Beau said.

"You're right. They were amazing." She grabbed two handfuls of her hair at her temples. "How can I choose?"

Beau pulled her hand from her hair and slid his palm against hers. "Don't stress. We can make a list and narrow it down when we get home. Then, you can have a few days to pray about it."

Her hand in his relaxed. "You're right. I don't

have to make a decision right now. I mean, Olivia is still begging me not to move out."

Beau pulled onto the main road and headed toward Dawson and Olivia's. "That doesn't surprise me one bit. Living with her best friend is probably a dream she's had since she was little."

An unexpected silence settled in the cab, and Beau glanced over at Anna. She was staring out the windshield, wearing an expression he couldn't read. "A penny for your thoughts?"

His words jerked her out of her trance, and she smiled. "How about a kiss?"

Beau leaned over the console and pressed a quick kiss to her lips that only left him wanting more. Little tastes of her only ignited his hunger.

"I was just thinking the houses are too big. It's just me, and while I do need lots of closet space, those houses are too much."

Beau tightened his grip on her hand. "Well, you'll have a family one day."

She cut her gaze over to him, studying his expression as he focused on the road. "What do you mean?"

Great. His palm was sweating, and he couldn't pry it out of hers without making things weird. "I know this is a lot of assuming on my part, but I live at the shop. It's fine for me now, but I could afford to buy a house when the time comes."

Anna sat up straighter, turning toward him in her seat. "Beau Lawrence, speak in plain language."

He lifted her hand and pressed his lips against her soft knuckles. "I'm trying to have a talk about our future, and you're making me very nervous."

Anna let out a small gasp, but he couldn't look at her. He'd lose all of his courage.

"This is big, isn't it?" she asked.

"Yep. About as big as it gets," Beau confirmed. He was having a premeditated talk with his girlfriend about the future. Their future. "But don't feel like you have to make a decision about a house with me in mind. Just because I'm hoping to be a part of your life for the foreseeable future doesn't mean you shouldn't pick the exact house that *you* want."

"Are you serious? I am one hundred percent thinking about you when I make decisions. I have been for months!"

"But you're just getting your independence, and—"

Anna leaned over the console until her face was only a few inches from him. "I don't need any more independence. I know I have that now. I need *you*."

Oh boy. His heart was running a marathon in his chest, and Beau was trapped inside the small cab of his truck. "Here's my take on where we live one day. I want a place where I can protect you and provide for you. I want to love you and cherish you, and I don't care one bit about what the house looks like."

He paused, and Anna spoke up. “I feel like there’s a but coming.”

“But I’d like to have room to grow our family,” he added.

Anna jerked back to her seat and squealed. “Ahhh! You’re joking!”

Beau gripped the wheel. “Good grief. What are you doing? What’s wrong?”

“I’m happy! I’ve never been so happy in my life! Beau, I want a future with you. I want it all. Let’s do more than house hunt together. Let’s buy one.”

“Are you sure? It’s only been a few months. What if—”

“What if everything isn’t perfect? What if we have fights and disagree? What if we work together to make the future we both want? What if it’s perfectly imperfect, and we love it?”

Beau jerked the truck into the nearest vacant lot and shifted into park.

“What are you—”

Wrapping a hand behind her head, he pulled her in for a kiss that did nothing to settle his wild pulse. They formed to each other, fitting perfectly together.

He never saw her coming, but Anna crashed into his life and changed everything for the better.

She pulled back long enough to take a few steadying breaths. “I know how big of a deal this is for you.”

He brushed a hair behind her ear and trailed his

thumb down her jaw. "It's not. It feels right with you. I don't want to pressure you into anything."

"I never feel pressured with you," she said. "I can finally be myself."

"Good, because I don't want you to be anyone else."

She pressed another quick kiss to his lips. "I tried to save my old life, but I was better off walking away from it. You love me so much that I don't care who doesn't anymore. I'm not trying to fix what doesn't work. I'm ready for what comes next."

She grabbed his large hand and enclosed it in both of hers. "This is worth fighting for, and I know my place now. It's with you."

Beau shook his head and fought a smile. "I don't have a ring yet."

"You already proposed once," she joked.

Remembering their first kiss from the restaurant in Freedom had his smile growing wider. "Yeah, but this time it'll be real."

Man, it was hard to wrap his head around how fully Anna had consumed his life, but he wouldn't change a thing.

"I promise I'll be ridiculously excited whenever you decide to ask."

Beau pulled the truck back onto the road. "But you already know it's coming, and you're taking all the guesswork out of it. Most guys don't know exactly what the woman is going to say when they ask."

Anna scrunched her nose. "Then why are they asking?"

She was still laughing when Beau's headlights landed on a strange car in Dawson and Olivia's driveway. "You expecting company?"

Anna sat up straighter to take a look. "Someone's on the porch."

A thin woman got to her feet, leaving the rocking chair swinging behind her.

He turned to Anna as he shifted the truck into park. "Did you know Brittany was coming?"

Anna's lips pinched together as she shook her head slowly. "I haven't talked to her since before Christmas, and I don't know how she knows I live here."

Great. Another surprise.

Beau pulled his phone out of his pocket. "Stay put for just a second."

"Who are you calling?"

"Dawson. It's his house, and I think the police need a formal report about this anyway."

Anna nodded and turned to where Brittany waited on the porch. "I think you're right."

CHAPTER 43
ANNA

Brittany waited on the porch with her arms wrapped around her middle. A thin layer of snow covered her car. How long had she been waiting?

Anna reached for the door handle, but Beau rested a hand on her arm.

"We have to be careful," he reminded her.

"I know. I don't think she would hurt me." Though, how much did she know about Brittany? They'd lost touch over the last few months, and she'd never explained her spur of the moment visits before.

Showing up at Dawson and Olivia's house was another breach of privacy. Anna had mentioned that she was staying with her friend, Olivia, but she most definitely hadn't given out the address.

Beau's lips pressed together into a thin line. The

wrinkle of worry between his brows deepened. “I don’t like this.”

“We’re not going to find out why she’s here by sitting in the truck. I need to talk to her.”

Beau sighed but reached for his door.

She had the freedom to make her own decisions, but this one affected Beau too. Was she sailing them into a storm?

Anna pulled her coat tighter around her as they approached the porch. Beau took his place dutifully at her side. The warmth of his body seeped into her side.

“Brittany. What are you doing here?” Anna asked, mustering every ounce of care and concern she’d been holding onto for weeks.

Shivering, Brittany just stared at her feet. She had to be freezing.

Anna unlocked the door and ushered Brittany inside. “Let’s get you warmed up.”

After taking her coat and leading Brittany to the couch, Anna made them all some hot tea while Beau started the fire.

While she prepared the kettle, Anna silently prayed for guidance and discernment. She couldn’t help Brittany if she didn’t want to open up about what she needed.

When Anna returned with mugs of hot tea, Brittany continued to stare into the fire. Beau sat in the recliner, but he remained on the edge of the seat.

Anna gently handed Brittany the tea. "Here. This should warm you up. How long have you been waiting?"

Brittany broke her trance and looked up at Anna. "A few hours."

"Why didn't you call me? I would have come sooner."

Brittany inhaled a shaky breath. "I don't know. I —I don't know why I'm here."

Anna sat beside Brittany on the couch. Resting a hand on Brittany's shoulder, she whispered, "It's okay. Maybe we can figure that out together."

Brittany took a few more stuttering breaths, but they didn't even out. Instead, the shaking grew worse until her entire body convulsed. "I'm just... lost."

The tears came immediately, and Anna wrapped her arms around her friend. The emotions she'd been hiding for months broke free in gut-wrenching sobs.

Anna caught sight of Beau over Brittany's head. His head was bowed and his eyes were closed. Was he praying? Probably. He didn't have much experience with emotions, and if she knew Beau, he was asking for guidance in a situation he wasn't equipped to handle.

"I...I should just quit. I should just end it all, and this pain would go away," Brittany said, loud and sorrowful through her tears.

Anna tightened her hold. "No. Listen to me. We can do this together. I can't promise to have all the answers, but I know someone who does."

Brittany's eyes widened. "Really? Who?"

"God. Our Heavenly Father. He's the only one who knows us inside and out. He knows your struggles, and I believe He led you here for help. Let me try my best."

Brittany shook her head. "You don't understand."

"Help me understand. I want to," Anna begged.

Brittany's chin quivered as she tried to gather the courage to speak. "You'll hate me."

"I can promise you that I won't hate you," Anna swore.

Sniffing, Brittany grabbed a tissue from a box on the end table. "I went to your wedding."

The wedding that never actually happened. It wasn't Anna's wedding because she never married Dean. Her life had changed so much since then. Everything had fallen into place just as it was meant to—hard times and all.

"I invited you, but you never said you were coming. I'm sorry I didn't see you there. When I heard about what Dean did, I just...ran."

"I didn't see you either, but I met your mother."

No. Anna's mom had been on a rampage that day. Olivia and Everly said Catherine screamed at everyone in her path after Anna left.

"What did she say?" Anna asked.

"I introduced myself because I was looking for you. She was furious with you for not staying, but when she found out I was your friend, she offered me a lot of money to...find you."

The hit stung. Anna knew her mom was mad at her, but hiring someone—a friend—to spy on her was a breach of privacy. She'd needed space, but her mother wouldn't allow it. Her mom had to have Anna under her control at all times.

"I'm guessing you took that offer?" Anna asked.

"I'm sorry," Brittany sputtered. "I haven't been able to keep a job with any of the designers you guided me to, and I thought I didn't have anything to lose."

"What do you mean?"

"I don't have a job. My parents haven't called me in years. I don't have friends. It's just me, and I betrayed the only friend I had."

Anna squeezed Brittany's hand. "I'm still your friend. I understand why you did what you did. My mother can be intimidating, so even if you hadn't been vulnerable, she might have still been able to convince you to do it."

"But I shouldn't have said yes. You were my friend, and I snuck around looking for you. Then I gave her the information. It felt wrong at the time, and I did it anyway. I'm so sorry."

"I forgive you. Brittany, I forgive you. Do you understand what that means?"

Brittany wiped at her tear-stained face. "No. I don't. Why would you do that?"

"Because we all make mistakes. You did what you thought was right at the time, and you didn't know you could just come to me. If you needed money, I would have helped you. If you needed a friend, I would have been there for you. I'm here for you now."

"I...I stopped taking my medicine," Brittany said, low and thick as she held onto Anna's hand.

"You don't have to tell me what you take the medicine for. I love you no matter what it is, but I am here for you if you need support."

"I didn't think I deserved to feel normal after what I've done. Then I felt ugly on the inside after what I did."

Anna took the mug of tea from Brittany's hand and set it on the end table. Wrapping Brittany in a tight embrace, she focused on breathing deeply and evenly. "Listen to me carefully. You are not ugly, and you are not your mistakes or a diagnosis. You are human and flawed, but you are loved unconditionally by a Father who created you in His image." Her breath rattled in her chest as she fought to keep control of the tears. "Can I pray with you?"

Brittany hesitated, then gave a small nod.

Anna bowed her head and closed her eyes, keeping a firm hold on Brittany's hand.

"Father, I humble myself before You for my friend, Brittany. She's lost and scared, but You are the one who can comfort us when we are alone and afraid. Please wrap Your loving arms around her. Let her feel your presence as she meets You in her darkest hour. I also pray that You will show me how to be a good friend to her. Thank You for the forgiveness You offer us whenever we come to You with our sins. In the name of Jesus Christ I pray. Amen."

Brittany raised her head and sniffed. "I don't understand that."

"It's okay. You don't have to right away. It's still hard for me to wrap my head around too."

Brittany fidgeted with her fingers in her lap. "I just got scared whenever you would stop responding to me. You were all I had, and even though I needed the money your mom gave me, I was still alone."

"You don't have to be. You have me. But I have to ask, why did you come to the wedding without telling me?"

Brittany crumpled the tissue in her hand and straightened it back out again. "Because I designed your dress, and I wanted to surprise you by telling you in person."

"You did? TrueBlue didn't mention the designer, even when I asked. I had no idea it was you."

The dress was gorgeous. When TrueBlue sent her the design to approve, Anna loved it immediately. Brittany hadn't even mentioned a partnership with the boutique.

"I asked them not to tell you because I wanted to be the one to tell you. I was so excited because I made it especially for you. I thought it would be the big break I needed too, but after you didn't wear it at the wedding, they cut all ties with me."

"And your beautiful dress was never seen. Brittany, I'm so sorry. I love that dress. It was perfect."

Brittany's tears began anew. "Nothing ever works out for me."

Anna clasped her hands at her chest. "Please don't give up. You are extremely talented, and I believe in you."

The front door opened, and Dawson entered wearing his full police uniform. Though he usually wore a friendly expression, his jaw was set as he looked from Brittany to Anna.

"Everything okay here?" he asked.

Brittany tensed beside Anna. "You—"

"He's our friend," Anna quickly said. "This is Dawson, Olivia's husband. He lives here, and they're letting me stay for a while until I find a place of my own."

Beau stood and jerked his head toward the kitchen. "Let's give them some privacy."

Dawson offered a hand to Brittany. "It's nice to meet you. Anna told us about you."

"I'm sorry for showing up unannounced," Brittany said.

"It's okay. Any friend of Anna's is welcome here," Dawson assured.

When the men left the room, Brittany wiped at her face again. "I should return the money your mom gave me."

"Actually, I have an idea. Your decisions are up to you, but I'd like to talk about some ways you can use that money."

CHAPTER 44
BEAU

Beau's phone dinged in his pocket. After wiping his hands on a grease rag, he pulled it out to read the message.

Anna: I have good news!

To Anna, good news could mean anything from finding a new moisturizer that smelled like coconuts and sunscreen to winning a huge case at the law firm.

Beau typed out a question, trying to manage his expectations for whatever the good news might be.

Beau: What's the good news?

Anna: We'll be there in fifteen.

That meant she was leaving her house, and Brittany was probably with her. After Anna bought a house, she asked Brittany to move in, and the two had been inseparable.

Beau glanced down at his grease-smeared T-shirt and jeans. Shoot. He needed a shower. Anna knew his job was dirty, but cleaning up a little before she showed up was the only polite thing to do since he wouldn't be able to keep his distance once she was within his reach.

Shouting toward the next garage bay, Beau headed for the back. "Tim! I'll be back in ten!"

"Tell Anna hi!" Tim answered.

Breaking into a jog, he headed for his apartment in the back. He'd beat this timer dozens of times before when Anna gave him a warning, and ten minutes later, he was back in the garage without a single grease smear on him.

"Lookin' sharp!" Gage said with a punch to Beau's shoulder.

"Shut up. You'd shower too if your girlfriend wore fancy clothes. Hadley works on a ranch."

Anna's car pulled into the lot, and she and Brittany both hopped out as soon as the tires stopped rolling.

Having Brittany in Blackwater was the best thing for both women. Anna was happy to have a friend and roommate, and Brittany was almost unrecognizable from the sad girl who'd shown up in town four months ago.

Anna's heels clapped against the concrete as she made her way to Beau. Her smile hit him like a line-drive to the chest as usual, and he opened his arms seconds before she barreled into him.

"I can't believe it!" Anna squealed as she wrapped her arms around his neck.

"It would be nice to know what you can't believe," Beau whispered against her temple before pressing a kiss to her soft skin.

Anna tilted her head up and pulled him down to kiss her. The connection was over before he knew it, leaving him wanting more.

"You tell him," Anna said, looking back at Brittany.

Brittany pressed her glasses higher on her nose before clasping her hands at her chest. "The fall release was a hit when we posted it on the website today, and we already have fifty orders."

Beau's eyes widened. "That was today? And you have fifty orders already?"

Anna gripped his wrist with both of her hands. "We decided to do a soft release. We didn't tell many people, but the reception was amazing, and it's already spreading all over social media. Three journalists have requested interviews with us already."

Beau glanced from Anna to Brittany and back to Anna. "Wow. That's amazing."

"What's amazing?" Olivia asked as she entered the garage. "What did I miss?"

"The fall release is a hit!" Brittany shouted.

Anna pulled out her phone and tapped on the screen. "Actually, we have fifty-five orders." She pressed a hand to her forehead. "How are we going to fill these orders?"

Brittany rested a hand on Anna's shoulder. "Relax. We planned for this, remember? We already approved five potential hires, and we have plenty of time to fulfill orders."

"I know. I just can't believe it. I knew your designs were amazing, and I'm so glad everyone else is seeing them too."

Brittany shook her head. "I couldn't have gotten started without your help. You're the one person who believed in me."

"And me!" Olivia wrapped Brittany in a bear hug. "You're awesome. I knew it. I called it first!"

Seeing Brittany accepted by their friends was the answer to Anna's prayers, and she'd poured a ton of her energy into getting Brittany's designs out into the world. It was also nice to see Brittany using the money she got from Catherine to build her own business.

Beau leaned back against the toolbox and watched Anna glow. Just when he thought he couldn't love her more, she showed him just how selfless and encouraging she could be.

The three women chattered on about designs and the growth of the business, and Beau took the opportunity to do a little research. Pulling out the top drawer of the toolbox, he grabbed a combination wrench and lifted Anna's hand.

Lifting the wrench to her ring finger, he measured the width. It was too big. He picked up another and did the same until the open end of the wrench bracketed the base of her finger perfectly.

Anna was still talking, oblivious to what he was doing. How much could he get away with?

Olivia noticed his attention on Anna's ring finger, but she didn't say anything. Her smile widened as she tried not to look his way.

While Anna gestured with her other hand, Beau pulled the ring out of his pocket and slid it onto her finger. Liv had been right about Anna's size. It fit perfectly.

Beau's heart pounded in his chest. He'd been carrying around the ring for weeks, but when would he get the nerve to ask her?

He slid the ring off just as Brittany gasped.

Anna looked down and spotted the diamond he still held at the tip of her finger. When she froze, so did he.

"Is that what I think it is?" she whispered.

Beau glanced down at the ring. "An engagement ring."

"Yes!" Olivia shouted.

Beau glared at his sister. "No one asked you."

Olivia covered her mouth, then waved. "Sorry. Continue."

Lowering to one knee, Beau looked at Anna who was already crying. "Anna, I love you with all my heart. You're the best person I've ever met, and you're way too good for me."

"It's true," Olivia whispered.

He poised the ring at the tip of Anna's finger. "Will you marry me?"

"Yes! A thousand times yes!"

Beau shot to his feet and slipped the ring on her finger. How could this be real life? He'd been so content to be alone that happiness like this hadn't seemed real. Anna had turned his world upside down, and he'd be thanking her for it until they were old and gray.

He slid his arms around her and pressed his mouth to hers. Fireworks lit up his entire body as Anna kissed him back. Every move they made was a silent promise to each other. Through better or worse. Through sickness and health. In good times and bad.

He had the rest of his life to love her, and he wouldn't waste a single opportunity.

EPILOGUE

ANNA

Anna rubbed a fingertip against the satin bow covering the stems of her bouquet. Her friends huddled in the small church entryway as they waited to step into the aisle.

A new song began, and Everly Lawson touched Bella's shoulder. "When the door opens. Wait two seconds, then go."

Bella nodded and faced the door with a smile just as it opened. As if the infant sensed her presence, baby Ariana cried from somewhere in the crowd.

The beautiful song filled the church as one by one Anna's friends made their way to the front of the sanctuary.

When the ladies were gone, Everly closed the doors and turned to Anna and Mr. Lawrence. "Ready?"

"I've never been so ready in my life," Anna confessed. She wanted to spring to where Beau waited and skip to the part where she became his wife.

Mr. Lawrence patted his hand over Anna's. "Thank you for letting me be a part of this day. I've watched you grow into a wonderful woman, and I consider you my daughter already." Beau's dad pressed his weathered lips together and glanced down. "My son is blessed to have you in his life, and my daughter is too."

Anna wrapped her arms around Mr. Lawrence's neck. "Thank you for being there for me when you didn't have to."

Beau and Olivia's dad had been a better father than Anna's to her, and it was only fitting that he walk with her down the aisle.

Her parents had been invited, but they'd quietly declined. Their absence still stung, but she continued to pray the relationship between them would soften one day. Until then, she'd done her best to mend fences, but she couldn't force them back into her life.

The small wedding was nothing like the lavish wedding she'd always planned, but it was perfect. The day wasn't about anything other than binding Beau and her together forever.

Her brother and his family had flown all the way from France to attend, and she'd been able to spend the last week getting to know her nieces and nephews. She was wearing a beautiful dress that Brittany designed, her friends were all gathered in one place to celebrate, and everything was as perfect as possible.

The Wedding March began, and Everly let out a little squeal. "That's your cue."

She squeezed Mr. Lawrence's arm, and he patted her hand. This was it. She was marrying Beau Lawrence, and she couldn't be happier.

As soon as the doors opened, she locked in on Beau waiting at the other end of the room. His shoulders swelled, and his mouth opened slightly as he caught sight of her.

Yep. That was her man—the only one in the world that God had made specifically for her.

Despite Everly's careful instruction, Anna's pace quickened. What was the point in drawing it out when she just wanted to finally be married to him?

Stopping at the end of the aisle, she waited impatiently as Mr. Lawrence gave her away. As soon as her hand was in Beau's, she held on with everything she had. They had a lifetime ahead of them, and it all started now.

BONUS EPILOGUE

ZACH

If Zach Wilson ever saw another pen, he might stab himself in the eye with it. How many papers could they really make him sign?

The sweaty man with a red beard and fat fingers slid another page across the table to Zach. "This one outlines the dates and times you will meet with your parole agent."

"And I have to sign it? Why do I have to sign it if it's just information?"

The big guy's expression didn't change. "We will make a copy for you to take with you."

Zach scribbled his signature on the line with enough force to tear the paper in a couple of places. "Great. I'll add these dates to my schedule."

With his lips pressed into a thin line, Zach handed over the papers. "That all?"

The man—Joe, if his name badge was

correct—reached behind him to grab a stack of papers. "These are the conditions of your parole. I assume these have been explained to you."

"Yep. They said I could walk around outside as long as I don't kill anybody else."

Joe actually rolled his eyes. It was official, he was human.

Zach took the papers and rolled them up before stuffing them into the top of his backpack. It was amazing how few things he'd kept over the last three years.

Well, it wasn't much of a surprise since no one had brought him a single cent since he'd been at Wyoming State Penitentiary. Any money he had before the lock-up was long gone.

"Anything else?" Zach asked, clasping his hands on the desk.

Joe jerked his head toward the door, and that was as much of a farewell as Zach would get.

The guard who'd been in charge of escorting Zach to the admin building opened the door and pointed the way toward the exit. When he opened the door and Zach stepped out, he was greeted by a boring gray sky and a cold wind.

A bus waited at the far end of the sidewalk. That was his ticket to freedom.

Ha! Freedom was a myth. He'd been a slave to the system way too long to think he was free now.

His parole agent's job was to "supervise" him for the foreseeable future.

Just what Zach needed—another person who wanted to control him. Dad, uncle, brother, teacher, principal, boss, officer, judge. Someone was always trying to tell him what to do.

A car door shut, and Zach looked over as he hiked his backpack onto his shoulder.

He'd been thinking this whole release thing was a dream anyway. Now he knew it for sure. There was no way Lauren Vincent just happened to be hanging out at the pen the morning of his release.

Her long hair streamed in the icy wind, and she seemed to move in slow motion as she rounded the front of the van.

Of course she was driving a minivan. Lauren was the oldest thirty-year-old he'd ever met. She was as straight-laced, high-strung, and as by-the-book as they came.

She was everything he wasn't. Dressed in a pink top and white pants, she was a firework of color against the concrete buildings of the compound.

Zach changed course and headed her way. Just like every time he saw her, a glimpse of the night she'd almost died flashed in his mind.

The cold. Her cries. The screams. He couldn't forget it no matter how hard he tried.

When she was close enough to hear him, he stopped walking. "What are you doing here?"

Lauren pushed her sunglasses onto her head and leveled him with a look that dared him to mess with her. "No one else is coming for you."

Great. She'd gone out of her way to pick him up from his prison release. She truly was a saint.

Too bad he was the king of ruining good things.

Funny she would show up today, since she was the reason he was locked up in the first place. It wasn't her fault. He'd chosen the wrong day to try to be the hero.

Shaking his head, he stared her down. "You shouldn't be here."

"Yeah, well, neither should you," she spat back.

See? That's where she was wrong. Guys like him did belong in prison. He'd bet the shoes on his feet he'd be back within six months.

He jerked his chin at her vehicle. "Go home."

Instead of turning around and doing as he said, she crossed her arms over her chest and jutted her hip out to the side. "No one else is coming to pick you up. Get in the van."

Zach crossed his arms and stared down at her with a look that had made men three times her size cower. "You're not the boss of me."

Lauren quirked one brow. Why did he like it when she did that?

No. You're not allowed to like her.

Real life didn't give second chances or happy

endings to the devil. Real life chewed him up and spit him out over and over.

Nothing made sense when it came to Lauren Vincent. She'd almost died because of him, but she was the only visitor he'd had in three years.

Worse than that, the sick feeling he got whenever he saw her was getting worse, not better. It was probably guilt or shame or something else he'd never experienced before, but how was he to know?

Instead of exploring the uneasy feelings she gave him, he narrowed his eyes and glanced toward the van. "Is there candy inside?"

Lauren rolled her eyes and reached into her jacket pocket. She pulled out a Snickers bar and shoved it at his chest.

"You are an angel." He tore the wrapper off and bit off a quarter of the snack.

When she didn't move or say anything, Zach pointed the candy bar at her. "Wait. Are you trying to butter me up?"

Her shoulders sank slightly. "I have a proposition for you."

"Good. It's been a while."

Her open hand hit his chest before he had a chance to regret his poor choice of words.

"Ow. Rude."

"Not that kind of proposition," she said. "I need your help."

Zach spread his arms out, showcasing everything he owned. The white T-shirt and gym pants he wore were given to him yesterday, and his backpack wasn't even half full. "I'm not in a position to help anyone, sweetheart."

She jerked her thumb at the vehicle. "Just get in. We'll talk about it on the way home."

"I don't have a home."

Lauren hung her head. She'd clearly underestimated his situation. "Just get in. I'll make some phone calls."

"What kind of phone calls could you make to get me a place to live? Any chance you have a connection for cars too because I don't have one."

Lauren turned around and headed back toward the van. "I'm not your fairy godmother, Zach."

He was following her before he even realized his feet were moving. "Nah. More like an angel."

She pointed a finger toward the passenger side of the van. "You do the sitting. I'll do the talking."

Zach bit his tongue between his teeth as Lauren bossed him around. At least he'd have an entertaining ride back to Blackwater.

LOVE UNDERCOVER

LOVE IN BLACKWATER BOOK 6

He once saved her life. Now she needs him to help save someone else.

Zach Wilson never meant for things to go so far. Abducting Lauren Vincent was an attempt to get answers—until his brother took things too far. Sparing Lauren was the only right thing Zach has ever done... but one good decision doesn't erase a lifetime of bad ones. And yet, who is the only person waiting for him when he gets out of prison? The woman he hurt the most.

Lauren has spent years haunted by that night—and by the man who saved her. She doesn't know why he did it, but she's never forgotten that Zach is the reason she's still breathing. Now, she needs his help again. Her cousin has been missing for years, and

Zach is the only one with the connections to find him.

Living next door while helping with repairs, Zach tries to keep his distance, but Lauren sees glimpses of the man he could be—the honorable man he tries to hide from the world. Despite his reluctance to help her if it means risking her safety, she's not afraid to risk everything to find her cousin.

As danger closes in, will they find answers, love, and redemption before it's too late?

WANT MORE FROM MANDI BLAKE?

Blackwater Ranch Series

The Harding brothers are tough as nails, but they fall hard for the strong women who wrangle their hearts. Through heartbreaks, reunions, and celebrations, the Hardings will fight for love and the future of the ranch.

Wolf Creek Ranch Series

These cowboys know how to treat a lady and never back down when things get tough. Through secrets, revenge, forgiveness, and redemption, the men of Wolf Creek Ranch will have to fight for love, and they'll do anything to protect the women who steal their hearts.

Love in Blackwater Series

If you loved the Blackwater Ranch Series and the Wolf Creek Ranch Series, get ready to fall in love all over again as more of your friends fall in love.

Unfailing Love Series

Visit Carson, Georgia and fall in love with the swoonworthy friends who will give you all the feels as they fall for the women who steal their hearts.

The Heroes of Freedom Ridge Series

Visit Freedom and enjoy the faith, friendships, and

forever-afters in this Christmas town nestled in the Colorado Rockies.

The Christmas in Redemption Ridge Series

If you loved the best-selling Heroes of Freedom Ridge Series, you'll love this spin-off series with all new characters and traditions, but the same magic of community and romance readers love.

ABOUT THE AUTHOR

Mandi Blake was born and raised in Alabama where she lives with her husband and daughter, but her southern heart loves to travel. Reading has been her favorite hobby for as long as she can remember, but writing is her passion. She loves a good happily ever after in her sweet Christian romance books and loves to see her characters' relationships grow closer to God and each other.